AMISH CHRISTMAS COLLECTION

A Plain and Simple Christmas
& Naomi's Gift

A

Kauffman

AMISH CHRISTMAS COLLECTION

A Plain and Simple Christmas
& Naomi's Gift

Amy Clipston

ZONDERVAN®

ZONDERVAN.com/
AUTHORTRACKER
follow your favorite authors

ZONDERVAN

Plain and Simple Christmas/Naomi's Gift
Copyright © 2012 by Amy Clipston

This title is also available as a Zondervan ebook.
Visit www.zondervan.com/ebooks.

Requests for information should be addressed to:

Zondervan, *Grand Rapids, Michigan* 49530

ISBN 978-0-310-31876-7

Cover design: ThinkPen Design, Inc.
Cover photography: Shutterstock®
Interior photography: Shutterstock®
Interior design: Beth Shagene, Melissa Elenbaas

Printed in the United States of America

12 13 14 15 16 17 /DCI/ 21 20 19 18 17 16 15 14 13 12 11 10 9 8 7 6 5 4 3 2 1

Glossary

ack: Oh
aenti: aunt
appeditlich: delicious
bedauerlich: sad
boppli: baby
bopplin: babies
bruder: brother
bruderskinner: nieces/nephews
daed: father
danki: Thank you
dat: dad
Dietsch: Pennsylvania Dutch, the Amish
    language (a German dialect)
dochder: daughter
dochdern: daughters
eiferich: excited
Englisher: a non-Amish person
fraa: wife
Frehlicher Grischtdaag!: Merry Christmas!
freind: friend

freinden: friends
freindschaft: relative
froh: happy
gegisch: silly
gern gschehne: You're welcome
grossdaddi: grandfather
grossdochdern: granddaughters
Grischtdaag: Christmas
grossmammi: grandmother
Gude mariye: Good morning
gut: good
Gut nacht: Good night
Ich liebe dich: I love you
kapp: prayer covering or cap
kind: child
kinner: children
kinskind: grandchild
kinskinner: grandchildren
kumm: come
liewe: love, a term of endearment
maedel: young woman
mamm: mom
mei: my
mutter: mother
naerfich: nervous
narrisch: crazy
onkel: uncle
Ordnung: unwritten book of Amish rules

rumspringe: running around time
schee: pretty
schtupp: family room
schweschder: sister
Was iss letz?: What's wrong?
Willkumm heemet: Welcome home
Wie geht's: How do you do? or Good day!
wunderbaar: wonderful
ya: yes

Families in *A Kauffman Amish Christmas*

(boldface are parents)

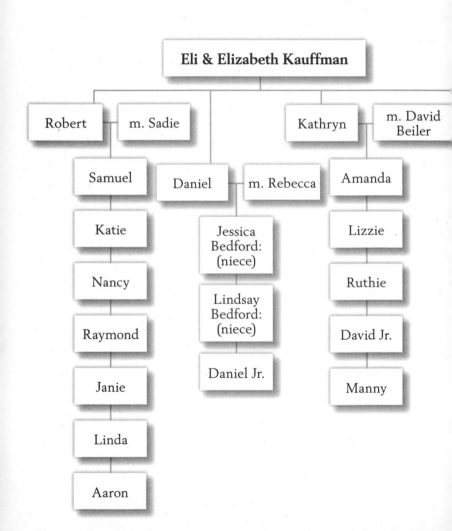

Eli & Elizabeth Kauffman

Robert — m. Sadie

Kathryn — m. David Beiler

Samuel

Daniel — m. Rebecca

Amanda

Katie

Jessica Bedford: (niece)

Lizzie

Nancy

Lindsay Bedford: (niece)

Ruthie

Raymond

Daniel Jr.

David Jr.

Janie

Manny

Linda

Aaron

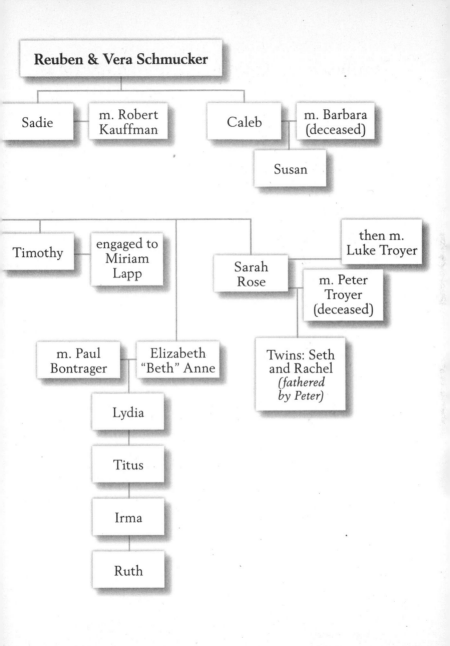

Reuben & Vera Schmucker

Sadie — m. Robert Kauffman

Caleb — m. Barbara (deceased)

Susan

Timothy — engaged to Miriam Lapp

Sarah Rose — then m. Luke Troyer

m. Peter Troyer (deceased)

m. Paul Bontrager — Elizabeth "Beth" Anne

Twins: Seth and Rachel *(fathered by Peter)*

Lydia

Titus

Irma

Ruth

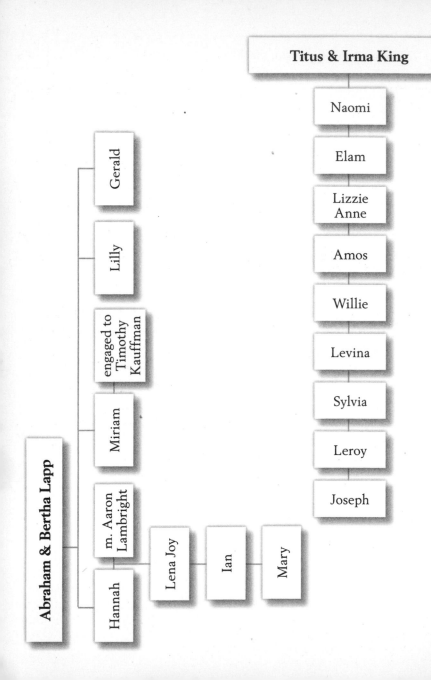

Titus & Irma King

- Naomi
- Elam
- Lizzie Anne
- Amos
- Willie
- Levina
- Sylvia
- Leroy
- Joseph

Abraham & Bertha Lapp

- Gerald
- Lilly
- Miriam — engaged to Timothy Kauffman
- Hannah — m. Aaron Lambright
  - Lena Joy
  - Ian
  - Mary

Note to the Reader

While this novel is set against the real backdrop of Lancaster County, Pennsylvania, the characters are fictional. There is no intended resemblance between the characters in this book and any real members of the Amish and Mennonite communities. As with any work of fiction, I've taken license in some areas of research as a means to create the necessary circumstances for my characters. My research was thorough; however, it would be impossible to be completely accurate in details and description, since each and every community differs. Therefore, any inaccuracies in the Amish and Mennonite lifestyles portrayed in this book are completely due to fictional license.

A Plain & Simple Christmas

*With love and appreciation for my godparents,
Joseph and Trudy Janitz.*

*Uncle Joe—You live on in the precious memories
you left behind.*

*Aunt Trudy—Thank you for all you do for our family.
We love you!*

CHAPTER 1

Anna Mae McDonough closed her eyes and folded her hands across her protruding belly. A tiny bump responded to the touch and she smiled.

"Thank you, Lord, for this bountiful meal on this beautiful Thanksgiving Day," her husband's smooth voice said. "And thank you for all of the blessings we have—our home and our wonderful life together." Kellan paused and Anna Mae glanced up, just as he squeezed her hand.

"Thank you, Lord," Kellan continued, "most of all for our baby who will be here in January. Amen."

"Amen," Anna Mae whispered, squeezing his hand. "Happy Thanksgiving, Kellan."

"Happy Thanksgiving, Annie," he said, his brown eyes filling with warmth.

Butterflies fluttered in her stomach in response to his loving gaze. "It's hard to believe this is our third Thanksgiving in Baltimore."

He filled his plate with slices of turkey and passed her the platter. "Time has flown since I found you in that bakery."

Her smile faded, and she rested her hands on her belly. Memories of Lancaster County crashed down on her.

Holidays spent with her four siblings and their families were chaotic, with children running around the room screaming. Anna Mae would find herself in the kitchen laughing and gossiping with her mother, three sisters, her sister-in-law, and nieces.

Tears filled her eyes as she glanced around her small, empty, quiet house. Kellan's only sister lived clear across the country in Los Angeles. Anna Mae had only met her sister-in-law once, and that was at their wedding three years ago. Kellan's father had died eight years ago, and his mother had abandoned him and his sister when he was ten years old. The only family they had was each other.

And sometimes the silence on holidays was deafening to Anna Mae.

"I'm sorry." Kellan leaned over, taking her hands in his. "I didn't mean to upset you by bringing up Lancaster."

"It's okay," she whispered. She swiped her hand across her wet cheek and forced a smile. "I cherish these times with you and wouldn't give them up for anything." And it was the truth. She'd never for one second regretted leaving her community to build a life with Kellan.

The baby kicked, and she looked down at her belly. Tears clouded her vision as she contemplated her newborn growing up without a host of relatives to love him or her.

"What is it, Annie?" Kellan asked. "I can tell by your expression that you're stewing on something. This delicious dinner is going to get cold if you don't fill your plate soon."

"It's just—" Her voice broke when she met his loving gaze. She cleared her throat and took a deep, ragged breath, hoping to stop the threatening tears. "I have so many memories of holidays and birthdays with my siblings and cousins." She rubbed her belly. "Our baby won't know any of them, and my family won't know our baby."

Kellan frowned and shook his head. "You're upset because it's been so long since you've been together as a family. Maybe after the baby is born, you can see them again."

"Leaning forward, she took his warm hands in hers. "You're probably right, but I wish I could have it all—you *and* my family."

"You can have it all." He shrugged and lifted his glass of Coke. "I've told you I have no objections to seeing your family. You name the time, and we'll go up there and visit them. I can take vacation anytime I want. That's the beauty of being the owner of McDonough Chevrolet. I can take time off and leave it in the hands of my capable staff."

"You know it's not that simple with my father." Despite her sudden loss of appetite, Anna Mae filled her plate with turkey, gravy, stuffing, a homemade roll, and homemade cranberry sauce. Thoughts of her father rolled through her mind. She knew she was at fault for not reaching out more. However, she'd wanted to build a new life without the emotional complications of dealing with the shunning.

"I don't get that whole shunning thing." He shook his head. "They say it's because they love you, but how is cutting off your child showing her you love her?"

"They shun in order to prevent members from leaving the community. When a member leaves, it's emotionally painful for the member's family." With her eyes trained on her plate, she cut some turkey and moved the piece through the gravy. "*Daed's* the bishop for the district, the religious leader. It's his job to keep us on the right path and enforce the rules of the *Ordnung*."

"But we go to our own church. Why isn't that good enough for him and the rest of the community? Why do they have to punish you for leaving?"

Sighing, Anna Mae looked up at him. "Kellan, my family is only following the traditions of the Amish that have come before them. The Amish beliefs and traditions go back a few hundred years. Shunning isn't punishment. They want their children to keep the traditions they've learned from their parents. They respect other Christians and don't believe that other ways of living are wrong. The Amish don't judge others or think their way is the only way. However, they want to keep their children within the community. They love me and want me to come back."

He glowered. "Without me."

She touched his hands. "I'm not going to go back. I just miss my family. I miss seeing them and spending time with them."

Kellan chewed more turkey, his eyes concentrating on his meal. He then looked at her. "How about we go visit them for Christmas? We can just show up and surprise them."

Anna Mae shook her head. "That wouldn't be wise. *Daed* wouldn't take kindly to a surprise visit. I'm certain he loves me, but he's very hurt that I left. I'm sure he thinks I rejected him and my mother."

Kellan's expression brightened. "What if one of your sisters helped you plan it?"

Anna Mae considered his suggestion and then shook her head. "I can't see one of them deliberately going behind my father's back. They'd be sure to tell him before I arrived, and that would make for a very uncomfortable and short visit."

He grinned. "I bet I know someone who would be happy to help you."

"Who?"

"Your brother David's wife."

"Kathryn." Anna Mae nodded, a knot developing in her throat at the thought of her sister-in-law. "She was the most supportive of my relationship with you. She seemed to be the only one in the family who understood why I left. She might consider planning a surprise visit. Kathryn was always known for speaking her mind, despite the consequences."

"Why don't you write her a letter and tell her how you're feeling?"

"Maybe I will." Anna Mae bit her lip, hoping to stop the threatening tears. "I miss her."

"Let's enjoy this delicious meal. After we're done eating, I'll clean up while you write a letter to Kathryn."

"Okay." Anna Mae tried to keep the conversation light while they ate.

After finishing off the meal with pumpkin pie and coffee, Kellan stood and gathered up the dishes. "I'll take care of this. You go write that letter."

"No. Let me help you." Anna Mae rose and reached for his mug.

"Anna Mae," he began with mock annoyance, "I'll take care of the dishes. Go write to Kathryn so you can rest easy tonight. The baby doesn't need the stress you're feeling about your family. Writing to Kathryn will ease your mind."

Stepping around the table, Anna Mae brushed her lips against Kellan's warm cheek. "I don't deserve you."

He set the dishes on the table and swept Anna Mae into his muscular arms. "Actually, I'm the one who doesn't deserve you." He kissed her lips, slow and easy, and then smiled down while brushing back a wisp of light brown hair that had escaped her bun. Even though she now lived an English lifestyle, she always wore her hair up. Some parts of her upbringing were still comfortable to her. "You're so sweet and loyal. I'll never understand how your family could shun you."

"Kellan, I already explained—"

"I know, I know." He held her close and whispered into her ear. "No matter what happens with our family, I love you. Don't forget that."

"I love you too." She closed her eyes, silently thanking God for her wonderful husband.

He let go of the embrace. "Go write your letter. I'll get the dishes under control."

"Thank you." After retrieving her favorite stationery from the roll-top desk, Anna Mae settled into Kellan's easy chair.

At a loss for how to begin the letter, she stared across the room at her favorite wedding portrait of her and Kellan, standing together at the altar of his church. Clad in a simple white dress, Anna Mae stood holding a small bouquet of flowers while clutching Kellan's arm. Her dress and the ceremony were both very different from an Amish wedding, but Anna Mae had wanted to fit into Kellan's English world. After all, she'd broken every Amish rule by leaving her community and marrying him. It was both the happiest and saddest day in her life. Only Kellan's sister and a handful of his friends and employees attended. She'd wished her family would've come, but they had objected to her leaving and did not condone their union. Anna Mae was cut off from the family when she left, even though leaving was her choice.

Closing her eyes, Anna Mae thought back to that fateful day when she'd met Kellan McDonough. It had been four years ago when Kellan had stepped into the Kauffman Amish Bakery in Bird-in-Hand, Pennsylvania, where Anna Mae worked with her sister-in-law Kathryn and Kathryn's relatives.

Anna Mae was twenty-three and had joined the Amish church the previous spring. After a few months of instruction covering the *Ordnung*, the unwritten rules of the Amish, she'd been baptized and had taken a public vow to live by the Amish beliefs. All three of her sisters were married, but Anna Mae had all but given up on finding a mate. She'd been certain she'd become an old maid, working in the bakery and making quilts for auction until she was too old and frail to work.

However, her life had changed irrevocably when a handsome English customer approached her and asked her to sit on the porch with him and share a slice of chocolate cake. Anna Mae hesitated, but Kathryn nudged her forward, telling Anna Mae to relish a much-needed break.

The customer introduced himself as Kellan McDonough, a car dealership owner from Baltimore in town visiting old friends. Kellan's soft-spoken demeanor and easy sense of humor intrigued Anna Mae. She was more comfortable chatting with her new friend than she'd ever felt with the young Amish men in her community.

Their conversation on the porch lasted an hour, ending only when Beth Anne, Kathryn's sister, came looking for Anna Mae. When Kellan said goodbye and shook Anna Mae's hand, a spark ignited between them.

Kellan visited Anna Mae at the bakery every day for the next week and then wrote her letters after he returned to Baltimore. Six months later, he visited her again, and six months after that he proposed to her.

"Annie?" Kellan's concerned voice brought her back to the present. "You all right?"

She opened her eyes and found him standing in the doorway to the kitchen with a pot in one hand and a dishtowel in the other. "Yes, I'm fine," she said. "I was just losing myself in memories."

He dried the pot with the towel. "Good ones, I hope."

She smiled. "The best."

"Do you need anything, like a drink or a snack?"

She groaned. "If I eat anything else, I'll explode. Thank you, though."

"You call me if you need anything."

"I will. Love you." She lifted her pen.

"Love you too." He retreated into the kitchen.

Taking a deep breath, Anna Mae began to write. Once she completed the letter, she signed and sealed it. After addressing the envelope, she closed her eyes and whispered a prayer, asking God to somehow reunite her with her family for Christmas.

CHAPTER 2

Walking up her long driveway, Kathryn Beiler smiled as her middle daughters prattled on about their day at school.

"Naomi told Millie that Danny likes her, but really Danny likes Rebecca," Lizzie said.

"But I heard that Rebecca likes Johnny, and so I—" Ruthie chimed in.

"Will you two take a breath?" Amanda snapped. "You've been yakking ever since you got home. I'm getting a headache." At the age of fourteen, she was Kathryn's oldest child and had already graduated from eighth grade. She now helped out at the bakery with Kathryn.

"Girls," Kathryn said, trying to suppress a laugh. "There's no need for bickering."

Kathryn's two boys, David Jr. and Manny, pushed each other and she gave them a stern warning look before glancing at the stack of envelopes in Amanda's hands. "Did you grab the mail from the box?"

"*Ya, Mamm.*" Amanda gave her the stack. "I think it's mostly bills, but I saw a letter mixed in with them. Looks like it's from Baltimore. Who do we know in Baltimore?"

"Baltimore?" Kathryn wracked her brain. "I'm not certain." Examining the letters, she gasped when she read the return address—*McDonough*.

"What is it, *Mamm*?" Amanda asked, craning her neck to read the envelope.

"Just an old friend." Kathryn shoved the envelopes into the pocket of her apron as she stepped into the foyer. She nodded toward the kitchen. "Boys, please set the table. Girls, you can start on supper. The stew is prepared in the refrigerator. Your *dat* will be home shortly."

While the children tended to supper, Kathryn slipped into the family room, dropping her bag and the stack of letters onto the sofa. She sank into her husband's favorite chair and opened the envelope from Baltimore. Tears filled her eyes as she read the beautiful script written by her youngest sister-in-law.

Dear Kathryn,

I'm sure you're wondering why you're receiving this letter since you only expect a Christmas card from me. However, this year I'm hoping you'll receive more than a card.

I've been thinking about you a lot lately. Actually, I've been thinking of you, my brother, my parents, and the rest of our family. I feel as if I have a hole in my heart since I no longer have everyone in my life. While I know it was my decision to leave the community, it wasn't my decision to be cut off from my family.

Although I'm no longer Amish, Kellan and I are living a Christian life together. However, I would like to come back to visit and be a part of the family. Kellan's only family is his sister who lives in California, and we haven't seen her since our wedding three years ago. Without an extended family, the holidays are too quiet in our little house. I miss the chaos of our Beiler gatherings. Also, Kellan and I have exciting news to share: we're expecting our first child in January, and we want our baby to know my family.

I know it's a lot to ask, but would you please help me find a way to see the family this Christmas? Kellan and I would love to travel to Lancaster County and share the Christmas meal with you, David, and the rest of the Beiler family. You were the only one who understood why I left, so I know you could convince the rest of the family that I want to be a part of Christmas this year.

Please consider my idea and write me back. Even if you don't think it's a possibility for us to visit, would you please let me know how everyone is? How are my parents doing? Does my father ever speak of me?

I look forward to hearing from you soon.

Blessings to you and your family,
Anna Mae

Kathryn read the letter three times with tears trickling down her cheeks. Memories swirled through her mind. Anna Mae was going to be a mother! What a blessing. Oh, how she missed her sister-in-law!

"*Aenti* Anna Mae," a voice said.

Kathryn's eyes cut to the doorway where Amanda stood, her arms folded across her thin frame and her blue eyes confident. "That letter is from *Aenti* Anna Mae," Amanda said.

Kathryn nodded. "*Ya.*"

Amanda lowered herself into the chair across from her. "What does it say?"

Kathryn paused, considering if she should share the letter or not. She knew the contents might upset David, since he'd felt caught between his father and Anna Mae when she'd decided to leave. However, Amanda was old enough to understand the situation, giving Kathryn no reason to distrust her.

"If I tell you," Kathryn began, "you must promise to keep this to yourself, Amanda. Your *dat* may not be happy when he finds out."

"So you're going to keep it from him?" Her brow furrowed with disapproval. "Is that the right thing to do?"

Kathryn smiled, both proud of her daughter's honesty and embarrassed by her own perceived dishonesty. "You're right. It's not right for me to keep this from your *dat*, but I need to figure out the best time to tell him. It's up to me to decide when to tell him, not you. Understand?"

"*Ya.*" Her daughter shrugged. "I don't understand why it should matter, but I promise not to share it with anyone."

"Anna Mae and her husband want to visit for Christmas."

Amanda grinned. "That's *wunderbaar*! We haven't seen *Aenti* Anna Mae for three years. Manny was just a baby when she left."

"Shhh," Kathryn hissed. "You can't say it too loud. If Lizzie or Ruthie overhear, you know what will happen."

Amanda rolled her eyes. "The whole district will know by tomorrow morning."

Kathryn clicked her tongue. "Now, now, you were just like them when you were around eleven."

"I doubt that," Amanda muttered. Her expression brightened. "Back to the letter. What exactly did she say?"

"She asked if I would help her plan a visit for Christmas. She and her husband are expecting a baby in January and they want the family to know their baby. It sounds like a *wunderbaar* idea, but your *Grossdaddi* Beiler won't be as open to it as we are."

"Because *Aenti* Anna Mae was shunned for leaving and marrying an Englisher."

"That's exactly right." Kathryn folded the letter and slipped it into the envelope.

Amanda shook her head, and the ties on her prayer *kapp* fluttered around her neck. "It's sad. She should be allowed to come for Christmas."

"She can visit, but your *grossdaddi* won't be as welcoming as the rest of us. It will be uncomfortable at best."

The back door opened and banged shut, followed by a chorus of children's voices yelling, "*Dat!*"

Kathryn dropped the letter into the pocket of her apron and gave Amanda a hard look. "Remember, this is our secret, *ya?*"

Winking, Amanda stood. "What letter? I have no idea what you're talking about."

Kathryn shook her head and swallowed a chuckle. She hoped the ease of her daughter's fib wasn't a glimpse into the future of her approaching *rumspringe*. She followed Amanda into the kitchen, where David stood surrounded by his children, smiling and nodding while they shared the details of their day.

He turned his gaze to Kathryn and his smile deepened,

causing her heart to warm. His smile still thrilled her, even after fifteen years of marriage.

She smiled in return and rested her hands on her apron, silently debating her choice to conceal the letter.

The children continued chatting, and David nodded while moving past them to the doorway. "*Wie geht's?*" he whispered, before brushing his lips across hers.

"*Gut,*" she said. "How are you?"

"Tired." He removed his hat and hung it on a peg on the wall. He brushed back his sandy blond hair, which was matted from the hat.

Kathryn crossed the kitchen and checked the stew on the stove. "It looks like supper is ready. Everyone go wash up."

The children filed out of the kitchen, chattering away in Pennsylvania *Dietsch* as Kathryn stirred the stew, savoring the aroma.

"How was your day?" she asked.

"*Gut.* The store was busy, which always makes my father happy. People always need farming supplies, no matter the time of year or the weather." He leaned over the pot. "Stew?"

"*Ya.*" She continued to stir it. "Your favorite."

"*Danki.*" He inhaled a deep breath. "Smells *appeditlich.* How was your day?"

"*Gut,*" she said. "The English customers love to come into the bakery this time of year and get desserts for their Christmas parties. We were busy all day long."

David snatched a spoon from the counter and sampled the stew. "Like I said, *appeditlich.* You make the best stew in Lancaster County."

She smiled. "You tend to exaggerate."

"No, I don't." He dropped the spoon into the sink and then moved behind her.

Hands encircled her waist, and she yelped. Looking up behind her, she found David leaning down. His lips brushed her neck, and she giggled while shivers danced up her spine.

"What has gotten into you, David Beiler?" she asked, placing her hands on his.

He turned her toward him and pulled her into a warm hug. "Isn't a man allowed to miss his *fraa*?" He leaned down to kiss her again, and then stopped when gagging noises erupted across the room.

Kathryn glanced over to her older son, David Jr., holding his neck while feigning to choke. His siblings surrounded him, and giggles erupted among the group of five children.

"I guess we'll have to continue this later," Kathryn whispered to David with a grin.

"*Ya*, I suppose so." David stepped over to the sink and washed his hands, while Kathryn and the children brought the food to the table.

Kathryn sat at the table surrounded by her children and across from her husband. When they all bowed their heads in silent prayer, she thanked God for the bountiful blessings in her life, including her family.

Then she sent up a special prayer, asking God to lead her toward a solution to making Anna Mae and her husband welcome for Christmas.

The following morning, Kathryn stood in the doorway separating the kitchen from the front of the bakery and observed her mother straightening the counter, placing sample containers in a row, and humming her favorite hymn.

She glanced behind her at her sister Beth Anne and daughter Amanda chatting while icing a chocolate cake.

Spotting no customers in the bakery, Kathryn sidled up to her mother. "Can I help you?" she asked.

"No, *danki*, I think that about covers it." Elizabeth stood up straight. "I believe the cakes and cookies are well stocked. It may be just as busy today as it was yesterday."

"*Ya*. I was telling David just last night how busy we've been." Kathryn placed her hand on her apron.

Elizabeth's eyes filled with concern. "What's on your mind, Kathryn? You look like the weight of the world is sitting on your shoulders."

Kathryn pulled the letter from her pocket. "I received this yesterday."

Elizabeth took the letter and read it. "Anna Mae is pregnant. What a blessing! And she wants to come and visit." She smiled. "What did David say about it?"

"I didn't tell him." Kathryn busied herself by straightening a row of individually wrapped cookies to avoid her *mamm's* stunned stare.

"Why not?" Elizabeth chuckled. "You're never one to keep silent about things. What's stopping you this time?"

Sighing, Kathryn looked up. "I know he'll think it's a bad idea to invite Anna Mae. He'll say her visit will open family wounds that he wants kept closed. You know how his *dat* gets about this subject."

Amanda appeared in the doorway. "But it's *Grischtdaag*! *Aenti* Anna Mae is our family, and the holidays are about family. Jesus tells us to love one another and forgive each other. *Grossdaddi* needs to remember that."

"He knows that, Amanda," Kathryn said. "You know as well as I do that he preaches about love and forgiveness, but he's in a complicated position because he's the bishop."

"But it's *Grischtdaag, Mamm,*" Amanda repeated with more emphasis on the word. "Can't our family put the shunning behind us for that?" Amanda's face transformed to her best "puppy dog face," as her father called it. "Please, *Mamm.* Please."

Grimacing, Kathryn glanced at her mother, who cupped her hand to her mouth and chuckled.

Kathryn turned back to her daughter. "Fine. You win. I'll talk to your *dat*, but I can't make any promises about what will happen."

Amanda squealed and threw her arms around Kathryn's neck, jerking her into a hug.

"You're the master of manipulation, Amanda Joy," Kathryn said, hugging her daughter close. "I feel sorry for the boys in our community when you start courting."

Amanda giggled and then danced back into the kitchen.

Kathryn shook her head. "She's a handful."

"*Ya,*" Elizabeth said, looping an arm around Kathryn's shoulder. "She reminds me of you at that age. You knew how to get just what you wanted too." Her expression became serious. "You're doing the right thing by discussing it with David. Tell him how you feel and how much more complete *Grischtdaag* will be with his youngest *schweschder* back with the family."

"I just hope he'll listen," Kathryn whispered.

"He loves you." Elizabeth patted her back. "He'll listen."

That evening Kathryn ran a brush through her waist-length golden hair while watching David lounge on the bed reading his Bible.

"I can feel your stare," he said without looking up. "What's on your mind, Katie?"

She cleared her throat and set the brush on the dresser her father had made as a wedding gift for her and David years ago. "I wanted to share something with you."

David closed the Bible and set it on the night table. "What is it?"

She plucked Anna Mae's letter from the dresser and handed it to him. "Please read this with an open heart and mind."

He raised his eyebrows in curiosity and took the letter. Kathryn held her breath while David scanned it.

Sighing, he glanced up and handed the paper back to her. "You know as well as I do that this would be a bad idea."

"But she's your *schweschder*, David. She's family. Isn't *Grischtdaag* about celebrating the birth of our Savior as a family?"

"She left the faith. As my father said, she made her choice." He lifted his Bible and flipped it open.

She placed the letter on the bureau and then climbed under the quilts next to him in the bed. "David, there's no harm in her visiting."

David closed the Bible and set it on his nightstand before facing her. A frown creased his handsome face and forehead. "I don't have to tell you that it's much more complicated than a simple visit. None of your siblings left the community, so you have no idea how it affected our family."

"That's not fair," Kathryn said with a frown. "I was here when she left. I saw how much it hurt us all. You know I love her like I love my own sisters."

"You're right. That wasn't a fair statement for me to make." He sighed. "I'm sorry. Her leaving was very painful for my parents. It's as if she became a stranger to my parents. She's no longer following our traditions. You know that if she came to visit, my father would be very upset."

"But it's been three years. Isn't it time for the family to heal? Life is so short. We saw that firsthand when my sister Sarah lost her husband in the fire at the furniture store. We never know when the Lord may call us home." She gave him her best pleading look, the one that usually got him to change his mind. "We had a lot of fun working together at the bakery. When she left, she also left a void in my life and a hole in my heart. I'm sure you feel the same way and miss her too."

"Of course I miss her." He snuggled down under the covers and pulled Kathryn close. "Let's not argue about this, Katie. You know that it's not a good idea to invite my sister for *Grischtdaag*. Maybe we can take the *kinner* and see her in the spring. We could take the train down. The *kinner* would love it."

Kathryn inhaled his comforting scent, soap mixed with his spicy deodorant. "*Ya*, they would love it." *But it's not the same as Grischtdaag!*

"We'll plan a trip," he said, his voice softening. "In the spring. *Ya*, it will be *gut*, and it won't involve my father and his temper."

She nodded, though she wasn't convinced waiting until the spring would help heal the family. She listened to his breathing as it changed, slowing down and deepening. Her mind swirled with ideas of how she could arrange to invite Anna Mae without alienating David. Surely he would change his mind when his sister was standing in front of him.

Although she was going against her husband's wishes, she couldn't shake the feeling that it was God's will for Anna Mae to come and see the family again.

Kathryn's thoughts turned to the time of Anna Mae's decision to leave the community. Oh, how Mary Rose, Anna Mae's mother, had cried. Mary Rose had begged Anna Mae to stay, promising that Anna Mae would find a nice Amish man to marry. However, Anna Mae had insisted that Kellan was the love of her life and she was meant to marry him.

Mary Rose had taken to her bed for a week after Anna Mae left. She'd said that the pain of seeing her daughter leave had debilitated her.

Wouldn't it be God's will for Mary Rose to see her daughter again and know that she was well and happy with her English husband?

Kathryn waited until she was certain David was in a deep sleep and then she wiggled out of his grasp, gingerly rose from the bed, and plucked the letter from the bureau. She took the kerosene lamp from the nightstand, lit it, and tiptoed down to the kitchen.

She fished her stationery from the desk and sat at the table. Closing her eyes, she sent up a silent prayer for the right words. She then poised her pen and began to write a letter to Anna Mae.

Opening the mailbox, Anna Mae fished out a stack of envelopes from inside and leafed through them.

"Bills, bills, bills," she mumbled with a sigh. They always came near the first of the month. But when Anna Mae came to a plain white envelope with pretty penmanship, her heart fluttered. She read the return address, squealed with delight, and hugged the envelope to her chest.

Kathryn had answered!

Anna Mae rushed into the house, dropped her bag on the kitchen table, and tore the envelope open. Lowering herself into a chair, she read the letter.

Dear Anna Mae,

I was overjoyed to receive your letter. It seems like only yesterday that you were with my sisters and me in the bakery, making cookies and cakes while laughing and sharing stories about our friends in the community.

How wunderbaar that God will soon bless you with your first baby! You and Kellan must be overjoyed! I'm so very happy for you and will keep you and your baby in my prayers.

*My mamm, sisters, nieces, and I stay busy these days.
The bakery is very busy right now during the holidays,
and we're still a favorite tourist stop during the spring,
summer, and fall.*

*The family is all doing well. Amanda is fourteen,
Ruthie is twelve, Lizzie is ten, Junior is eight, and Manny
is four. David says he wants more, but we'll have to wait
and see what the Lord has in store for us. Your mamm and
dat are in good health, as are your siblings, nieces, and
nephews. Our family is very blessed.*

*It would be wunderbaar to have you and Kellan come
for Grischtdaag! I can't think of a better time of year for
the family to reunite. Would you like me to work out the
details for you? How many days would you and Kellan
like to stay? Do you know where you'd like to stay? Of
course, you're welcome to stay with us, but you might
be more comfortable at the Paradise Bed and Breakfast.
Perhaps you'd like to stay there instead?*

I look forward to hearing from you soon.

> *God's blessing to you and your family,*
> *Kathryn*

Anna Mae read and reread the letter until she'd nearly committed it to memory. Tears spilled from her eyes while she remembered the time she'd spent at the bakery with Kathryn, Kathryn's sisters, her nieces, and Kathryn's *mamm*, Elizabeth. Those were some of the best memories she cherished from Lancaster County.

Glancing at the clock, Anna Mae realized Kellan would be home for supper in an hour. She folded the letter and put it back into the envelope and then into the pocket of her sweater. She then hoisted herself from the chair, headed to the refrigerator, and rooted around until she found a pack of steaks, Kellan's favorite. After marinating the steaks in his favorite barbeque sauce, she placed them in the oven set to broil and stuck a couple of potatoes in the microwave.

Anna Mae was preparing a green salad when Kellan entered the kitchen clad in one of his best suits.

"How was your day?" he asked before kissing her cheek. Leaning down, he cupped his hand to her belly. "And how was your day, Lug Nut?"

"Lug Nut? How can you be so sure it's a boy?" she asked with a chuckle.

He shrugged. "Just a hunch."

She smiled, rubbing her belly. "We had a good day. The quilting circle at church was a lot of fun. We caught each other up on the latest church news and also got a lot accomplished for our quilt drive. How was your day?"

"It was good. Busy. Sales have gone up this month, which makes everyone at the dealership happy." He breathed in the aroma emanating from the stove and moaned. "Steak?" He eyed her with suspicion. "What are you up to, Annie?"

"Nothing." She gave him her best innocent smile and carried the salad bowl to the table. "I thought you might like to have your favorite tonight."

His lips curled into a grin. "Is that so?" He retrieved plates and utensils and set the table. "You seem to be scheming over something. I know when you're fibbing. Steak is always an ulterior motive for something."

"Maybe I prepared your favorite meal because I love you."

Anna Mae brought the steak and potatoes to the table while Kellan gathered the condiments and glasses of water for them.

After saying grace, they began to eat.

"I can tell by the expression on your pretty face that you're excited to share something with me," he said, cutting up his steak. "What's up?"

"I've been dying to tell you. I have good news!" Anna Mae fished the letter from her pocket. "I received this today."

While he read the letter, she smiled, thinking of her upcoming trip to Lancaster County at Christmas. A bump on her belly drew her attention to the unborn baby. She rested her hand on her abdomen and smiled while rubbing the location of the movement. She longed to give her child the gift of knowing her family in Lancaster. The trip was for her baby and the baby's future as a member of the Beiler family.

Kellan looked up and placed the letter on the table beside his plate. His expression was cautious. "I guess this means you want to go to Lancaster for Christmas. That's what *Grischtdaag* is, right? Christmas?"

"Yes, that's right. *Grischtdaag* is Christmas." Anna Mae nodded toward her belly. "I want to do this for our baby. Now is the best time to try to make amends."

He gave a tentative smile. "It sounds like a great idea, but I want you to be sure this is what you want. I don't want you to get hurt. Your father used some harsh words when you left. I'll never forget his words to you, Annie. He said you were no longer his daughter if you left."

She moved her hand over her abdomen in response to more kicks. "He didn't mean that. He said it out of anger, hurt, and disappointment. I was his only child to leave the faith and the community."

Kellan's eyes moved to her belly and a smile curved his lips. "Is he moving?"

She nodded. "I think *she's* doing somersaults." She gave a grin.

"I bet my boy likes steak. He's a chip off the old block." He placed his hand on her belly, and she covered it with her hand. "Wow." His grin widened as he met her gaze. "He does like steak. He's telling you to make it more often, Mommy."

"Yes, maybe she does like steak, Daddy. Girls can like steak too." Leaning over, she brushed her lips against his.

"I love you," he said, his smile fading. "That's why I support this trip, but I also don't want your family to hurt you—especially now."

"But you encouraged me to write the letter. Why are you changing your mind?"

"I thought about it more and I keep remembering how your father behaved when you left. I'm nervous about it." He nodded toward her belly. "Your family could get you upset and then something could happen to him or her." He shook his head, frowning. "Maybe we should wait until the summer or even next fall. By then the baby will be older, and traveling will be easier for us. If we wait, then we don't have to risk you getting upset and something happening to you or the baby."

"I doubt anything bad will happen. I have a good feeling that this trip will go well, and I'll get my family back." She lifted his hands and intertwined her fingers with his. "Please don't change your mind about this. It's really important to me. Please do this for me. Let me see my family and try to rebuild a relationship with them."

He sighed, brushing back a lock of her hair with the fingers of his free hand. "Tomorrow you see the doctor, and you can get her opinion. If she says it's safe for you to travel, then I'll go to make you happy. But if your family upsets you, then I'll bring you home immediately."

"It's a deal." She kissed his cheek. "Thank you. If the doctor says it's safe, then I'll call Kathryn and see what I can arrange."

"I need you to make me one promise, though." He grimaced. "Just don't make me stay at your father's house."

She laughed. "I promise I won't."

❦

Kathryn handed the customer her change and her bag of pastries. "Thank you. Have a nice day."

As the woman walked toward the door, the bakery phone began to ring. Kathryn picked up the phone and cradled it between her ear and her neck.

"Good afternoon," she said. "Kauffman Amish Bakery."

"Hello," a hesitant voice said. "May I please speak with Kathryn?"

"This is she." Kathryn absently straightened packages of cookies on the counter. "How may I help you?"

"Kathryn," the voice said. "This is Anna Mae."

Kathryn gasped and sank onto a stool behind her. "Oh my goodness! Anna Mae! *Wie geht's?*"

"I'm doing pretty well," Anna Mae said. "How are you?"

"*Gut.*" Kathryn glanced across the bakery showroom, glad

to find it empty of customers. "I was so glad to hear from you. Congratulations on your baby!"

"Thank you. I was delighted that you answered. I'm glad everyone is well." She paused, as if gathering her thoughts. "Has my father asked about me or mentioned me at all?"

Kathryn bit her lip, debating what to say. She didn't want to lie, but the truth wouldn't be easy to swallow.

"It's okay," Anna Mae said quickly. "I didn't think he had. You don't need to smooth it over."

"I'm sorry," Kathryn said. "I wish I had better news about him, but no, he hasn't said anything to me. He may have said something to David."

"I doubt it. How's my *mamm*?"

"She's *gut*." Kathryn fingered her apron while she spoke. "She splits her time between helping care for her *kinskinner* and working in the farm store."

Anna Mae sniffed. "I'm so glad to hear it." Her voice quavered, and she cleared her throat. "I'm glad your *kinner* are doing well. I bet they're all getting so big."

"*Ya*." Kathryn chuckled. "David wants ten. I'm leaving it in the Lord's hands."

Anna Mae asked about her three sisters, and Kathryn gave her an update on their lives.

"So much has changed in three years," Anna Mae said. "I feel like I've been gone for a lifetime."

"It hasn't been that long." Kathryn glanced at the doorway and found her mother watching her with a smile. "Are you and Kellan still considering coming for *Grischtdaag*?"

"I saw my doctor yesterday, and she said that it's safe for

me to travel. So, I really want to come." Her voice was small, unsure.

Kathryn paused, considering her husband's disapproval. Still, Kathryn believed it was God's will for the family to heal. "Do you want me to work out the details for you?" she asked, the words flowing despite her hesitation.

"Yes, please."

Kathryn ran her fingers over the edge of the counter. "When will you arrive?"

"The Wednesday before Christmas."

"That sounds perfect." Kathryn found a notepad and pen by the phone. "Give me your phone number so we can keep in touch." She wrote down the number as Anna Mae rattled it off. "I'll see what I can arrange."

"*Danki.*" Anna Mae's voice shook again. "It means more than you know."

They chatted about the weather and then hung up. Standing, Kathryn turned and found Amanda and her mother with expectant expressions.

"I guess that was *Aenti* Anna Mae?" Amanda asked.

"*Ya*, it was." Kathryn sat back on the stool.

"And she's coming for *Grischtdaag*?" Amanda clasped her hands together, her eyes glistening with hope.

"She wants to come." Kathryn glanced at Elizabeth, hoping for an answer, a reason to go against David's wishes.

Elizabeth's eyes assessed her. "And you think it's a bad idea?"

Kathryn blew out a frustrated sigh. "David is against it."

"What?" Amanda gasped. "*Dat* doesn't want to see *Aenti* Anna Mae? Why?"

"It's complicated, Amanda," Kathryn said, folding her hands over her apron. "We've already discussed this."

"*Grossdaddi* will understand," Amanda said. "He'll welcome her back and the family will all be together again." Amanda looked between Kathryn and Elizabeth. "Besides, everyone is happy when someone is expecting a baby. *Grossdaddi* will be so happy to see her that he'll forget all about how disappointed he was when she left."

Elizabeth looped her arm around Amanda and pulled her into a hug. "You're such a smart *maedel*."

Kathryn studied her mother's eyes. "So you would go against *Dat* if you believed something in your heart?"

Elizabeth shrugged. "Depending upon the circumstance, maybe."

"And in this circumstance?" Amanda asked.

Elizabeth winked. "One of my English customers once said it's easier to ask for forgiveness than to get permission."

Kathryn glanced at Amanda. "Don't say anything to your siblings or *Dat*. I need to figure this out by myself before your *dat* finds out about it."

"But is that right, *Mamm*?" Amanda folded her arms and frowned. "Shouldn't *Dat* know about this? *Aenti* Anna Mae is his *schweschder*."

Kathryn gave Amanda a stern look.

Amanda sighed. "Fine. My lips are sealed," she grumbled and marched back into the kitchen.

"What am I teaching *mei dochder*?" Kathryn muttered, rubbing her temple.

Elizabeth touched her arm. "You're teaching her to follow her heart when she feels God speaking to her. If Anna Mae is meant to come here, then the plans will fall together and all will work out the way God wants it to."

Kathryn shook her head and grimaced. "I pray you're right."

Later that evening, Kathryn placed the last clean dish in the cabinet and thanked the girls for helping clean up after supper. The girls ran upstairs to take their baths and get ready for bed.

The back door opened and slammed, and David entered the kitchen and sighed. "Chores are done. It's been a long day," he said, sitting at the kitchen table. "It feels good to relax."

"*Ya*," she whispered. She grabbed two glasses of water and sat across from him. Thoughts swirled through her mind like a tornado. Guilt weighed down on her, feeling like a stone sitting on her chest and stealing her breath. How could she possibly deceive the man who'd been her best friend and confidante since she was a child?

"Is something wrong, Katie?" he asked, lifting his glass. "You seem preoccupied." He took a long drink.

Kathryn cleared her throat. "I spoke to Anna Mae today."

His eyes widened with shock. "You spoke to her? What do you mean?"

She took a sip of water and cleared her throat. "She called the bakery."

"How is she?"

"She's doing *gut*." She traced the condensation on the glass with her fingertip. "She and Kellan still want to come and

visit for *Grischtdaag*. I told her it sounded like a nice idea."
She inhaled a breath, awaiting his response.

"Katie." Reaching over, he took her hand in his. "You
know it's a bad idea. I told you we'll go visit her in the spring,
and that's what we'll do. Forget any plans for their coming
for *Grischtdaag*. It just won't work out the way you'd like."

"But David, it's *Grischtdaag*. The family should be
together."

"You know as well as I do that having Anna Mae and her
husband here would just upset my *dat*. We don't want that at
Grischtdaag. We'll go to Baltimore and visit Anna Mae in the
spring and discuss inviting her back another time. We'll have
to warn my *daed* about it and prepare for the visit. Having
them just drop in would cause problems that I'm not ready
to face."

"But I really feel that this is the time to invite her," she
said slowly, choosing her words as best she could. "It feels
like God is leading me to this. I feel it strongly in my heart,
David. I'm not just making this decision lightly. It's coming
from the very depths of my soul."

"I'm too tired to discuss this now, Katie." He yawned.
"The store was busy all day long, and I'm ready to read the
Bible and relax. We'll go see my *schweschder* in the spring.
That's it. It's decided." He stood. "This discussion is over." He
started for the door.

"Wait." Kathryn stood and took a deep breath. "I'm not
finished."

Turning, he raised his eyebrows.

"You read the letter," she said. "Anna Mae and Kellan
are expecting their first child. They want to rebuild their

relationship with the family for the child's sake." She stepped over to him. "Surely you can understand that."

He frowned. "I've already told you that we'll visit her in the spring. You need to let this go. A Christmas visit is not a good idea. There's nothing else to discuss."

"But David—"

He grimaced. "There's nothing else to discuss, Kathryn." He turned and crossed the room, and Kathryn's resentment simmered in her soul.

Glowering, she snatched the glasses from the table and washed them. David had a knack for deciding when a discussion was over, whether she was finished making her case or not. David had no problem walking away when they'd had a heated debate. He would let it go, not discussing it any further. He would probably be reticent the rest of the evening, but by tomorrow he'd be past it, acting as if the disagreement had never happened. However, Kathryn would hang onto her resentment, mulling the problem over and over again in her mind and thinking of everything she should've said to him to make her case.

She knew tonight would be one of those nights when she'd go to bed and lie awake for hours, probably most of the night. While drying the glasses, she contemplated Anna Mae. Kathryn's heart had swelled at the sound of Anna Mae's voice. She had sounded so hopeful on the phone, so desperate to be reunited with her family.

How could a family reunion at Christmastime be wrong? Wasn't that the best time of year for a family to work out issues and become one again? Besides, Anna Mae was building bridges for her unborn child. Surely David understood that!

David's concern regarding his father's temper was valid. Henry Beiler was a strict bishop who stuck to the rules and expected the district, especially his family, to follow suit.

While Henry was a stickler for the Amish way, he also had a big heart. She'd seen him drop whatever he was doing to help a family in need. He'd organized more than one barn raising, and he had also spent long hours helping Kathryn's father and brothers rebuild the furniture store after it burned down. Kathryn loved and respected her father-in-law, and she believed that deep down he missed his youngest daughter and would be overjoyed to see her come back at Christmas. Why couldn't David see that?

Kathryn placed the clean glasses into the cabinet and squeezed her eyes shut. She wished she knew the right answer. Was inviting Anna Mae to Christmas against her husband's wishes a mistake? Was it a sin to make the plans behind her husband's back? Of course it was, since she'd have to lie to David in order to arrange for Anna Mae to come. Lying was always a sin.

But was not revealing the whole truth a lie?

She rubbed her temples. Of course it was a lie. She'd punished her children more than once for leaving out important details in their stories, telling them they'd lied.

Kathryn folded her hands. She needed a sign. She needed God to reveal the right answer to her.

Gnawing her lower lip, she sent up a silent prayer to God, asking—no pleading with Him—for a sign, a clear-cut sign, that inviting Anna Mae was the right decision for the Beiler family's Christmas.

CHAPTER 4

Saturday morning, Kathryn wiped down the counter in the large, open bakery kitchen. When a flurry of Pennsylvania *Dietsch* floated in from the front of the store, she moved to the doorway and found her mother-in-law, Mary Rose, chatting with her mother and Amanda.

Kathryn approached Mary Rose and hugged her. "*Wie geht's?*"

"*Gut.*" Mary Rose smiled. "How are you?"

"*Gut.* What brings you out here?" Kathryn asked.

"I wanted to see how you all were doing." She glanced toward Elizabeth. "David told me the bakery has been hectic with Englishers coming in for goodies for their Christmas parties. I'm glad to hear the bakery is staying so busy."

"*Ya,* it has been busy. You've come by during a lull today. We had a rush earlier." Elizabeth gestured toward the kitchen. "Can I get you some coffee and a piece of chocolate cake?"

Mary Rose brightened. "That sounds *wunderbaar. Danki.*"

Elizabeth touched Amanda's arm. "Will you help me?"

"*Ya,*" Amanda said, following her into the kitchen.

Kathryn gestured toward one of the small tables across from the counter. "Let's have a seat. It's nice and quiet now, so we can talk for a while." She led Mary Rose to the table. "How's Henry doing?" she asked as she sat.

"Oh, he's *gut*," Mary Rose said, lowering herself into a chair. "He's been busy at the store. I'm sure David has told you that they've had a nonstop stream of customers the past week."

"*Ya*, he has." Kathryn ran her fingers over the cool wooden table. "I'm glad to hear it."

Mary Rose's gaze focused across the room and her smile faded. "Can I tell you something, Kathryn?"

"Of course. *Was iss letz?*"

"Nothing's wrong, but there's something I want to share with you because I know you'll understand." Mary Rose sighed and looked at Kathryn. "Lately, I can't stop thinking about Anna Mae. I've dreamed of her nearly every night the past week. I can't stop worrying about her."

Kathryn cupped her hand to her mouth to squelch the gasp bubbling up from her throat. Was this the sign from God she'd prayed for?

Mary Rose, unaffected by Kathryn's reaction, kept talking. "I want to know how she is. Is she *froh* with her life with Kellan in Baltimore? Does she need anything? Does she miss us? Does she have any *kinner*? If so, will I ever know them?"

"Have you tried to contact her lately?" Kathryn asked, hoping to conceal her shock at Mary Rose's revelation.

Mary Rose shook her head, tears glistening in her brown eyes. "Not since last *Grischtdaag*. She sends me a card with a short letter every year and I send her one in return."

"Have you ever considered inviting her for *Grischtdaag*?" Kathryn bit her lip, hoping Mary Rose would say yes.

Frowning, Mary Rose shook her head. "Henry wouldn't hear of it."

"But we're permitted to see those who are shunned. You know that."

"You know your father-in-law." Mary Rose's voice quavered, and she cleared her throat and wiped her eyes. "He would only agree to see her if she were coming back to make things right with the church. I believe her love for Kellan is strong and she's left the Amish church for good. I just wish I could see her again. No matter what, she's my *dochder*, and I miss her terribly."

Kathryn traced the wood grain on the table. "What if she came to visit you? How do you think Henry would react?"

Mary Rose's expression was pensive. "If Anna Mae were to come here, Henry would have to face her, wouldn't he?" Her expression fell. "But she won't come. After what Henry said to her, she has no reason to come back."

"Unless she misses you as much as you miss her." Kathryn raised her eyebrows in response to Mary Rose's surprised expression.

Elizabeth sidled up to the table balancing a tray of four cups of coffee with Amanda in tow, holding a tray with a chocolate cake, forks, and napkins. While Amanda set out the cake and place settings, Elizabeth added a mug at each setting.

"Enjoy," Elizabeth said as she sat across from Mary Rose.

Mary Rose forked some chocolate cake into her mouth and moaned. "This is *wunderbaar*. *Danki*, Elizabeth."

Kathryn ate a moist piece of cake and sipped the coffee while Elizabeth and Mary Rose discussed the weather, their families, and upcoming holidays. Their conversation was only background noise to the thoughts whirling through her mind. Mary Rose's eyes had spoken volumes of the emotions in her soul for Anna Mae—sadness, regret, love, and worry.

Was this the sign from God that Kathryn had been waiting for?

Yes! Absolutely it was!

The answer was right before Kathryn—she needed to arrange for Anna Mae to visit at Christmas. God was giving her the direction, and she needed to let Him use her to heal the Beiler family.

Kathryn tried her best to appear interested in the idle conversation around her, nodding and smiling at the appropriate times. However, internally, she was swallowing her excitement and anticipation. She couldn't wait to call her friends in Paradise and see if their bed and breakfast was available the week of Christmas.

She needed to be discreet with the plans so David didn't find out before Anna Mae arrived. Because if he did . . .

"Kathryn?" a voice asked.

Kathryn looked up and found her mother-in-law's brown eyes studying her.

"Are you okay?" Mary Rose asked.

"*Ya.*" Kathryn cleared her throat, hoping to appear casual. "I was just thinking about everything I have to do before *Grischtdaag.*" In her peripheral vision, Kathryn spotted her mother giving her a skeptical look. Elizabeth was always a master at reading her children's expressions and their true emotions.

"I reckon I'd better be going," Mary Rose said. "*Danki* for a lovely visit and delicious food." She stood and gathered her dirty mug, fork, and napkin.

Amanda rose and took the items from her and set them on the table. "Just leave it, *Grossmammi*. I'll take care of it." She hugged her. "I'm glad you came to see us."

Mary Rose kissed Amanda's head. "Oh, *danki*, Amanda. You're such a sweet *maedel*." Looping her arm around Amanda's shoulders, they started for the door.

Kathryn followed them to the door. "It was *wunderbaar* to see you, *Mamm*. We'll visit you soon." She gave her a quick hug, and while Amanda and Elizabeth said their goodbyes, Kathryn hurried back to the table and loaded a tray with the dirty forks, mugs, and napkins.

Kathryn was washing the mugs and forks when Elizabeth came up behind her.

"What was really on your mind during Mary Rose's visit?" Elizabeth asked.

Wiping her hands on a rag, Kathryn faced her. "I think God spoke to me today."

Elizabeth raised her eyebrows. "When?"

"While you and Amanda were preparing the cake and coffee, Mary Rose spilled her heart to me, telling me how much she's been thinking of Anna Mae and wishing she could see her and know she was doing well."

Elizabeth gasped. "Oh my."

Kathryn dropped the rag on the counter and grasped Elizabeth's sleeves. "This is the sign I prayed for. I asked God to give me a sign that I'm doing the right thing by helping Anna Mae come for a visit. This was the sign, *Mamm*. He answered me, and I'm going to listen."

Elizabeth smiled. "So it seems that God does bless this visit from Anna Mae."

"I guess so," Kathryn said. "Would you walk out front with me?" She led her mother to the front counter. "Do you think I should make a reservation for them at the Paradise B&B so they have privacy? They may want to get away from the family at night and be alone."

Elizabeth nodded and fished the phone book from the pile of papers on the desk. "That's a great idea. I'll find the number for you." She pointed out the number, and Kathryn's heart pounded as she dialed.

While the phone rang, she hoped David would forgive her for going behind his back and that God would lead the family to a joyous reconciliation in honor of His Son's birth.

On Sunday, Kathryn carried a pitcher of water from her sister-in-law Vera Zook's kitchen to the large family room where the rows of tables were set for the noon meal after the church service. Keeping with tradition, the service had been held in the large room with the moveable walls pushed out in order to accommodate the backless benches for the members of the church district. Families within the district took turns hosting the services every other Sunday during the year. A schedule was set up in advance so that each family would know when it was their turn.

After the four-hour service, the benches were transformed into tables, and the women retired to the kitchen to prepare the food and serve the men first. Each family provided a dish.

Pennsylvania *Dietsch* echoed throughout the room as Kathryn made her way around, refilling cups and nodding to friends and family. Her eyes moved to a small table in the back of the room, off on its own away from the crowd, where an English couple, friends of her sister Beth Anne, sat chatting.

That's where Anna Mae and Kellan would sit—by themselves, away from the family.

The thought came to Kathryn before she could stop it. Her thoughts had been with Anna Mae during the service. Instead of concentrating on the bishop and ministers who had been preaching the Word, Kathryn found herself glancing over toward the English couple sitting in the back, off by themselves, during the service.

If Anna Mae and Kellan were to visit and attend a service, they too would sit alone, away from the family, like strangers —perhaps not strangers, but more like visitors instead of members of the family.

Finding her pitcher empty, Kathryn stepped back into the kitchen where Anna Mae's three sisters, Barbie, Vera, and Fannie, were flittering around the kitchen, preparing to bring out the cakes and cookies for dessert. Kathryn wondered how they would react to seeing their youngest sister again. Would they welcome her with open arms despite the pain of her leaving? Or would they be standoffish, giving her a mere nod and cold greeting when she arrived?

"Kathryn," Vera said, holding out a plate of cookies. "Would you take these out?"

"Of course," Kathryn said, taking the dish. She paused. "Have you heard from Anna Mae lately?"

Vera stopped and her eyes widened with surprise. "No, I haven't heard from her since last Christmas. She always sends me a card. Have you?"

Kathryn nodded. "I have."

"You have?" Vera asked. She turned to her sisters. "Fannie! Barbie! Kathryn's heard from Anna Mae."

The three sisters surrounded Kathryn.

Vera asked, "How is Anna Mae?"

"When did you hear from her?" Fannie demanded.

"Is she happy with that English man?" Barbie chimed in.

"She's doing well," Kathryn said, gripping the plate. "She and Kellan are very happy and are expecting their first baby."

The three sisters gasped and then fired off more questions about Anna Mae's life. Kathryn held up her hand, and they stopped speaking.

"The baby is due in January," Kathryn said. "Anna Mae and Kellan are both doing well. She said she misses the family and would like to reconnect with everyone for the sake of the baby." Kathryn bit her bottom lip, debating how much to share. "She wants to come visit."

"Oh." Barbie frowned. "I don't know how *Daed* would react to that."

Fannie nodded. "Probably not a good idea."

"I think it would be *wunderbaar gut*," Vera said. "When does she want to come?"

"She's still working out the details," Kathryn said.

"She should wait until after the baby is born," Fannie said while Barbie nodded in agreement. "That would help smooth things over with *Daed*."

"*Ya*," Barbie added.

"I disagree," Vera said, touching Kathryn's arm. "Any time would be *gut*. Her visit might be awkward, but it would start to mend some fences."

Kathryn glanced down at the cookies. "I better get these out to the men before they start complaining." She stepped out into the family room with Vera in tow.

"Does Anna Mae want to come soon?" Vera whispered.

Kathryn nodded. "*Ya*. Very soon."

Vera raised her eyebrows in question. "How soon?"

"For Christmas," Kathryn said.

Vera patted her arm. "Tell her to come. *Daed* and my siblings may be against her visit, but it would heal my *mamm's* broken heart."

Kathryn smiled. "I'll do that."

Later that evening, Kathryn waited until David was snoring before she padded downstairs to the kitchen and found her stationery in the drawer. In the light of the gas lantern, she wrote a letter to Anna Mae, outlining the plans for her trip. After signing it, she sealed it in the envelope and addressed it. She then placed it in the pocket of her apron hanging on the peg in the kitchen and tiptoed up to bed.

As she snuggled down under the covers next to David, Kathryn whispered a prayer to God, telling Him that she hoped she was honoring His wishes and asking Him to use her as He saw fit to bring the Beiler family back together for Christmas.

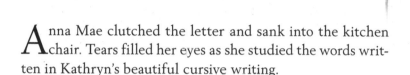

CHAPTER 5

Anna Mae clutched the letter and sank into the kitchen chair. Tears filled her eyes as she studied the words written in Kathryn's beautiful cursive writing.

Dear Anna Mae,

    I hope this letter finds you and Kellan well. Please know you're in my daily prayers.

    As I'm writing to you, my heart is filled with excitement. After we talked last week I prayed and asked God to show me a sign that I was doing His will by helping you plan a trip here for Christmas. The next day I received the message from God that I'd been hoping for when your mamm came to visit me at the bakery.

    Anna Mae, your mamm shared with me that you've been on her mind and in her heart for some time now. She said she thinks of you constantly, wondering if you're gut and froh with your life in Baltimore. She shared with me that she would love to see you, and I know that's what God would want.

    Today I attended church at your sister Vera's home, and I spoke to her about your possible visit. Vera was

excited and told me that having you visit would be a
wunderbaar way to help bring the family back together.
She said that while the visit may be strained at first,
having you here would begin to mend fences.

I've arranged for you and Kellan to stay at the
Paradise Inn Bed and Breakfast from December 22–24,
checking out on Christmas morning. You are welcome
to have dinner with us that first night, and from there
we will make arrangements to see the rest of the family.
Please let me know if that will be convenient for you.

I'm keeping your visit a secret. Only my mamm
Amanda, and Vera know that you're planning to come,
and we'll keep it to ourselves until you get here. As I said
above, I know that your initial arrival may be awkward,
but I'll be by your side to help work through that. Once
your parents see you and find out that you're expecting
a baby, they will be willing to work things out in order to
have you, Kellan, and the baby in their life.

I can't wait to hug you and talk to you in person.

In His Name,
Kathryn

She reread the letter and sniffed, tears flowing from her eyes.

"Annie?" Kellan crossed the kitchen and crouched beside her chair. "Honey, what's wrong?" He wiped tears from her hot cheeks with the tip of his finger.

"*Mamm* misses me," she whispered, holding out the letter to him. "She misses me like I miss her. And my sister Vera wants to see me too. I miss my sisters so much."

While he read the letter, Anna Mae rubbed her abdomen and lost herself in memories of her family—the delicious smell of freshly baked bread in her mother's kitchen, the roar of her brother and cousins roughhousing in the yard, the *clip-clop* of horses coming up the lane with buggies packed with visitors. She wanted her child to experience all of that—all she loved and missed about being Amish.

Kellan met her gaze and kissed her cheek. "I'm so happy for you. I hope this visit gives you the peace and love you need from your family. If God sent Kathryn a sign, He is also sending us a sign that we need to go."

"Thank you! I'm so glad you agree!" She wrapped her arms around his neck, and he shifted his weight and chuckled.

"You're going to sweep me off my feet again, Annie." He took her hands in his and smiled. "You nearly knocked me over."

"I'm going to write her back tonight and tell her that we'll be there on the twenty-second." She hoisted herself from the chair and crossed the kitchen. "I only have a couple weeks until we go. I have so much to do." She fished a notepad and pen from a drawer and began a list. "We'll have to bring gifts for all of the children. I'm not quite sure what, though." She jotted down ideas for gifts, including candies and small toys.

"Gifts for all of the kids?" Kellan stood behind her. "How can we buy for all your relatives, Annie? Aren't there hundreds of kids now?"

Glancing up, she laughed. "I don't expect hundreds, but, yes, there are many children in the Beiler family. And I'll bring them little gifts, like candy and small toys. Don't worry; I won't break our budget. I'll visit the Dollar Mart in town after my quilting circle meeting." She jotted a few more things down on the list and then looked up. "Maybe we can run to the store tonight after supper. I think they're open late, and I'll need your help with the bags."

A smile spread across his lips. "I have an idea. How about we go to our favorite steak place and then go shopping?"

"Steak and shrimp?" She glanced down at her abdomen. "How does that sound, Butterbean?"

"Butterbean?" Kellan raised an eyebrow.

"I thought it was a cuter name than Lug Nut. I think Lug Nut sounds like a boy, and Butterbean could be a boy or a girl." She rubbed her belly. "Let me get my purse and we can head out." She kissed his cheek on her way to the hall.

Her heart skipped a beat as she thought of seeing her family again. She couldn't wait to hug her mother, Kathryn, and her sisters. And she hoped her father would be happy to see her too.

Thursday evening, Kathryn slipped the letter into her apron pocket and pulled plates from the cabinet in preparation for supper. A smile turned up the corners of her lips as she placed a bag of rolls onto the table. In less than two weeks, she would see her sister-in-law for the first time in three years, and her visit would bring the Beiler family together once again. The plan would come together solely due to Kathryn's efforts. If she were a proud person, Kathryn would gloat.

The letter outlined Anna Mae's plans. She and Kellan would check in at the Paradise B&B the afternoon of Wednesday, December 22, and have dinner with Kathryn and her family that night. Depending on how they were received, they would stay till Christmas, visiting and reconnecting with family and friends.

Kathryn's smile deepened. Mary Rose, Vera, and some of the other relatives would be ecstatic when they saw Anna Mae, and they would have Kathryn to thank for it.

But how would David feel about her going against his wishes? Would he feel betrayed? Her smile transformed to a frown, for she knew the answer to those questions. David hadn't mentioned Anna Mae since their last strained conversation. He would certainly be angry when Anna Mae arrived at their home, but she believed in her heart that he would forgive her soon after seeing his sister.

The back door squeaked open, revealing David entering the kitchen. He crossed the room to the sink and washed his hands. "The *kinner* are on their way in from the barn."

"I bet they're hungry," she said, placing a block of cheese on the table. She then grabbed a pot of soup from the stove. "I made some chicken noodle soup. It's cold out there, *ya?*"

"*Ya,*" he said, drying his hands. "It's hard to believe *Grischtdaag* is only a few weeks away. The boys were just discussing what gifts they hope to find on the table Christmas morning. It feels like only yesterday it was summer. Where did the year go?"

"I don't know." Kathryn grabbed a stack of bowls. "It seems like the years pass by quicker, the older we get." She yanked open the drawer and reached for a handful of spoons and then placed the bowls and utensils on the table.

He snickered. "*Ya.* Some days I feel eighty instead of almost forty." Stopping her on her way back to the table, he pulled her into his arms and brushed his lips across hers, sending her stomach into a wild swirl. "But then you make me feel young again."

Kathryn wrapped her arms around his neck and inhaled his scent, earth mixed with soap. "*Ich liebe dich*, David." *And please forgive me for planning your sister's visit behind your back.*

He took her face in his hands and his eyes were full of love. "Katie, I thank God for you and our *kinner* every day. This year I'm most thankful for you and our life together."

She swallowed as the guilt of her secrecy rained down on her, then forced a smile. "*Danki.* I thank God for you daily too." *And I hope you'll still trust me after Anna Mae's visit.*

His eyes studied hers. "You all right?"

"*Ya.*" She turned toward the counter. "I was just thinking about everything I need to do before *Grischtdaag*. I must get to the market. I'll need to see if Nina Janitz can take me shopping." She rooted around in a drawer in search of a notepad and a pencil. "I have to make a list."

"Katie." David took her hands in his. "Look at me."

She met his gaze, her heart pounding with a mixture of guilt and anxiety. "*Ya?*"

He traced her face, from forehead to chin, with his fingertip. "*Was iss letz, mei liewe?*"

"Nothing's wrong," she said, her voice quavering.

His brown eyes continued to probe hers, and her mouth dried. How was it that he could read her so well? She searched for something to say to change the subject.

"I wonder what's taking the *kinner* so long," she said. "Should you go check on them? Amanda and Lizzie are upstairs working on a sewing project. I'll go call them again." She started for the stairs, and he took her arm and pulled her back.

"Wait," he said, looking concerned. "If something is bothering you, you can tell me. There should be no secrets between a man and his *fraa*."

She sighed. She had to tell him the truth, and now was the appropriate time. "David, I just wish you would reconsider your thoughts on Anna Mae's visit."

His concerned look transformed to a grimace. "I told you that this subject was closed. We'll go visit her in the spring. Now, please drop it."

She scowled. "Why can't we discuss it? Why must you tell me when the subject is closed without my input?"

He raised his hand to his temple, pinching his forehead. "I'm tired of having this argument, Kathryn."

She jammed her hands on her hips. "I am too. I want you to listen to me. I think it's a *gut* idea. Christmas is the best time for a family reunion. Why can't you even consider it?"

He gritted his teeth. "Because I know how painful it will be for my parents, and I don't want to ruin Christmas for them. It would be more appropriate if we waited until spring to visit Anna Mae and Kellan. Once we visit with them, then we can pave the way for my parents to see them. I know what's best for my family, Kathryn."

"You do?"

"*Mamm? Daed?*" a little voice asked. "Why are you fighting?"

Kathryn turned to find Lizzie standing in the doorway, her brown eyes wide with fear. Amanda moved up behind her and placed her hand on Lizzie's shoulder, and Kathryn's heart sank. She'd managed to scare her daughter by arguing with David.

"Everything's fine," Kathryn said. "Dinner is ready."

The back door opened and slammed with a bang, and David Jr., Manny, and Ruthie marched into the kitchen, chattering away about Christmas and what toys they hoped to receive while hanging their wraps and coats on the pegs.

"Wash up, please," Kathryn said, feeling David's eyes boring into her. Ignoring his stare, she brought a pitcher of water to the table. "Did you and Lizzie finish that dress you were working on?" she asked Amanda.

"We're almost done," Amanda said, placing cups at each table setting while Lizzie distributed the plates and bowls. "Lizzie is doing a *wunderbaar* job. She'll be making her own dresses soon."

David glared up at Kathryn while she poured water into his cup and she averted her eyes by concentrating on not spilling. Once the table was set, Kathryn sat between Amanda and Lizzie while the rest of the children took their spot at the table. David gave her one last hard look before bowing his head in silent prayer. A chill of worry coursed through her.

Kathryn bowed her head. She thanked God for the wonderful blessings of her family and home and then she asked Him to guide Anna Mae's visit. She prayed the Lord would open her father-in-law's heart so he would welcome Anna Mae and Kellan home to Lancaster County.

But most of all, she prayed that David would forgive her and understand why she defied his wishes and helped plan Anna Mae's trip.

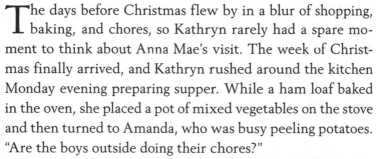

CHAPTER 6

The days before Christmas flew by in a blur of shopping, baking, and chores, so Kathryn rarely had a spare moment to think about Anna Mae's visit. The week of Christmas finally arrived, and Kathryn rushed around the kitchen Monday evening preparing supper. While a ham loaf baked in the oven, she placed a pot of mixed vegetables on the stove and then turned to Amanda, who was busy peeling potatoes. "Are the boys outside doing their chores?"

"*Ya*. Lizzie and Ruthie are upstairs cleaning our room," Amanda said, her pretty face scowling. "*Mamm*, I wanted to speak with you about something in private."

Kathryn raised her eyebrows with curiosity while wiping her hands on a towel. "What's on your mind?"

Amanda glanced across the kitchen. "I don't want anyone to hear us."

"You just said that the boys were outside and your sisters are upstairs, so I'm certain we're alone." Kathryn leaned against the counter. "*Was iss letz?*"

Amanda glanced back toward the door. "Let's go into the *schtupp*."

Kathryn followed her into the family room and stood near the doorway. "What's bothering you?"

Amanda lowered her slight body onto the sofa.

"I'm worried about what's going to happen this week." Amanda wrung her hands. "*Daed* might get really angry that *Aenti* Anna Mae is coming."

Kathryn smiled. "Everything will be fine once he sees his sister. Trust me." A door closed, and Kathryn assumed the boys had come in from the barn.

"But he should know the truth." Amanda's eyes were full of determination.

"*Ya*, you're right." Kathryn nodded. "He'll know the truth soon enough. It's going to be a surprise."

"I think you're wrong not to tell him. I feel like I'm holding in a horrible lie by not telling *Daed*, and lying is a sin." Amanda shook her head. "I think *Daed* has a right to know that *Aenti* Anna Mae is coming—" She stopped speaking and her eyes grew wide while her cheeks flushed a deep rose.

"What did you say, Amanda Joy?" David's gruff voice rumbled from behind Kathryn, causing her to jump.

Kathryn spun around and her mouth dried. David was glowering at her from the doorway.

"What did Amanda say about *mei schweschder*?" he asked, his brown eyes slicing through her with indignation.

Kathryn inwardly shuddered. Feigning indifference, she kept her expression serene. "She was discussing when our company would arrive," she said, standing up straighter and mustering all of the courage she could find inside herself. "Amanda was telling me that she thinks you have a right to know that Anna Mae and Kellan are going to join us for

Christmas this year." The truth was now out in the open. She felt a mixture of relief and anxiety at the opportunity to finally say the words out loud.

David's expression hardened. "Kathryn, how many times do we have to discuss this?" His voice was low and full of frustration and fury. "I've already told you that I am against this visit. I can't think of how I could make it more clear to you."

"You've made yourself perfectly clear. However, the plans have been made." She looked at Amanda, who was studying her hands in her lap. "Amanda, our company will arrive sometime Wednesday afternoon."

Amanda met her gaze with a worried expression, and Kathryn smiled, hoping to calm her. Ruthie and Lizzie entered the family room with wide smiles on their faces.

"Company?" Ruthie asked.

"Who's coming?" Lizzie chimed in.

"Your *Aenti* Anna Mae and *Onkel* Kellan from Baltimore are coming to spend Christmas with us," Kathryn said, ignoring the feel of David's angry stare boring into her. "*Aenti* Anna Mae is your *dat's* youngest *schweschder.*"

"The one who was shunned?" Ruthie asked.

"*Ya.*" Kathryn nodded. "That's right."

"Are they staying here?" Lizzie asked while sinking down onto the sofa next to Amanda.

"They can sleep in my bed with me," Ruthie said, walking over to Kathryn.

Kathryn smiled. "That's very thoughtful, Ruthie, but they're staying at a bed and breakfast in Paradise."

"But we'll see them, *ya*?" Ruthie asked.

"*Ya*, we will see them," Kathryn said. She pushed a lock of hair back from where it had fallen from beneath her prayer *kapp* while avoiding David's eyes. "They'll be visiting for a few days."

"Kathryn," David said, his calmness forced. "Kathryn, please look at me."

"*Ya*." She turned to him, finding disappointment and hurt reflecting in his eyes. Guilt and determination battled inside her. While she knew keeping the information from him was wrong, she was certain she was doing God's will. God was using her to heal the family, and David needed to understand that.

His frown deepened. "We will discuss this later at length."

Kathryn nodded while forcing a smile. "I'm certain we will."

"Call me when supper is ready," David said, stomping through the family room toward the stairs.

Kathryn glanced at Lizzie. "Would you and Ruthie please set the table?" While her two younger daughters headed for the kitchen, she turned to Amanda. "Now he knows."

Amanda nodded, her cheeks still glowing red. "He was very angry. I made it worse, didn't I?"

Kathryn shook her head. "No, you didn't make it worse, but this wasn't the way I wanted him to find out."

Amanda's lower lip quivered, and her eyes filled with tears. "I'm sorry, *Mamm*."

Kathryn touched Amanda's arm. "You didn't do anything wrong. You were right to talk to me about it if it bothered you."

"I didn't know he was standing there until it was too late,"

Amanda said with a sniff. "He must've come in quietly and heard us talking."

"I'm certain he did." Kathryn gestured toward the door. "Come help me make the dumplings. The ham loaf smells like it's almost done."

Amanda stood and walked with her toward the kitchen. Kathryn was certain that David would be quiet during supper and leave the discussion of Anna Mae's visit for bedtime. Dread filled Kathryn at the thought of facing him. She hoped David would understand why she'd gone against his wishes.

Kathryn ran a brush through her waist-length hair and studied her reflection. Clad in her nightgown, she glanced toward the door for the fourth time. The clock on the wall told her it was nearly nine, David's daily bedtime.

He'd barely spoken to her during supper and had only given terse answers to her lame attempts at fostering a conversation. Instead of conversing with her, he'd spoken to the children about their day. After supper, David had disappeared outside with Junior, which they often did in the evenings. However, she'd heard Junior come back into the house and disappear into his room awhile ago, but she'd not seen David.

Stepping over to the window, she moved the dark green shade and peeked outside. The barn and backfield were dark with no sign of a lantern.

The bedroom door squeaked open and banged shut, and Kathryn jumped with a start.

"Sorry," David mumbled, scowling. "I didn't mean to

slam it." He stepped over to his bureau and pulled off his suspenders.

Her heart pounded as she sat on the edge of the bed. "Where were you?"

"In the barn," he muttered, shucking off his shirt.

She pushed an errant lock of golden blonde hair behind her shoulder. "What were you doing in the barn?"

"Thinking." He changed into his pajama pants. "Actually, trying to figure something out."

The tension between them was suffocating her. She had to apologize to him and make things right. She took a deep breath. "David, I—"

"Would you like to know what I was trying to figure out?"

"David, please—"

He stood before her and held a hand up to keep her from talking. "Let me finish."

Knowing she wasn't going to earn a chance to speak her mind, Kathryn crossed her arms in front of her chest. "Go on."

"I was trying to figure out why you would go behind my back and do something I'd asked you not to do, especially after we'd discussed it several times." Still glowering, he pulled up a chair and sat before her. "I'd asked you not to invite Anna Mae. I told you, no I *promised* you, that we would visit her this spring. I also said that once we visited her and Kellan, we would make plans for her to come back to the community to visit the family. From what I remember, you said that would be a *gut* plan."

Kathryn opened her mouth to defend herself, and he again held up his hand to stop her.

"Please let me finish." He sat up straight. "What I've been trying to figure out is why you went against my wishes. What makes it even worse is that you not only broke a promise and went behind my back, but you involved our *kinner* in your lies." He shook his head, disappointment clouding his handsome face. "What hurts the most is that you lied. In our fifteen years of marriage, I never once lied to you or went behind your back. You've always been the one person I've trusted most, the one I knew I could count on."

Shaking his head, he paused. "Now, I'm trying to figure out who you are. The *maedel* I married would have never lied to me, not like this. You knew how serious I was about this and how much I was against inviting Anna Mae home during the holidays. This is going to cause a huge blowup with my *daed*, and I'm not prepared to deal with that."

The knot forming in her throat choked off her words for a moment. She cleared her throat before she tried to speak again. "David, I've never lied to you before," she began, her voice trembling with guilt. "You're the most important person in my life, aside from our *kinner*. You know that and you know me." She pointed to her chest. "You know my heart."

"But we talked about it over and over again. I told you more than once that it was not a *gut* plan. We decided that we would wait until spring. Why did you go back on your word?"

"I never agreed to spring." She reached for him, and he stood, backing away from her touch. "David, will you let me explain?"

Folding his arms, he leaned back against the wall and scowled. "I'm listening."

She stood in front of him. "I know in my heart that what I'm doing is right. It's God's will that Anna Mae and Kellan are coming here." She took his hand in hers. "God spoke to me."

He raised an eyebrow with curiosity. "What do you mean?"

"I prayed about it and asked Him to give me a sign." Hot tears spilled from her eyes. "The very next day, your *mamm* came to the bakery and told me she's been thinking of Anna Mae and Kellan and wondering how they're doing. She was near tears and said she longed to see Anna Mae again. She said she had to know if Anna Mae was happy with her life with Kellan." She squeezed his hand. "That was the sign from God I needed. That was how I knew what I was doing was right."

He considered her words and his frown deepened. "A sign from God?" He snorted with disbelief. "I don't know about that, Kathryn. God has a plan, and it's His plan. He doesn't need to send us signs."

"*Ya*, He does! You have to believe me. I never meant to hurt you and I don't want to ever lose your trust in me." More tears splattered her cheeks. "Can't you see that? Can't you see I did this for you and our family? This is what God wants me to do."

"I don't believe God has to send us signs for us to do His work. His rules for how we should live our lives are contained in the Bible. Whether you believe He sent a sign or not doesn't matter. You deliberately went against my wishes, and I'm angry and hurt." His expression remained hard as stone. "Why did you keep your secret from me?"

"I followed my heart because I didn't want you to talk me out of it. I wanted to do it, no matter what you said." She cleared her throat. "I wanted to do it for Mary Rose. I can't imagine how I would feel if one of our *kinner* had moved away and left the community. I would worry about her too. Your *mamm* has a right to meet her future grandchild."

He shook his head. "That's not for you to decide. Now Christmas is going to be a disaster."

"That's not true." Kathryn wiped her tears. "Vera agrees that this visit is a good idea too. She thinks it'll be good for your parents."

His eyes widened. "You told Vera?" He frowned. "Who else have you told?"

"My mother knows too," she whispered.

He threw his hands up. "Why don't you just paint a sign on the side of the barn so that the whole district knows!"

"David," she hissed. "You're going to wake the *kinner*!"

"Why not tell them too?" he continued, his voice booming off the walls. "The rest of the district already knows." He started toward the door. "I'll go tell my father now."

"David!" Kathryn rushed after him and pulled him back. "Now you're acting *narrisch*!"

"I'm *narrisch*?" He snorted with sarcasm. "I'm not seeing signs from God involving everyone but my spouse in secret plans." He shook his head. "I especially don't like that you involved Amanda. I don't want you to teach our *dochdern* to defy their future husbands."

Kathryn shook her head. He didn't comprehend her motive, and she couldn't think of anything else to say to try to get through to him. "You don't understand why I did this at all, do you?"

"No, I don't." He folded his arms across his wide chest. "What will this visit entail? I know she's arriving Wednesday and staying in Paradise. What else have you planned without my knowledge?"

"We're hosting them for supper Wednesday. Thursday night we'll also invite your parents."

He raised an eyebrow. "I'm sure your mother supports all of this."

"She also believes it's God's will for our family to heal." She reached for his arm, but he stepped away from her touch. "I truly believe that, David. That's why I did it. My best intentions were for our family. I didn't want to cause you to be upset with me."

"You know my *daed*." He frowned. "He won't be as *eiferich* as the rest of the Beilers."

"We can all pray for his heart to be opened and warmed by the sight of his youngest *dochder* and his future grandchild."

"This is going to be a huge mistake." He shook his head and started for the door.

"Where are you going?" she asked.

"Downstairs to read my Bible and think," he said.

"But it's after nine," she said.

"I'm not ready to sleep. You go ahead to bed," he said.

She watched him disappear into the hallway and close the door behind him. Sighing, she climbed into bed. For the first time in their sixteen years of marriage, she was going to bed alone. Ironically, Kathryn's plans for bringing the family together had seemed to tear David and her apart. Tears filled her eyes at the thought of the chasm she'd put between herself and her husband.

Shivering, she pulled the quilt up to her chin and closed her eyes, hoping somehow Christmas would turn out better than David expected.

CHAPTER 7

Anna Mae's stomach fluttered as their burgundy Chevrolet Equinox took another winding hill. She gripped the door handle as more snow flurries peppered the windshield.

"You okay?" Kellan reached over and covered her hand with his warm palm.

"Don't you think you should slow down?" she asked. "The snow is picking up."

"We're fine," he said with a confident smile. "I know how to drive in snow. You forget I went to college in Maine. This is nothing compared to the blizzards I saw up there."

"I hear it's going to snow most of the week and may be pretty bad on Christmas." Anna Mae turned to him. "Now, you remember that Amish Christmases are different from English Christmases. They don't put up a tree or include Santa. They may do a little bit of decorating with poinsettias and candles, but you won't see any Christmas lights. To the Amish, it's more about family and Jesus' birth, not Santa and gifts."

Kellan nodded. "I remember that. You've explained it to me before."

"And they have First Christmas and Second Christmas,"

she reminisced. "In our family, we received our gifts on Christmas morning. My mother set up the table especially for the kids, and it was called the Christmas table. She put our names by each place setting and placed our gifts on the plate. We visited our extended family on Second Christmas, which was the twenty-sixth, and shared a huge meal. It was so much fun playing with all of our cousins. My grandparents would give each of us a little gift, like candy."

"Sounds like a lot of visiting," Kellan commented.

Anna Mae laughed. "Since Amish families are so large, they have lots of get-togethers. Some have their Christmas dinners as early as Thanksgiving." She shifted in the seat and a sharp pain radiated through her abdomen, causing her to suck in a breath.

"Are you all right?" Kellan's voice was full of alarm.

Anna Mae took short, quick breaths until the discomfort subsided. "I'm fine. Thank you." She heaved a sigh of relief. "It's gone now. No worries." She smiled, in spite of his distressed expression.

"I was concerned about your traveling this close to the due date," he said, his eyes trained on the road. "The doctor said the risk of preterm labor or complications goes up after week thirty."

Anna Mae rubbed her abdomen. "Yes, but she gave us permission to go on this trip since we're within ninety miles of her office. We're only about eighty miles from home, so if something should happen, we can get back to the hospital quickly. I'm sure we'll be fine."

He negotiated another sharp turn. "Promise me that you'll tell me if you start feeling different or if the pain becomes more frequent. I'll get you to Lancaster General in the blink of an eye."

She settled back in the seat. "I'm sure that won't be necessary, but I promise I will. I think Butterbean has several weeks before she decides to make her entrance into the world."

The SUV rounded another corner and a brick colonial home came into view. A large sign with the words "Paradise Bed & Breakfast" stood by the sweeping enclosed porch facing the road. A cobblestone pathway led from the sidewalk to the front door. White Christmas lights outlined the home, and a tree decorated with silver and blue ornaments and white lights sat by a large window in the enclosed porch.

Kellan steered into the gravel parking area next to the house and nosed the SUV up to the wall. "Here we are," he said. "It was nice of them to agree to an early check-in. We'll get rid of our luggage and then we can do whatever you'd like. This is your trip, Annie."

He climbed from the truck and then came around to her side of the vehicle. Opening her door, he offered his hand.

"I'm fine," she said, struggling to hoist herself from the seat.

"Are you?" He laughed and took her hand. Lifting her up, he smirked. "Now you're fine."

She gave him a mock glare. "I could've done it myself."

"And how long would that have taken you? I don't have that kind of time. The reservation is only for three nights." His grin was wicked.

"Ha, ha," she muttered. Glancing down, she spotted her purse on the floorboard of the SUV and swallowed a groan.

"I'll get it." He handed her the purse, then kissed her cheek. "Go on inside. I'll get the bags."

Anna Mae schlepped up the cobblestone path, silently wishing she'd worn her boots instead of these stupid, uncomfortable loafers that had become too tight in the last week. It seemed everything was too tight, even her maternity clothes. She quickly changed her mind about her due date and hoped Butterbean would make his or her appearance soon. However, she did hope it wasn't *too* soon.

The tiny flakes of snow kissed her warm cheeks, and she inhaled the moist air. It smelled like home. She smiled to herself. Three years had been too long to stay away.

Kellan weaved past her with a bag over his shoulder and a suitcase trailing behind him, the wheels scraping the cobblestones. He held the door open, and Anna Mae stepped into a hallway lined with a steep staircase, loveseat, and bookshelves. Kellan directed Anna Mae to the loveseat and set the luggage down next to her before stepping into the kitchen and greeting the bed and breakfast owners.

The older couple led Kellan and Anna Mae to a large bedroom located off the hallway, and Anna Mae was thankful to not have to climb the long staircase.

While Anna Mae freshened up, Kellan brought in the rest of their luggage. Once they were settled in the room, Kellan took Anna Mae's hand and led her back to the SUV, where he helped her climb in.

Kellan hopped into the driver's seat and fastened his safety belt. "So, where are we going?" he asked, turning the key and bringing the engine back to life with a purr.

"Let's head toward Bird-in-Hand," she said, her heart thumping at the thought.

He grinned. "To the site where I first laid eyes on your beautiful face?"

She nodded.

"I still remember the way." He put the SUV in reverse and backed out of the parking space. He then steered it toward the main road.

They rode in silence with the only sound coming from the quiet hum of the engine, the occasional whisper of windshield wipers clearing away the flurries, and the Christmas music singing softly through the speakers.

Anna Mae stared out the window while memories danced through her mind. Excitement and anxiety coursed through her while they drove.

As they turned onto Gibbons Road, her heart raced. Soon she would see her sister-in-law for the first time in three years. Would their reunion be as wonderful as she'd dreamed? What if she felt awkward and out of place? What if they had nothing to discuss and they merely stood in silence, studying each other and thinking of how different they had become?

She said a silent prayer that her family would welcome her and be happy to see her.

Kellan's warm hand covered hers. "It'll be fine, Annie. They'll be so happy to see you that they'll all cry. You'll see."

She squeezed his hand. "You always seem to read my mind."

He lifted her hand to his lips and kissed it. "That's my job, dear." He nodded toward the windshield. "Here we are."

Anna Mae's stomach flip-flopped as they pulled into the parking lot of the bakery. It looked just as she remembered. The large white clapboard farmhouse sat near the road and included a sweeping wraparound porch. A sign with "Kauffman Amish Bakery" in old-fashioned letters hung above the door.

Out behind the building was a fenced-in play area where in the warmer months the Kauffman grandchildren would run around, play tag, and climb on a huge wooden swing set. Beyond it was a fenced pasture dotted with patches of snow. A few of the large Kauffman family farmhouses and barns were set back beyond the pasture. The dirt road leading to the other homes was roped off with a sign declaring "Private Property—No Trespassing."

A large paved parking lot sat adjacent to the building. Kellan steered the SUV into a parking space near the entrance of the bakery and put the truck in park. He then pulled the keys from the ignition and faced Anna Mae.

"Ready?" he asked.

Anna Mae sucked in a deep breath, her heart pounding against her ribcage. "I guess I'm as ready as I'll ever be." She gripped the door handle.

"Hey." Kellan touched her shoulder, and she faced him. "Don't forget what I told you before we came here. No matter what happens with your family, I'll always love you. What matters is that we have each other." He touched her belly. "We're a family whether your father accepts you back or not."

She touched his face. "Thank you for bringing me here. I couldn't do it without you."

He kissed her hand. "You're stronger than you think,

Annie." He squeezed her hand. "Let's go in. I'm sure the Kauffmans are anxious to see you."

Anna Mae grasped Kellan's hand as they made their way through the swirling snow flurries to the front door of the bakery.

Her pulse quickened when he opened the door, and the little bell chimed, announcing their arrival. She breathed in the delicious scents of freshly baked bread and chocolate. She glanced around the bakery, which looked just as it had three years ago, with the long counter filled with pastries and the array of shelves and displays packed with Amish Country souvenirs. A half-dozen small tables, each with four chairs, sat by the window, welcoming tourists to sit and enjoy their pastries.

She spotted Kathryn, Elizabeth, and a pretty teenager who resembled Kathryn standing by the counter.

"Anna Mae!" Kathryn cried, meeting her gaze. Kathryn looked exactly as Anna Mae recalled. She had the same golden blonde hair pulled tight in a bun under her prayer covering. Her eyes were still a deep shade of powder blue, and her skin was as clear and porcelain as a doll. She rushed across the bakery with her mother and the girl in tow and engulfed Anna Mae in her arms.

Anna Mae held onto her sister-in-law as tears spilled from her eyes. She inhaled Kathryn's scent—lilac mixed with cinnamon—and smiled.

Stepping back from the hug, Kathryn studied Anna Mae. "Let me look at you. You're still *schee*." She gestured to Anna Mae's stomach. "You look *wunderbaar*!" She turned to Elizabeth. "*Mamm*, doesn't she look lovely?"

The three women began prattling away in Pennsylvania *Dietsch*, and Anna Mae looked between them, trying to resurrect her fluency. The words clicked through her mind, and she suddenly felt as if she'd never left. Her first language fit like her favorite winter gloves. She answered in *Dietsch* their questions about how her trip had gone.

Anna Mae looked at the girl. "Amanda," she said. "You're so *schee*. You look just like your *mamm*!"

"*Danki*," Amanda said.

Anna Mae took Kellan's hand and pulled him to her side. "You'll have to speak English for Kellan. We don't speak *Dietsch* at home."

Kathryn and Elizabeth exchanged smiles.

Anna Mae nodded toward them. "Kellan, you remember Kathryn, Elizabeth, and Amanda, right?"

He shook their hands. "It's so good to see you again. You all look well."

Elizabeth smiled. "I can tell you're taking good care of Anna Mae. Thank you."

Anna Mae hugged Elizabeth and then Amanda.

"You're all grown up," Anna Mae said to Amanda. "I bet you don't even remember me."

"Of course I remember you, *Aenti* Anna Mae," her niece said. "You're the *aenti* who used to play dolls with me when I stayed at *grossmammi's* house."

"That's right." Anna Mae touched her shoulder. "I'm glad you remember that."

"Let's all sit down and visit." Elizabeth pointed toward a table with chairs on the other side of the bakery. "Amanda and I will grab some drinks and snacks."

Looping her arm around Anna Mae's shoulders, Kathryn steered her toward the table. "Does the bakery look the same to you?"

"Oh yes," Anna Mae said, scanning the shelves of pastries and mementos. "I feel as if I never left."

"Do you miss it?" Kellan asked.

Anna Mae shrugged. "It's hard to say. I do, but I don't. I don't regret leaving, but I do miss my family." She smiled up at Kathryn, who squeezed her shoulder.

"We miss you too." She gestured toward the chairs. "Please sit. I want to hear all about the *boppli*. Do you know if you're having a boy or a girl?"

Anna Mae shook her head. "No, we decided we want to be surprised. Kellan is sure we're having a boy, but I think there's a possibility it may be a girl."

"When are you due?" Kathryn asked.

"January fifteen," Anna Mae said, sinking into the chair. "But some days it feels sooner."

"Oh?" Kathryn raised her eyebrows. "Was it smart for you to travel so close to your due date?"

"See?" Kellan tapped the table. "I'm not the only one who is concerned about you, Annie."

Anna Mae frowned at Kathryn. "Don't encourage him. He worries too much."

"That's my job." Kellan slipped off his coat. "Do you need help taking off your wrap?"

"No, I'm fine, thank you." Anna Mae pulled off her cloak. "To answer your question, the doctor gave me permission to travel. I shouldn't have any problems, and we're only about eighty miles from home. If something were to happen, we can get back to the hospital quickly." She glanced at Kathryn, who was smiling. "What is it?"

"You're glowing, Anna Mae." Reaching over, Kathryn squeezed her hand. "You look so *wunderbaar*, so *froh*. Your *mamm* is going to be thrilled. Tell me all about your life in Baltimore."

Anna Mae shared stories about the car dealership and her quilting ministry at church. Soon, Elizabeth and Amanda joined them with mugs of hot chocolate and cookies. Anna Mae enjoyed the warm cookies while Kathryn, Elizabeth, and Amanda filled Anna Mae and Kellan in on the latest community news.

When Anna Mae yawned, Kellan rubbed her shoulder. "I think you've had too much excitement. We should go back to the room, so you can rest before dinner." He nodded toward her belly. "He needs his rest too, you know."

Anna Mae shook her head. "You coddle me too much."

"Enjoy it now," Kathryn said with a laugh. "The focus will be on the baby once he's here."

"I'm sure that's how it will be." Anna Mae turned to Kellan. "A nap sounds like a wonderful idea. I am tired from the trip."

"I hope you can still join us for dinner," Kathryn said. "Tonight you can see our family before you visit with everyone else. David will be so anxious to see you, and the *kinner* are excited too."

"Do David and the *kinner* know we're here?" Anna Mae asked.

Amanda frowned. "He overheard my *mamm* and me talking about your visit Monday night. I didn't mean for him to hear, but at the same time, I felt like he needed to know."

"It's okay." Anna Mae smiled and then turned to Kathryn. "Is David okay with it? The visit, I mean."

Kathryn gave a slight shrug. "He was upset at first when he found out I'd planned it without his consent. He's concerned that your parents aren't going to take it well, but I believe that this visit is going to heal some family wounds." Reaching over, she touched Anna Mae's hand. "I think it will go just fine."

"Do my parents know we're here?" Anna Mae asked, praying that they were happy if they did know.

Kathryn shook her head. "No, but my family and Vera know. Before we try to see the rest of the family, we thought it best that you see how things go with *Daed* first."

"That's a good plan, but I would like to try to see my sisters too." Anna Mae turned to Kellan. "I guess we'll head back to the bed and breakfast for now."

"Sounds good." He looked at Kathryn. "What time should we be at your house for supper?"

"Five o'clock." Kathryn stood. "Does that sound *gut*?"

"Sounds fine. Can we bring anything?" he asked.

Kathryn waved off the question. "Don't be silly. We'll have plenty to eat. You just be sure Anna Mae takes a *gut* nap so she can enjoy our company."

"I'll get a good rest. Don't you worry about that." Anna took Kathryn's hands in hers. "Thank you for everything. It's so good to be here with you again. It's been too long."

"*Ya*, it has." Kathryn hugged her. "I look forward to seeing you in a few hours."

"Me too." Anna Mae took Kellan's hand and started for the door. "We'll see you later."

"You rest up now," Kathryn called. "I don't want you in the hospital while you're here."

"I will," Anna Mae promised. Stepping outside, she noticed that the snow flurries had picked up.

Kellan hooked his arm into hers as they headed for the truck. "You better tell me if you get too tired out. I don't want anything happening to you."

"I'll be fine." She rested her head on his shoulder. "Don't worry about me."

❦

That evening Anna Mae and Kellan walked up the front path toward David and Kathryn's farmhouse. She grasped his hand and stopped him before they reached the door. "Let's wait a minute before we go in."

"You look beautiful." He brushed a lock of hair back from her face. "You have nothing to be nervous about, Annie. They're your family, and Kathryn invited you to come."

Smiling, she swiped a snowflake that had landed on his nose. "I'm sure visiting with my family won't be the most exciting way for you to spend your time off, but it means a lot to me. Thank you. Or maybe I should say *danki*."

"How do you say you're welcome?" he asked.

Anna Mae smiled. "*Gern gschehne.*"

He pulled her into his arms. "*Gern gschehne.*" He brushed his lips against hers, and courage surged through her.

"*Danki,*" she said. "I needed that. Now let's go see my

brother and his family." Taking his hand in hers, Anna Mae climbed the porch steps and knocked on the door.

Voices sounded on the other side of the door before it opened, revealing four children, two boys and two girls, staring wide-eyed at Anna Mae and Kellan. All four were blonde like Kathryn. The girls were miniature versions of Amanda, and the boys reminded Anna Mae of her brother as a child.

"You're our English aunt!" a little girl said.

"*Aenti* Anna Mae," the other girl said.

Amanda marched toward them, frowning at her siblings. "Lizzie, Ruthie, Junior, and Manny," she snapped. "Please step back and let *Aenti* Anna Mae and *Onkel* Kellan come into the house." After the children backed away from the door, she turned to Anna Mae. "They're excited to see you. Please come in."

Kellan held the door and Anna Mae stepped in. The warmth from the fireplace seeped beneath her wrap while the aroma of roasted turkey and potatoes caused her stomach to growl.

The children swarmed around her, asking questions and rattling off their names. Tears filled Anna Mae's eyes as she spoke with them. It warmed her heart to be with her family again.

"Anna Mae," a voice bellowed above the chorus of children's voices.

Glancing up, Anna Mae found her brother David studying her, his brown eyes glistening. He looked just as she remembered: he was tall but stocky with his sandy blond hair cut in a traditional Amish bowl cut. His beard had grown longer during the past few years. Although a few lines around his eyes revealed he was closing in on forty, he still wore youthfulness in his face.

"David," she whispered, stepping over to him. "How are you?"

He nodded and gave a little smile. "I'm *gut*. How are you?"

Tears spilled from her eyes. "It's so good to see you."

"*Ya*," he said, his voice thick. "It's *gut* to see you too." He then looked at Kellan. "How are you?"

"I'm doing well." Kellan shook his hand. "How are you?"

"*Gut, gut.*" David gestured toward the family room. "Please come in." He glanced toward the children. "Go wash up. It's time to eat." He then looked back at Anna Mae. "Kathryn told me that you're expecting your baby soon. Congratulations."

"Thank you," Anna Mae said. "We're very excited." She took Kellan's hand in hers. "It's a dream come true. God has finally seen fit to make us parents."

David nodded. "That's *gut*. How are things in Baltimore?"

"Going well," Anna Mae said. "I work part-time in the office at Kellan's Chevrolet dealership, and I also run a quilting ministry at our church. Both keep me busy." She rubbed her abdomen in response to a kick. "Of course, I'll have to cut back after the baby is born." She touched David's arm. "How about you? Are you still working for *Daed* at the farm supply store?"

David absently pulled on his beard. "*Ya*, I am. We keep very busy."

"How are *Mamm* and *Daed*?" she asked.

"Doing *gut*." David shook his head. "*Daed* is the same. Still stubborn. *Mamm* is still a sweet angel and hasn't changed a bit."

"*Wie geht's?*" Kathryn came around the corner from the kitchen and hugged Anna Mae and shook Kellan's hand. "I hope you both brought your appetite." She gestured toward the table. "Everything is ready for you."

They sat at the table with the family, and Anna Mae silently marveled that Kathryn hadn't asked them to sit at a separate table alone since she was shunned. It warmed her heart that Kathryn and David included them as part of the family.

During dinner Anna Mae, Kathryn, and David reminisced about relatives and old friends. Anna Mae also listened to stories told by her nieces and nephews about their friends and school. They laughed so much that her abdomen and lower back were sore by the end of the meal.

After supper, they sat in the family room and ate cookies and talked about old times until nearly nine o'clock.

When Anna Mae began to yawn, Kellan stood and placed his hand on her shoulder. "I think you've had enough excitement for tonight," he said, rubbing her shoulder. "You should get some rest, and we'll visit again tomorrow."

Anna Mae covered his hand with hers. "You're probably right." She glanced over at Kathryn. "Everything was *wunderbaar.* Thank you so much for arranging this visit."

"Don't be silly," Kathryn said, waving off the comment. "It was no problem at all. We're just glad you're here." She took David's hand in hers and looked at him. "Right, David?"

"*Ya.*" He smiled at Anna Mae. "We're very happy you're here."

Anna Mae and Kellan stood and collected their coats.

They then hugged and kissed the children before heading for the door.

"You must join us for supper again tomorrow night," Kathryn said. "We'll have some guests along with you."

Anna Mae's heart leapt in her chest. "My parents?"

"*Ya.*" Kathryn nodded. "It will be fine. Have faith."

Anna Mae looked at her brother. "How do you think *Daed* will take my visit?"

"I pray it goes well." David's expression didn't mirror the certainty of his words.

"Same time tomorrow night?" Kathryn asked.

"That sounds perfect." Anna Mae hugged Kathryn and shook David's hand before she and Kellan headed to the SUV.

While they drove down the road, Anna Mae sniffed back tears. Overwhelmed by the emotion of seeing her brother and his family again, she began to sob.

"Hey, Annie," Kellan cooed, rubbing her arm. "Are you okay?"

"Yeah." She laughed in spite of herself. "I guess it's silly to be so happy to see my family that I cry, huh?"

"No, it's not. It makes perfect sense. I think your brother was feeling emotional too. He didn't cry, but he looked like he might when we first got there."

"I noticed it too." Anna Mae fished a tissue from the center console and wiped her eyes and nose. She pointed at an approaching intersection. "Turn right here and then take the second left."

"Yes, ma'am." Kellan negotiated the turns. "Where are you taking me?"

"You'll see." Anna Mae rubbed her abdomen as the familiar farmhouse came into view. She directed Kellan to turn onto a long driveway leading to the large home.

Memories flooded her mind—long hot days working in the garden, lazy summer nights spent sitting on the porch singing, winter evenings spent watching the snow from the front windows. Her whole childhood had played out in that very house. Her first Christmas, her first birthday, her first kiss from her childhood friend Daniel Yoder, her first heartbreak when Daniel told her he was in love with Linda Chupp—every significant childhood memory came from that farmhouse.

A light shone from the center window on the second floor. "He's still awake," she mumbled. "Probably reading from the Bible."

"Who?" he asked.

"My father," she whispered.

"Oh. Do you want to go up to the house?"

She shook her head. "No. I don't think he'd want to see me." Fresh tears splattered on her cheeks.

"Come here." He pulled her over to him and kissed the top of her head. "Don't cry. You don't know how tomorrow night is going to turn out. He may see you and break down in tears, realizing how much he missed you."

"I doubt it." She wiped her tears with the tissue.

Kellan rubbed her cheek with his thumb. "His heart will be full of joy when he sees you're carrying another grandchild for him. You mark my words."

A bump came from within her abdomen, and she giggled.

"What?" he asked, a smile growing on his handsome face.

"Feel this." She put his hand over the area where the kicks were plunking her. "I think Butterbean hears her daddy."

Kellan gave a little laugh. "See? Even our Junior agrees with me."

"Junior?" she asked with a chuckle.

"Yes, Junior," he continued. "You just see tomorrow night. His grandpa will be so thrilled to see you that he'll welcome us back into the family. Right, little buddy?" He kissed her and then put the SUV in reverse and backed out of the driveway. "Let's get you back to the room so you can get some rest. Tomorrow will be another exciting day."

Kathryn gently closed the door to Lizzie and Ruthie's room and then crossed the hall. Opening the door, she peeked in and found Junior and Manny snoring in their beds.

She tiptoed down the hallway with a smile and entered the bedroom. "They're all sleeping," she said.

David looked up from his Bible and nodded. "It was a long and exciting night for them," he said, placing the Bible on his bedside table.

Kathryn sat on the edge of the bed and took a deep breath. "Are you still angry with me about the visit?"

He sighed. "I'm still not convinced it's going to go well tomorrow. It was *gut* to see her and Kellan, but I don't think this is the right time."

She gave him a sad smile. "I respect your thoughts, but would you try to keep an open mind tomorrow?"

He shrugged. "I'm not certain it will help. You can't change my father."

"No, I can't, but I can pray." She nodded toward the Bible. "What were you reading?"

"I was reading in Colossians and a Scripture has been echoing in my mind: 'Bear with each other and forgive whatever grievances you may have against one another. Forgive as the Lord forgave you.'" He took her hands in his. "I'll remind my *daed* of that verse if I have to."

Kathryn nodded. "That sounds like a *gut* plan."

He frowned. "I just hope my *daed* listens."

"Have faith." She leaned over and brushed her lips against his. "I do."

The next morning, Anna Mae sat with Kellan at the long table in the formal dining room of the bed and breakfast. Platters of scrambled eggs, bacon, sausage links, buttered toast, and hash browns cluttered the center of the table.

Anna Mae sipped a glass of orange juice and listened as Richard and Sandra Sheppard, the innkeepers, discussed the day's weather. When a knock sounded on the door, Sandra excused herself and headed toward the kitchen.

Filling her plate with eggs and toast, Anna Mae contemplated the day, wondering what her siblings were doing and if she would get a chance to see them. Familiar female voices filled the kitchen, and her heart thumped.

Could it be?

"She's right in here," Sandra said, moving into the doorway to the dining room.

Anna Mae glanced over just as Vera stepped into the doorway and smiled. Fannie and Barbie followed with hesitant expressions.

Anna Mae gasped. *"Mei schweschdern."* Her heart filled with joy.

"Anna Mae!" Vera came toward her with her arms outstretched.

Anna Mae stood and Vera engulfed her in her arms. "It's so good to see you," Anna Mae said. "How did you know we were staying here?"

"Kathryn told me. I went to see her this morning and asked if you'd made it for your visit. You look *wunderbaar gut*!" Vera held her hands. "How are you?" She gestured toward Anna Mae's belly. "When are you due?"

"I'm doing well, and I'm due January fifteen." Anna Mae gestured toward Kellan. "You remember my husband, Kellan." She motioned toward her sisters. "Kellan, you remember Vera, Fannie, and Barbie."

While Fannie and Barbie stood back by the door, Vera held out her hand to him. "How are you?" she asked.

"Fine," he said, shaking her hand. He turned to Fannie and Barbie. "How are you?"

They nodded, muttering *gut* in unison.

Sandra appeared with a tray containing donuts, mugs, and a coffee pot. "Why don't you ladies join Kellan and Anna Mae?" She deposited the tray on the table.

"Thank you," Kellan said.

"We'll let you all visit," Sandra said, moving to the door.

"Please let us know if you need anything," Richard chimed in before following her into the kitchen.

"Thank you so much," Anna Mae said. She then gestured toward the chairs. "Please join us."

Vera sat next to Anna Mae while Fannie and Barbie sank into seats at the end of the table. Kellan poured each of them a cup of coffee.

"How are your children?" Anna Mae asked.

Vera prattled on about each of her seven children, and Anna Mae nodded and smiled. Anna Mae then shared information about her life in Baltimore and her work in Kellan's business and with the quilt ministry. She asked Fannie and Barbie about their families, and they gave her short updates. Anna Mae wished they would warm up to her like Vera had.

"Have you seen *Daed*?" Barbie asked while gripping her mug.

"No, not yet," Anna Mae said. She idly fingered her napkin. "We're having supper with *Mamm* and *Daed* at David's tonight." She glanced over at Kellan, who gave her an encouraging smile.

"Do you think that's a good idea?" Fannie asked, lifting her cup to her mouth.

Anna Mae glanced at Vera. "Well, I ..."

"I think it's a *wunderbaar* idea," Vera said. "This is the best time of year for a family to get together and work things out."

Barbie and Fannie exchanged looks of disbelief. Ignoring them, Vera updated Anna Mae on community news about friends who lived nearby.

"I would love to see everyone," Anna Mae said. "It would be nice to get the whole family together."

"It's too bad you just missed a church Sunday," Vera said. "That would be a good place to see everyone."

"We could always come back in the spring and plan to be here on a church Sunday," Kellan offered.

Anna Mae nodded. "That would be nice."

They chatted and shared stories for more than two hours.

When Vera glanced at the clock, she stood. "I guess we'd better go. I told Lydia we'd be back by noon. I better call the driver."

"Would you ladies like a ride somewhere?" Kellan offered, standing.

"Oh no," Barbie said. "We can call our driver to come and get us."

"Don't be silly," Kellan said. "Anna Mae can rest for a while, and I can take you back to your house."

Barbie and Fannie exchanged cautious glances and Vera scowled at them. She then smiled at Kellan. "Of course we would like a ride. *Danki*, Kellan."

Anna Mae stood next to Kellan. "I'll ride with you."

"No, you rest." Kellan kissed her forehead. "I'll take them. I'm sure we'll see them again soon. I'm going to run and get my coat and keys. I'll meet you in the kitchen."

Anna Mae's eyes filled with tears as she turned to Vera. "I hate to see you go."

"I promise we'll get together again soon." Vera hugged her. "*Ich liebe dich, mei schweschder,*" she whispered.

"I love you too," Anna Mae said, wiping her eyes. She turned to Barbie and Fannie, who gave her uncomfortable smiles. "It was so good to see you both."

"You and your family are in my prayers," Fannie said, touching Anna Mae's hand.

"*Ya,*" Barbie said with a nod. "May God bless you and your family."

Anna Mae followed them to the door where they met Kellan. She waved as they hurried off toward the truck. Tears trickled down her cheeks while she headed back into her room. It was wonderful to spend time with her sisters, but the cold manner in which Fannie and Barbie treated her was painful. Of course she'd expected it, but she'd hoped all of her siblings would've been warm like Vera and Kathryn.

Lying down on the bed, she hoped for a miracle, that her parents would receive her warmly too.

Anna Mae grasped Kellan's hand while they walked up the path to Kathryn's house later that evening. Her heart skittered with a mixture of anxiety and excitement when they reached the door. Taking a deep breath, she knocked and then pushed the door open to find her nieces and nephews gathered around her parents.

When her gaze met her mother's, Mary Rose stood and gasped. "Is that you, Anna Mae?" she asked in *Dietsch*. "Is this my Anna Mae?"

Anna Mae nodded. "*Ya*, it's me, *Mamm*. It's really me. Kellan and I came to see you for Christmas." She turned to her father and found him staring at her, a deep frown imprinted on his face.

Mary Rose rushed to the door. "Oh, my! It's a *Grischtdaag* miracle!" She gathered Anna Mae in her arms and wept. "God has answered my most fervent prayers."

"*Mamm*," Anna Mae whispered, her voice quavering. "It's so good to see you. I've missed you so much." Her mother smelled just as she'd remembered — vanilla mixed with strawberry.

"Oh, Anna Mae," Mary Rose said, taking her face in her

hands. "Let me look at you." She glanced down and gasped again. "You're expecting!"

"*Ya*," Anna Mae said. "It's our first."

"When are you due?" Mary Rose asked.

"January fifteen." She smiled at Kellan.

He held out his hand. "Mrs. Beiler, it's so good to see you. You look well."

"Oh, Kellan!" Mary Rose shook his hand. "Are you taking *gut* care of my *dochder*?"

"Yes, ma'am." Kellan looped his arm around Anna Mae's shoulders and beamed. "She's the light of my life. I'm so blessed to have her by my side."

Kathryn entered the room and rushed over to them. "Kellan! Anna Mae!" She held out her hands. "Hand me your coats, and let's head into the kitchen. Supper is ready. I made my famous meatloaf and rolls."

"It smells wonderful," Kellan said, handing her his coat. He then helped Anna Mae out of her wrap.

"*Kinner*," Kathryn called. "Go wash up and then get to the table. It's time to eat."

The children filed out of the room with Kathryn in tow.

Mary Rose squeezed Anna Mae's shoulders. "I've prayed for you every day since you left. Oh, you must tell me everything about your life in Baltimore."

"Of course." Anna Mae glanced over at her father and found him still scowling at her. With trembling legs, she cleared her throat and stepped over to him. "*Daed*," she said. "It's *gut* to see you. You look well."

Still glowering, he studied her, but said nothing in response.

"Sir," Kellan said, holding out his hand. "It's a pleasure to see you again."

Daed grunted and looked back at Anna Mae. "You will cover your head in this house. It's only proper." He turned to Mary Rose. "I will not eat at the same table as her." He stood and marched toward the kitchen.

Anna Mae cupped a hand to her mouth to stifle a gasp. She then closed her eyes and took deep breaths to stop her threatening tears. When she opened her eyes again, she found her mother and Kellan studying her.

"This was a mistake," Anna Mae whispered. "I never should've come." She met Kellan's concerned gaze. "You were right. I don't belong here."

"No, no. Don't say that. It's going to be okay," Mary Rose said quickly. "Your father is just hurt that you left, but he still loves you. Kathryn has a kerchief you can borrow. Your *daed* will come around. Just do as he asks, and everything will be okay. We can set up a small table in the kitchen for you and Kellan. It will be just fine." Her eyes pleaded with Anna Mae's. "Please don't leave. You just got here. I want to visit with you and get to know you again."

"I won't leave," Anna Mae said. "I promise."

"*Gut.*" Mary Rose headed out of the room. "I'll be right back."

Anna Mae turned to Kellan. "This was much worse than I thought. I never should've come here." Her voice was thick. "I thought for sure he would forgive me, but he won't. Did you see his eyes?" She sniffed as tears welled up in her eyes.

"Shh." Kellan placed a finger on her lips. "This wasn't a mistake. You've answered your mother's prayers, Annie.

You're supposed to be here. Your father may take a little longer to reach, but we have a few more days. Just give him time and trust God."

"I have a kerchief for you." Mary Rose appeared with a head covering. "Let me put this on you." She put the blue material over Anna Mae's head and tied it under her chin. "Now, let's go eat as a family."

Anna Mae and Kellan followed Mary Rose into the kitchen, where the family was gathered around the large table. In the corner was a smaller table with two chairs and place settings. Anna Mae glanced up at Kellan, who gave a tentative smile.

"It's okay," he whispered. "Just do as your father asks, and he'll come around." He took her hand and gently pulled her toward the table.

Anna Mae sank into a chair at the small table with Kellan sitting across from her. They followed her relatives' lead and bowed their heads in silent prayer, and Kellan took her hands in his. With her eyes closed, she silently thanked God for the many blessings in her life and asked Him to work on her father's heart.

When she heard the utensils hitting the dishes, she looked up and found the family filling their plates. Anna Mae turned toward the table and studied her parents. They looked exactly as she'd remembered them, except for maybe a few more wrinkles on their faces. Henry was still a brooding man with graying brown hair and a matching beard, while Mary Rose still had striking brown eyes and graying light brown hair peeking out from under her prayer *kapp*.

Kathryn rose and brought a platter of meatloaf, potatoes, and green beans over to Anna Mae and Kellan.

"I'm sorry about this little table," Kathryn muttered. "I tried to talk Henry out of it, but he insisted you sit over here."

Anna Mae forced a smile. "I expected it but had hoped for something more inviting." She filled her plate with the meatloaf.

"I'll sit with you." Kathryn frowned. "I think it's wrong for you to be here alone, and I don't care about the rules. You're my family."

"No." Anna Mae touched her hand. "I don't want to be the cause of problems between you and David."

Kathryn stuck out her chin. "I refuse to treat you like an outsider." She stepped over to the table and whispered something to David, who stared at her, frowning.

"She means business, huh?" Kellan whispered with a smile.

"Kathryn has always been known for speaking her mind and standing up for her convictions, sometimes to the chagrin of my brother," Anna Mae replied.

Kathryn returned, carrying a chair. She grabbed a dish and utensils from the adjacent table and then seated herself next to Anna Mae. "Your brother isn't too happy with me, but he'll have to get over it," she said. "You came to visit and I'm going to spend time with you."

Anna Mae glanced toward the table and found her mother smiling at her. She moved her eyes to her father, who continued to frown. Feeling a lump swelling in her throat, Anna Mae studied her glass of water.

Kathryn filled her plate with food. "Tell me what you did today."

"I had a surprise this morning," Anna Mae said. "My sisters came to see me at the bed and breakfast."

"Oh." Kathryn grinned. "What a nice surprise."

"Thank you for telling them where we're staying," Anna Mae said while filling her fork with meatloaf.

"*Gern gschehne*," Kathryn said. "How was your visit with them?"

Anna Mae explained how Vera was warm and Fannie and Barbie were cold.

Kathryn shook her head. "I'm sorry about that. They behaved the same way when I mentioned you might visit, and I'd hoped that Fannie and Barbie had come around. Still, it speaks volumes that they came to see you. That's a step in the right direction." She turned the conversation to the threat of a blizzard while they finished their meal.

After supper, David came over to their table. After giving Kathryn a hard look, he nodded at Anna Mae. "It's *gut* to see you." He then turned to Kellan. "Would you like to join me in the barn? It's sort of a tradition for men to stand around and chat after a meal, even in the cold weather."

Kellan glanced at Anna Mae, who smiled in response. He then looked at David. "Sure." He kissed Anna Mae on the head before following David out of the kitchen.

Glancing around, Anna Mae found that Henry had left the kitchen, and she assumed that he had already gone outside. The voices of her young nieces and nephews rose from the family room where they were playing games.

Anna Mae rose and began to pick up the plates.

"Don't be *narrisch*," Kathryn said, touching her hand. "I don't expect you to do dishes in your condition."

"I'm pregnant, not bedridden," Anna Mae said, carrying dishes to the sink.

Kathryn shook her head. "You may sit and watch me do the dishes, but you will not help. I won't hear of it." She turned to Mary Rose. "You sit with her and visit while Amanda and I do the dishes. You two have a lot of catching up to do."

Mary Rose sat across from Anna Mae and held her hands. "Tell me everything about Baltimore. Are you *froh*?"

Anna Mae smiled and nodded. "*Ya*, I am." She then told her mother all about her quilting ministry at the church and about her job working in the office at the dealership. She asked about her siblings, nieces, and nephews, and Mary Rose told her how they each were doing.

Mary Rose was in the middle of sharing a funny story about one of her nephews when Henry came through the door.

Avoiding eye contact with Anna Mae, he frowned at his wife. "It's time to go, Mary Rose," he grumbled. He started toward the door and then turned back to her. "Now."

Mary Rose's eyes were wide with shock. "Henry, do you see your youngest *dochder* sitting here? Don't you want to speak with her?"

He kept his eyes fixed on Mary Rose. "I said it's time to go. I'll be out front waiting for you in the buggy."

"Henry!" Mary Rose called after him. She turned to Anna Mae. "I'm sorry. I have to go."

"But, *Mamm*," Anna Mae began. "I came all this way to see you."

"I know." Mary Rose stood. "But you know your father." She hugged Kathryn. "Supper was *wunderbaar. Danki*." She then touched Anna Mae's shoulder. "Come and visit me before you leave."

Anna Mae stood with tears in her eyes. "You can't let him do this to me, *Mamm*. Kellan and I were hoping that we could be a family again. You have to stand up to *Daed*."

"He's the bishop." Mary Rose's eyes filled with tears. "I have to go. *Ich liebe dich, mei dochder*." She patted Anna Mae's hand and then rushed out of the kitchen.

"*Mamm*! *Mamm*!" Anna Mae started after her. "Please don't go."

"Anna Mae!" Kathryn grabbed Anna Mae's arm and pulled her back to the table. "Stop. Just let her go."

"What if I never see her again?" Anna Mae lowered herself into the chair.

"Shh." Kathryn sat beside her and rubbed her arm. "Trust God to heal the family."

Covering her face with her hands, Anna Mae dissolved into tears.

David leaned against the barn door and glanced up toward the sky. Large flurries twirled and danced to the ground, covering the pasture with a silver quilt. He glanced over at his English brother-in-law, who shivered and hugged his arms to his lanky body. "I hope you packed a warmer coat because I heard we're supposed to have a white Christmas this year," David said.

The door opened and slammed, and Henry marched down the porch steps.

"Here's *Daed*." David sent an uneasy glance Kellan's way as Henry moved toward them. "*Daed*, would you like to join—?"

"David, help me get my horse hitched up," Henry said, pushing past him into the barn.

David glanced at Kellan, who shrugged.

"*Daed*?" David followed him into the barn. "You're leaving?"

"*Ya*, I am." Henry led his horse from the stall. "I'd appreciate your help getting the horse readied."

David placed his hand on his arm to stop him. "Why are you going?"

Henry narrowed his eyes. "I think you know why." He pushed past David with the horse in tow.

David followed him out of the barn toward the buggy. "Why can't you stay and visit?"

Henry glanced at Kellan on his way to the buggy. "You know why." He hitched the horse to the buggy.

David glanced at Kellan and found him scowling.

"It's all right," David said. "I'll talk to him."

"There's no need to talk to me," Henry said. "I've already told your *mamm* to come out here so we can go home."

"You can't do that to *Mamm*," David said. "Didn't you see *Mamm's* face when she saw Anna Mae was here? This means so much to her. Taking her away from Anna Mae is wrong."

Henry faced him, shaking a finger in his face. "It's not your place to tell me what's right and what's wrong."

David threw his hands up in frustration. "Anna Mae made her decision to leave and was shunned. But you and I both know that shunning tradition dictates that we can't eat at the same table as she does and we can't conduct business with her. It says nothing about visiting with her, which is what we were doing in the house." He gestured toward the house. "Leaving isn't necessary, and it's not right to do that to *Mamm* or Anna Mae."

"You have no right to judge me, son." Henry finished hitching the horse and glanced toward the house. "It's written: 'for all have sinned and fall short of the glory of God, and are justified freely by his grace through the redemption that came by Christ Jesus.'"

David narrowed his eyes, challenging him. "What about that verse in Colossians: 'Bear with each other and forgive whatever grievances you may have against one another. Forgive as the Lord forgave you.'"

"Where's your *mamm*?" Henry asked, keeping his eyes averted from David's stare.

"You should go without her," David said, resentment bubbling up inside him. "I'll bring her home or she can stay here tonight."

"You stay out of this." Henry started toward the house. "I'll go find her."

David turned and found Kellan standing alone, his face rigid.

"I'm so sorry," David apologized. "I don't understand why he's making more of this than it is." David leaned against the barn door and watched the snowflakes land on the fence posts. "Anna Mae made her choice and he's not going to change that. It's obvious that you and Anna Mae are happy."

Kellan spoke slowly. "I know it was risky to come here, but Anna Mae really wanted to see her family again. I just hope this doesn't break her heart." He gave a slight nod toward the porch where Mary Rose and Henry were descending the steps. "I'll stay here until they've left," he said. "I don't want to cause any more trouble."

David stepped over toward his parents, and the hurt and sadness in his mother's eyes nearly broke his heart.

Before speaking in *Dietsch*, David took a deep breath, hoping to calm his frayed nerves. "You don't have to leave, *Daed*. No one will think less of you as a bishop if you visit with Anna Mae."

Mary Rose gave Henry a hopeful look, while Henry kept his eyes trained on the horse.

"I cannot stay here," Henry declared before climbing into the buggy.

David frowned, but he knew from his father's tone of voice that arguing would do no good. Bending down, he hugged Mary Rose. "I'm sorry the evening had to end this way," he whispered to her. "Kathryn had hoped that *Daed* would see the visit as an opportunity to mend the family."

"It's not your fault," she whispered. "Your *daed* is a stubborn old mule. *Gut nacht*." She then climbed into the buggy.

David stood alone as they rode off through the swirling flurries.

Anna Mae wiped her cheeks with a napkin. "I guess I was wrong to think my coming here would be a joyous reunion with my parents."

"No, you weren't wrong." Kathryn's eyes were full of concern. "I thought your *daed* would be so overwhelmed with happiness to see you that he would welcome you with a hug and a prayer of thanksgiving."

Anna Mae shook her head. "It's no use. He won't ever accept me."

"Don't say that." Kathryn rubbed Anna Mae's shoulder. "God will change his mind. I can feel it."

Kellan burst into the room, rushed to the table, and crouched beside Anna Mae. "Are you okay?" He took her hand in his.

Anna Mae nodded. "I'm fine. Just disappointed." The worry in his eyes caused hers to tear up again.

"I don't know what your father was saying in that Pennsylvania Dutch, but I could tell he was angry that we were here." He shook his head. "It doesn't make sense to me. You came to visit him, and he left in a huff."

"He's hurt that she left the faith," Kathryn said. "It's painful for a parent when the child leaves the community."

Kellan shook his head. "She was a grown woman and it was her choice. I didn't want to steal her away. I left it up to her, and she chose me."

"Let's not go through this all again," Anna Mae said. "What's done is done, and I let him and the rest of my family and the community down. I thought that by coming here we could work things out, but he couldn't stand to stay in the same house with me. He didn't want my mother to stay either. I couldn't convince her to stay and visit with me. She followed him outside."

"We should go home." Kellan stood. "We'll go back to the bed and breakfast and pack up our things."

"No," Anna Mae said with more force than she'd planned. "I can't give up now. I'm already here."

Kellan placed a hand on her abdomen. "But the baby. The stress your father is causing could hurt the baby."

"I'm feeling fine. I've been resting, so there's nothing to worry about." Anna Mae averted her eyes by staring at the wood grain of the table.

Kellan put a hand on her shoulder. "We should go home and plan to visit later, after the baby is here. Maybe next spring. The weather will be better and you and the baby will be ready to travel." He took her hand and lifted her to her feet. "Let's go say goodbye to everyone and head home."

Kathryn touched Kellan's shoulder. "Don't give up on Henry yet. He's a stubborn man, but he has a deep faith in God. Give him a chance to adjust to seeing you and Anna Mae together."

Kellan raked his hand through his brown hair and turned to Anna Mae.

She studied his eyes and silently prayed he'd agree with Kathryn. "We've come all this way," she whispered, taking his hands in hers. "Won't you give him another chance?"

"Give him another day," Kathryn said. "If it doesn't work out, then David and I will come and visit you this spring."

"You will?" Anna Mae smiled as joy filled her heart. "You'll come see us?"

"*Ya*, we will," she said. "David had suggested that we visit you this spring instead of you coming here for Christmas."

"Oh, that would be lovely!" Anna Mae hugged her. "We'd love to have you visit, right, Kellan?"

Kellan nodded. "Anytime you want to come, you're welcome in our home."

"I hope I didn't get you in too much trouble with David by coming out for Christmas," Anna Mae said. "I hate that you went against his wishes."

Kathryn shrugged. "It wasn't the first time that I followed my heart instead of David's suggestions."

Anna Mae laughed. "No, it certainly wasn't."

Kathryn's expression became serious. "Join us for lunch at your parents' house tomorrow at noon, and we'll try one more time. If it doesn't work out, then we'll take it from there. You've come too far to give up this easily."

"Lunch at my parents' house?" Anna Mae asked. "Who will be there?"

"Just David and our immediate family," Kathryn explained. "It's our turn with them since the rest of David's siblings planned to see them on other days to have their Christmas celebrations. You know how hectic it gets this time of year. We put our word in for Christmas Eve first."

Anna Mae nodded and let the words process. Christmas Eve with her parents. She could be strong; she could do this. She turned to Kellan. "Does that sound okay to you? We'll try lunch tomorrow."

Kellan sighed. "I'll go along with it on one condition."

Anna Mae nodded. "What's your condition?"

He put a fingertip under her chin and angled her face so

that she was staring directly into his warm eyes. "I won't stay here if the stress is too much for you and our baby. If things take a turn for the worse, then we will leave. Do you agree with me?"

Overwhelmed by the love in his eyes, Anna Mae nodded as more tears filled her eyes. "Yes," she whispered.

"Then we have a deal." He kissed the top of her head. "I'll let you ladies talk a few minutes while I go say goodbye to your brother. We shouldn't stay too late. You and the baby need your rest." He then headed out of the kitchen.

"He really loves you," Kathryn said.

Anna Mae sighed. "I just wish my father would see that."

David hung up his coat and blew out a sigh. Turning, he spotted Kellan coming from the kitchen. "How is Anna Mae?" he asked.

"As well as can be expected," Kellan said. "May I talk to you a minute?"

David waved his hand toward the quiet family room. The children had gone upstairs to get ready for bed. Sinking into a rocker, David patted the chair next to him. "Have a seat."

"Don't mind if I do." Kellan lowered himself onto the chair and jammed his hands in his pockets. "What a night, huh?"

David kept his eyes fixed on the flames crackling in the fireplace. "*Ya*, I reckon it has been."

"There's something I need to ask you," Kellan said.

David faced him. "What is it?"

"I didn't understand much of what your dad said out by

the barn earlier since he was speaking Pennsylvania Dutch. But, at the same time, I'm not stupid. From what I deduced, he wants Annie and me to leave, right?" Kellan's expression was serious but also sad.

Suddenly David felt as if he'd been transported back in time. Once again, he was trapped in the middle between his father's strict Amish ways and Anna Mae's choice to leave the community.

"You don't have to sugarcoat it, David," Kellan continued. "I'll take it like a man."

"My father wasn't happy you and Anna Mae were here," David began, facing him. "He didn't say that he wanted you to leave, but he did say he couldn't stay here."

"I told Annie that we should go home, but she's insisting on staying through tomorrow to see if she can smooth it over." Kellan shook his head, frowning. "I'm concerned the visit is going to be too stressful if it keeps going the way it is. While the doctor said that it was safe for us to make this trip, I'm worried the stress of all of this might hurt her or the baby."

David absently rubbed his beard as worry filled him. "I hadn't thought about that."

Kellan leaned back on the chair. "I just don't understand it. How can a father treat his child that way? It doesn't make sense to me. Annie made her choice when she married me and it was *her* choice. I didn't force her to leave your community. In fact, I asked her several times if she was certain she wanted to give up this life for me, and every time I asked, she insisted she was."

"I knew that *Daed* would have trouble welcoming Anna

Mae," David said. "I warned Kathryn, but she insisted on arranging this visit."

Kellan shook his head and held his hands palms up. "I don't understand it. Annie and I have been married almost three years. We're expecting our first child and we're happy. She's everything to me and she tells me I'm everything to her. She's not coming back here or going to join your church again, but she wants to be a part of the Beiler family. Why can't Henry accept that?"

David shook his head. "I don't think you understand my father's point of view. He was deeply hurt when Anna Mae left. We know that once a member of the community has left, it's rare that she comes back, and it's devastating for the parents. On top of that, it's more complicated than that for my father. He's the bishop, and I'm certain he feels like he failed as a father and leader of the church because she chose to leave."

"How is he a failure?" Kellan said. "He should be proud of his daughter. Anna Mae is a good wife and will be a wonderful mother too. She may live and worship God in a different way than the way she was raised, but all the most important elements of her faith are still there. The rest is just window dressing."

David nodded. "I see your point, but I also see my father's. It's not an easy situation at all."

Kellan sighed. "It just kills me to see Annie so upset. She came here with the best of intentions." He glanced at his watch. "I'm going to see if she's ready to head back to the room. I want to be sure she gets her sleep." He stood and headed into the kitchen.

David watched him leave, rubbing his beard in frustration. It was obvious that Kellan was a good Christian man who cared for his sister. But would his father ever acknowledge that fact?

He sighed and got up to poke at the fire. He'd done all he could. Now he had to leave the rest up to God.

CHAPTER 9

Mary Rose sat on the edge of the bed while thoughts of her beautiful Anna Mae swirled through her mind. How could Henry rebuff their daughter? Of course Mary Rose understood the importance of shunning, but Henry had gone way beyond what was expected of an Amish person, even a bishop. His behavior had been downright cruel, and it broke her heart to see Anna Mae so distraught.

Her eyes moved to the other side of the bedroom where Henry changed into his nightclothes. His silence had been deafening since they'd climbed into the buggy at David's house. It was bad enough that he'd insisted they leave David's home soon after supper, but the way he sat in silence after the incident was the icing on the cake. Resentment and disappointment surged within her.

"Go ahead and say it, Mary Rose," he grumbled, pulling on his nightshirt. "I know you're waiting to speak your mind."

"I don't understand you," she whispered, angry tears spilling down her cheeks. "Your youngest *dochder* comes back to see you and tell you that she's expecting her first *boppli*, and you treat her like an enemy. How could you, Henry Beiler?"

"You know the position I'm in as bishop." He crossed the room and climbed into bed.

She swiped her hand across her wet cheeks. "*Ya*, I do, but I also know you're a *gut daed* and a *gut* man. I expected you to treat her with love and respect, despite the fact that she left us. She's still our *dochder* no matter where she lives or whom she chooses as her husband. Kellan McDonough is a *gut* man, and he'll be a *gut daed*. We need to accept him as well as our *dochder* or we'll lose her and her *boppli*. Is that what you want? Do you want to lose Anna Mae altogether?"

"She made her choice when she left," he said, rolling onto his side and facing the wall.

"I want to be a part of her life." Mary Rose stood and crossed to his side of the bed. "You can't take her away from me."

"I'm sure you're just as hurt as I am that she left."

"Have you no heart, Henry?" Her voice shook with resentment. "Have you no feelings for your own *kinner*?"

"I never said I didn't love her," he muttered. "She left me. I mean, she left us, all of us. Our whole family. She hurt us all when she rejected us."

"That's not true. She never rejected us, Henry. She simply chose another life, but she's still our *dochder*."

His eyes closed and a snore escaped his chest.

"Don't you fall asleep on me!" Mary Rose's voice shook with renewed anger. "This conversation is not over, Henry. I want our *dochder* to be a part of our *Grischtdaag*, and you can't stop that." Turning, she stomped from the bedroom and down to the family room, where she curled up on the sofa and opened her Bible. Taking a deep breath, she prayed for guidance on how to deal with her stubborn husband.

While her eyes scanned the many verses, she thought of her beautiful Anna Mae. How her heart had swelled when she'd first laid eyes on her youngest *dochder*. While she'd never quite overcome the hurt and disappointment that Anna Mae had left to marry an Englisher, she felt at peace after seeing her again. Before she saw her father's rejection, Anna Mae's face had shone with happiness and joy.

And she was going to be a *mamm*! What a *wunderbaar* miracle!

Mary Rose could not understand why Henry was being so cruel to Anna Mae. He'd have been acting within the rules if he'd visited with their *dochder* and her husband for a few hours before they'd gone home.

Mary Rose let Henry's words turn over in her mind. He'd said that Anna Mae had hurt everyone when she'd rejected them. Was Henry nursing a broken heart? Could that be the reason for his anger toward Anna Mae?

Shaking her head with confusion and disgust, Mary Rose glanced back down at the Bible. She read along, trying to put her resentment out of her mind and concentrate on the Lord's Word.

A Scripture caught her eye, and she whispered it aloud, "Ephesians 4:2: Be completely humble and gentle; be patient, bearing with one another in love." She allowed the words to sink into her heart.

Why couldn't Henry remember this verse when he was with Anna Mae tonight? Henry should've remembered to be patient, humble, and gentle with their daughter. She was just as precious as their other children, even though she was no longer Amish.

Mary Rose stared at the verse until it struck her: she too needed to be gentle and patient, bearing with her husband in love even though she was exasperated by his stubbornness and hurt by his actions. Still, questions tumbled through her mind. She wanted to understand Henry's behavior, and she also longed to know how she could help him change.

While she loved Henry with all her heart, she couldn't let him hurt their daughter this way. Mary Rose was determined to have Anna Mae back in her life. She wanted to know and love her youngest grandchild. She needed more time with Anna Mae, and she needed to find a way to get it before it was too late.

She closed the Bible and set it on the end table. Then she lowered herself onto her side on the sofa and draped a quilt over her body. She recited her evening prayers, adding an extra one for Henry, asking the Lord to warm his heart toward their youngest child. She then asked God to keep Anna Mae in town long enough for Mary Rose to visit with her and bond with her.

Drifting off to sleep, Mary Rose dreamed that she was sitting on a porch with Anna Mae and her newborn child, laughing and chatting while the warm sun shone down on them.

Kathryn tiptoed down the hallway from Manny's room toward her bedroom. Stepping through the doorway, she found David staring out the window. Taking a deep breath, she walked over to him, hoping he wouldn't be angry with her for the incidents that had unfolded this evening.

"I'm sorry things didn't go better tonight with your *dat*," Kathryn said, crossing her arms over her chest. "You were right, and I was wrong to defy you. I was also foolish to assume that things would go smoothly."

"I was right about my father." Turning, he faced her, frowning. "And to make it worse, you put me in a bad position when you ate with her and Kellan."

Kathryn shrugged. "She's still family whether she's shunned or not."

"But you know the rules as well as I do. Your defiance doesn't reflect well on me or this family." He sighed. "I too had hoped things would've gone better."

She raised an eyebrow. "Are you saying I was right about having Anna Mae and Kellan visit?"

"I didn't say that," he began. "It was a disaster at best, and I'm still angry and hurt that you planned this behind my back. However, I do think it's time we tried to bring the family back together."

Kathryn suppressed a smile. David was finally starting to see things her way.

"Anna Mae's heart was in the right place, but the plan to reunite the Beiler family for *Grischtdaag* didn't work." Shaking his head, he frowned. "I don't think my *daed* can get over his hurt that quickly. She's the youngest, the baby. Imagine how we would feel if Manny left."

"I hope your *daed* gets over it soon because it's killing your *mamm*." She took his hand in hers.

He rubbed his beard, his brown eyes deep in thought. "I changed my mind about Kellan tonight."

"What do you mean?" Still holding his warm hands in hers, she led him to the bed, where they sat.

"He's a *gut* man and clearly loves my sister. We talked and it was obvious that he loves God and takes good care of Anna Mae." He shook his head. "I wish my father could see that. Maybe then he would accept them both as part of the family."

"All is not lost." Kathryn squeezed his hands in hers. "I've asked Anna Mae to join us at your parents' house tomorrow and we can try again."

David shook his head. "You should give up this idea of a Christmas miracle. It won't work."

"*Ya*, it will." She nodded with emphasis. "Didn't you see the joy in your *mamm's* eyes when she first saw Anna Mae? That was all I needed to see to know I made the right choice. Anna Mae was meant to come here. It's God's will."

David stood and walked over toward the window again. "I don't know, Katie. I don't think it's our place to decide God's will. My *daed* is going to become even angrier when he finds out Anna Mae and Kellan are still here. I'm certain he thinks that they headed home tonight. He'll be less than pleased if they show up for Christmas Eve lunch. He'll blow his top and possibly not speak to you or me for a very long time."

"Don't say that." Kathryn crossed the room to him. "Don't you believe in *Grischtdaag* miracles, David?" She placed her hand on his shoulder. "Remember our first *Grischtdaag* together as husband and wife when I told you we were going to have Amanda? That was a miracle."

"But this is different," David said. He stared out the window. "This isn't about having a child. This is about working out family differences. These problems run deep and can't be solved by sharing a dinner and telling the *Grischtdaag* story."

"Look at me." She cupped his face in her hands and turned it toward her. The worry in his deep brown eyes broke her heart. "I need you to trust me that this is going to work out. I need you to believe in a *Grischtdaag* miracle for the sake of our family. Please, David. For me."

A sad smile turned up the corners of his lips. "Your faith never ceases to amaze me, Katie. But this goes beyond your belief in signs and miracles. I don't think that there is an easy fix to this. I can't tell you that I believe in *Grischtdaag* miracles."

She sighed and ran her finger down his cheek. "I hope to prove you wrong, David Beiler, because I believe that there will be a miracle."

He nodded. "I hope you're right and I'm wrong."

Lounging on the bed in their room, Anna Mae rubbed her abdomen while watching a news reporter highlight details of a snowstorm that was headed toward Lancaster County that evening.

"Looks like we're going to get hit with quite a bit of snow," Kellan said, sinking onto the bed next to her. "It's a good thing we brought the SUV and not the car." He held up a plate of cookies he'd received from the innkeepers. "Want one?"

"No, thanks." Anna Mae cupped a hand to her mouth to

stifle a yawn. "I don't think I could eat another bite. Things with my dad ruined my appetite. I still can't believe how badly the evening went. I never imagined it would be that bad, but I guess I was kidding myself."

Reaching over, he touched her hand. "I'm sorry that things haven't worked out the way you'd planned. We can always go home tomorrow. If we leave early enough in the day, we'll still be able to enjoy Christmas Eve at home. I can light the fireplace and—"

"No." She shook her head, her eyes filling with tears. "Kathryn invited us for Christmas Eve lunch, and we have to go. I can't go home without giving my dad one more chance. After all, we came all this way. We've already discussed this. Why are you changing your mind now?"

"Okay, okay." He rubbed her arm. "I didn't mean to distress you. We'll try once more, but if your father upsets you again, then we'll head home. I can't stand to watch you grieve. It's too much for me."

She nodded, wiping her eyes. "I promise I'll leave if he upsets me, but you have to let me try once more."

"I will." He smiled. "I just want you to be happy. You know that." He placed the plate on the bedside table and then crossed to the window. Pushing back the shade, he glanced out. "Yup, it's snowing all right. I think we may have a full-fledged blizzard by morning."

Anna Mae opened her mouth to speak, but pressure like fire gripped her abdomen and lower back, stealing her breath. She gasped and clutched her belly.

"Annie?" Kellan rushed to her, dropping onto his knees in front of her. "Are you all right? Do you think labor is starting?"

She shook her head as the pain subsided. Taking deep breaths, she closed her eyes.

He held her hands. "Annie, let me call a doctor." He stood, but she latched onto his hand and pulled him back.

"I'm okay," she whispered, forcing a smile. "Probably false labor. If they're real labor pains, they'll get more regular. After all, I'm not due for three weeks."

A frown twisted Kellan's handsome face. "I think we should go home and you should see Dr. Trask."

"Sit." She pulled him down next to her on the bed and arranged the blankets around them. "Even if we went home, no one would see me unless my labor pains were coming every fifteen minutes." She smiled, his concern warming her soul. "There's no reason to rush home."

"As usual, you win." He kissed her forehead. "But you tell me if the pain gets worse and more frequent. If you start to feel bad, we will go home, Mrs. McDonough."

She snuggled up next to him and placed her head on his muscular chest. "Yes, Mr. McDonough." Closing her eyes, she sighed. "Good night, Kellan."

He encircled her with his arms. "Good night, Annie."

CHAPTER 10

Kathryn stepped into her mother-in-law's kitchen the following morning. The sound of her children's voices filled the room as they ran through the kitchen playing tag and laughing. Mary Rose stood by the stove, pulling out pots and pans.

Kathryn took a deep breath and hoped her plan would go well for lunch. Anna Mae and Kellan would arrive at noon as surprise guests.

Kathryn kissed Mary Rose's cheek. "Can you believe it's Christmas Eve already? Where did the year go?"

"*Ya*," Mary Rose muttered, frowning. "The year has flown by."

Kathryn's heart filled with sadness. "*Was iss letz?*" she asked even though she already knew the answer. "It's about Anna Mae, isn't it?" she whispered.

Mary Rose glanced around the kitchen and moved closer to Kathryn. "I didn't sleep much last night." Her cheeks flushed with embarrassment. "Henry and I had words and I slept on the sofa. He's still not speaking to me."

Dread filled Kathryn's gut. She'd prayed over and over last night and this morning that this dinner would go well and the family could finally begin to heal.

"Let's sit and talk." Kathryn took Mary Rose's hand and led her to the table. "I was worried after you left so abruptly."

Mary Rose sighed. "I was so excited to see Anna Mae. Having her back was an answer to my prayers, and seeing her pregnant was even more *wunderbaar.*" She scowled. "I never expected Henry to be so harsh. I expected him to be upset, but for him to drag me away from her was too much. I was so angry and disappointed last night. We both said some terrible things to each other. I couldn't stand to be in the same room with him, so I went downstairs and read my Bible for a while. Then I fell asleep on the sofa. This morning he barely said a word to me. I know he's upset, but I am too. I'm not going to act like nothing happened."

"I'm so sorry, *Mamm.*" Kathryn shook her head. "I never meant for Anna Mae's visit to cause so many problems."

Mary Rose's expression became curious. "I keep thinking about the conversation we had in the bakery that day when I told you about how much I missed Anna Mae. It seems too coincidental that she came for *Grischtdaag* after we talked. Did you have something to do with Anna Mae's visit?"

Kathryn studied Mary Rose's hopeful eyes. She knew that the best answer would be the truth, but she hoped it wouldn't upset Mary Rose even more. "If I told you that I did, would you be angry with me?"

"No, no!" Mary Rose shook her head with emphasis. "I would thank you. You helped answer my prayers."

"But is her visit more of a burden than a blessing?" Kathryn touched Mary Rose's hands.

"Oh, of course it is a blessing, Kathryn. You brought my *dochder* back into my life after three long years," Mary Rose said. "No, it didn't cause problems; it just brought to light what I already knew: that I have accepted Anna Mae's decision to leave, and Henry has not. This is something he and I may never agree upon." She tilted her head in question. "Tell me, how did the visit come about? Did you contact Anna Mae after you spoke with me?"

Kathryn shook her head. "No, actually, Anna Mae had contacted me before you and I spoke. She wrote me a letter about a month ago and asked if she could visit. I offered to help her coordinate the details, but I worried that it might not be a good idea because of how Henry could react. I prayed about it and asked God to lead me and use me as He saw fit. What you told me was the sign from God I needed to help Anna Mae plan out the details."

"Did David know?" Mary Rose asked.

Nodding, Kathryn grimaced. "*Ya*, but he was worried that things would go badly. I planned it all behind his back. He was upset when he found out I went on with the plans without his blessing. He and I don't see eye-to-eye about it, but we'll get past it."

Mary Rose's eyes filled with tears. "Tell me, has Anna Mae left to go home?"

Kathryn shook her head. She looked around the kitchen, and finding it empty, she leaned closer to Mary Rose and lowered her voice. "She's still here, and she and Kellan plan to join us for our Christmas Eve meal. However, it's a secret, and I don't think we should share it with *Daed*."

"I won't tell Henry." Mary Rose's eyes filled with excitement as tears trickled down her cheeks. "I'm so thankful that she didn't go home. Last night I prayed that I would see her again. I need more time to visit with her. A few hours weren't nearly enough. I've missed her so much."

"I know you have." Kathryn squeezed her hands. "And she wants more time with you. She was so disappointed when you left."

"I don't understand Henry." Grabbing a napkin, Mary Rose swiped her eyes and nose. "He told me that Anna Mae hurt us all when she left. I would bet she broke his heart, but he hasn't admitted it aloud yet. He needs to heal, not hold onto this anger he's been harboring for the past few years."

Kathryn nodded. "You're right."

"Last night I read my Bible and came across a verse that really spoke to me," Mary Rose continued. "It said: 'Be completely humble and gentle; be patient, bearing with one another in love.' I'm trying to be patient with him, but it's hard."

Kathryn gave a sad smile. "I truly believe God won't give up on Henry. He'll see us through this, and our family will be reunited."

"I hope so." Mary Rose sighed.

Kathryn stood. "We'd better start dinner before we run out of time."

"*Danki.*" Mary Rose pulled her into a hug. "You're a *wunderbaar dochder* and a *wunderbaar fraa* to my David."

"You know I'd do anything for our family," Kathryn said. She stepped over to the counter and grabbed the cookbook. Flipping through the pages, she sent up a silent prayer that dinner would go better today than it had last night.

Anna Mae rubbed her abdomen while Kellan steered the

SUV through the winding streets in the blowing snow. The street was a solid sheet of white, lined with trees donned with white powder, reminding her of garland. Her stomach somersaulted as the vehicle approached her parents' house. The whitewashed clapboard house stood like an apparition in the blowing snow. The roof was pure white, as were the lawn and walkway.

"I guess this is it," she whispered. "Whatever happens after we walk through that front door will affect my relationship with my parents forever."

Kellan squeezed her hand as the SUV bounced along the long gravel driveway toward the house. "Yes, it will, but that doesn't mean it will have a negative effect."

After parking the SUV next to the barn, he turned and faced her. Leaning forward, he brushed his lips against hers. "Let's go in there and wish them a Merry Christmas. I'll get the gifts from the trunk." He took the keys from the ignition and climbed from the vehicle.

Anna Mae unfastened her seatbelt and turned toward the door. As she leaned forward to exit the vehicle, a sharp pain radiated through her abdomen and stole her breath. She sucked in short, shallow breaths while gripping the door handle in vain as more fire shot from her lower back through her abdomen.

"Annie!" Kellan rushed around the SUV and pulled the door open, and she let her hands drop into her lap. He cupped her face in his hands, alarm glowing in his eyes. "Should I call nine-one-one?" He fished his cell phone from his pocket.

The pain deadened, and she took a ragged breath. "I think I'm okay."

He narrowed his eyes with suspicion. "I don't get that impression from the expression on your face."

She attempted to stand, and the pain flared. "Oh." She sat back in the seat, and the pain moved through her back. She ran her fingers up and down her lower back, which felt like it had been kicked by steel-toed boots. "Maybe I should wait a minute."

"Anna Mae!" a familiar voice called. "Are you going to come in or sit in the car all afternoon while the snow gets worse?"

Anna Mae glanced over at Kathryn hurrying through the snow with a cloak over her purple frock.

"She's having some pain," Kellan said. "I'm concerned she may be going into labor."

"What?" Kathryn's eyes rounded with excitement. "You're in labor?" She took Anna Mae's arm. "Let's get you inside."

Anna Mae swatted her hand away. "No, no. I'm not in labor. I just have some pangs now and then, but nothing regular." She lifted herself from the seat. "Just give me a minute and I can get into the house without any help."

Kellan shook his head. "Don't believe her. She's downplaying the pain I just witnessed. She looked like she was going to pass out from it."

Anna Mae shot Kellan the best serious expression she could conjure despite the dull pain in her abdomen. "I'm fine. Please get the gifts from the trunk and we'll head inside." She took Kathryn's extended arm and they started toward the back door. "I just need to rest when we get inside. I'm sure it's just the excitement of seeing everyone again." She bit her bottom lip. "Do my parents know we're here for lunch?"

"I told your mother." Kathryn smiled. She pulled a kerchief from her pocket. "Here. You'd better put this on so that you don't upset your *dat*."

"Good idea." Anna Mae arranged the kerchief on her head and tied it under her chin.

Kathryn smiled and hugged her. "I'm so glad you're here."

"*Danki*." Anna Mae held her and sniffed back threatening tears. "I am too."

"Ready?" Kathryn asked with a smile.

"As ready as I'll ever be." Anna Mae glanced back at Kellan. "Shall we go in?"

Holding the shopping bags, he gave a smile. "Absolutely."

Taking a deep breath, Anna Mae followed Kathryn into her parents' home. A rush of memories overcame her as she crossed the threshold. Family gatherings, birthdays, childhood memories flooded her mind and filled her heart with a mixture of happiness and longing for her childhood. She scanned the family room and it looked just as she remembered —an old sofa sat at one wall along with a few arm chairs, end tables, and a coffee table. Keeping with Amish tradition, the Christmas decorations included poinsettias on the mantel over a crackling fire along with a few decorative candles.

Kathryn took Anna Mae's hand and led her to an easy chair, where Anna Mae sat. Kellan sank down in a chair beside her and helped her hand out the candies and little toys she'd brought for her nieces and nephews, who rushed over to greet them.

Anna Mae was talking with Ruthie and Lizzie when she felt eyes studying her. Glancing up, she found her mother, tears spilling from her eyes, standing in the doorway to the kitchen watching her. Her father stood behind her, his eyes cold and his mouth creased in a deep frown. He gave her a hard stare and then disappeared back into the kitchen.

Anna Mae started to stand, but the ache in her back caused her to sink back into the chair.

"Don't get up," Mary Rose said. "I'll come to you." She held her hands out, and Anna Mae took them. "I'm so glad you're here, *Dochder*."

"Me too." Anna Mae smiled.

"Join us for Christmas Eve dinner, Anna Mae," Mary Rose said. She helped Anna Mae to her feet and steered her toward the kitchen with Kathryn in tow.

Stepping into the kitchen Anna Mae found her father sitting at the table next to David. When he met her gaze, he still frowned and looked away, causing her stomach to plummet. She turned to Kathryn, who gave a dismissive gesture as if reading her mind.

"Sit here," Kathryn said, pointing to a small table next to the larger table in the center of the room. "I'll sit with you."

"I will too," Mary Rose said.

Anna Mae's eyes widened with shock. "You'll sit with me?"

"Of course I will." Mary Rose's voice was confident. "You're my *dochder*." She patted the chair. "Have a seat, *mei liewe*, and Kathryn, the girls, and I will serve the meal."

"*Danki*." Anna Mae sank into a chair with Kellan beside her. She glanced over at her father and found him still glowering. He shot her mother a glare, but her mother continued helping Kathryn, Amanda, Ruthie, and Lizzie serve the traditional Amish Christmas meal, including chicken with stuffing, mashed potatoes, gravy, succotash, applesauce, buttered noodles, macaroni and cheese, salad, and pickles.

The delicious smells brought back happy Christmas memories and also caused Anna Mae's mouth to water.

Kellan took her hand and leaned close. "Have you had any more pain?" he whispered.

"No, not really," Anna Mae replied. She'd had some, but she didn't want to mention it to Kellan now. He'd just worry. And she longed to soak up the presence of her family, especially her mother.

During lunch, Kathryn, Amanda, and Mary Rose joined Anna Mae and Kellan, while the rest of David's family and Anna Mae's father sat at the kitchen table.

Anna Mae chatted during the meal, sharing stories of her life in Baltimore and enjoying the stories that Mary Rose, Kathryn, and Amanda told. She frequently looked over at her father, who would scowl and look away. David gave uncomfortable glances toward Anna Mae's table and looked as if he were straining to make conversation with his father, who wasn't responding much at all. However, Anna Mae tried in vain to smile and ignore the ache seeping through her lower back.

After they finished the meal, Mary Rose, Kathryn, and the girls cleared the dishes.

"For dessert we have fruit cake, shoo-fly pie, and butterscotch pudding," Kathryn said as she filled the sink with soapy water. "I thought we'd save them for later on since we enjoyed such a big meal."

"That sounds *gut*," Mary Rose said, gathering the dirty glasses.

While the boys and David left the table, Anna Mae sat with Kellan and watched her father exit the kitchen. The sight of his leaving without speaking to her sent anger and regret tangling within her belly.

The silence between her and her father was nearly as painful as the aching in her lower back. She had to make things right. She couldn't let her father treat her this way. Life was too short, and her child had a right to know his or her grandparents.

Now was the time to make things right with her father.

She hoisted herself from the chair and sucked in a breath when pain sliced through her abdomen.

"Annie?" Kellan rose and took her hand in his.

"I'm fine," she whispered, starting for the door.

He followed her. "Where are you going?"

"I can't take it anymore. I have to go talk to him." She passed David and the boys and started toward the back door, where she'd seen her father head. She assumed he had retreated to the barn, his favorite place to read his Bible and think. David opened his mouth to speak to her, but Anna Mae continued past him.

"What good will it do?" Kellan asked.

When she didn't respond, he took her arm and gently turned her toward him. "Annie, please answer me. I'm worried about you. You look really upset. Won't talking to your father just make it worse?"

Her voice trembled. "I can't stand the way he's ignoring me." She absently rubbed her back where the pain sizzled. "I need to work this out with him. I have to do it before we go home. If I don't, then I'll regret it for the rest of my life,

Kellan." She touched his cheek. "Don't you understand that? He's my dad, the only dad I'll ever have, and the only living grandfather our child will have."

Frowning, Kellan sighed. "You're not going to let this go, are you?"

"No." She sniffed and wiped her eyes.

"Okay, then we'll make a deal. I'll give you five minutes with him." He snatched her cloak from the peg on the wall by the door and draped it over her shoulders. "If you're not back in five, then I'm coming to get you. Understand?"

She nodded, hugging her cloak to her body. "Thank you."

She gripped the doorknob and trekked out into the blowing snow, stumbling twice on her way to barn. The large, fluffy flakes drenched her cloak and clung to her shawl.

Wrenching open the barn door, Anna Mae trudged into the barn, passing the horse stalls on her way to her father's workshop. The aroma of animals and leather seeped into her senses.

She spotted her father in the corner, sitting on a bench and reading the Bible. She stood in the doorway and studied him for a moment, her body trembling as the pain in her lower back increased anew. She leaned against the door frame and took a deep breath.

"*Daed*," she began, her voice small like a little girl. "*Daed*," she repeated with more force.

He looked up at her and his eyes narrowed before cutting back to the Bible.

"*Daed*, I have something I need to say." She kneaded her lower back with her fingers, hoping to curb some of the discomfort.

He continued reading without acknowledging her. She shivered, absently wondering if the cold was from the temperature of the air in the barn or from his treatment of her.

"Kellan and I came all this way to spend *Grischtdaag* with you, *Mamm*, and everyone else because we want to be a part of the family," she said. "While I made my choice to build a life with Kellan, I never chose to lose you. I'm still a Beiler by birth, and my child is also a Beiler. You can punish me for not staying Amish, but it's unfair to punish my innocent *boppli*."

Her body continued to shake, and the pain from her lower back slithered to her abdomen. She gripped the door frame for balance and took a deep breath.

Her father kept his eyes trained on the Bible.

"Are you going to even look at me?" she asked, her voice small and quiet, squelched by the pain moving down her legs. "I'm a person. I deserve a response."

He met her gaze and scowled. "You've said your piece. Now you may leave."

"That's it?" She shook her head in disbelief as angry tears splattered her cheeks. "I came out here in the blizzard to talk to you and all you can do is dismiss me?"

He stood. "If you won't leave, then I will." He moved past her and marched out of the barn.

Anna Mae covered her face with her hands and sobbed, the pain increasing in her back and abdomen. A few moments later, she heard Kellan calling her name.

"Annie?" Kellan's panicked voice echoed through the barn. "Where are you?"

Anna Mae wiped her eyes. "I'm back here," she said. "By the workshop."

Kellan jogged toward her. "What's going on? I saw your dad come back into the house."

Sobs stole her voice.

He pulled her into his arms. "Are you all right?"

She buried her face in his chest as her tears fell. He rubbed her back.

"That's it," he said. "We're leaving. Now." He took her hand and led her through the snow toward the SUV. "I'll go in to let Kathryn know we're going. You can call her at the bakery next week."

"No." She shook her head. "I want to say goodbye to them."

Pulling the keys from his coat pocket, he hit the unlock button. "You get in the truck, and I'll go get them."

"But—"

He opened the passenger door and gestured for her to climb in. "Please, Annie. It will be easier that way. You can say goodbye and then we'll go to the bed and breakfast and check out." His eyes softened. "You don't need this nonsense from your dad. We can spend Christmas Day at home tomorrow and put this mess behind us." He nodded toward her belly. "We have plenty of good things to look forward to, and that man is not going to steal our joy."

She sighed with defeat and climbed into the car, and he jogged through the blowing snow into the house.

Kellan marched into the house, rage roaring through his veins.

David glanced over from where he stood with Kathryn and Mary Rose, and his eyes widened. "What's wrong?"

"We're leaving," Kellan said. He jammed his thumb toward the door. "Anna's in the car already. Henry upset her, so we're leaving now. You can go say goodbye to Anna Mae. I need to speak with Mr. Beiler."

Kathryn and Mary Rose exchanged surprised expressions and then rushed out the front door.

"Where's your father?" Kellan asked David.

"In the kitchen." David followed him to the doorway.

Kellan found Henry standing with a glass of water in his hands.

"Mr. Beiler," Kellan began. "I'd like to have a word with you, man to man, in private."

Henry placed his glass on the counter and gave Kellan a cold look. "Follow me to the porch."

Kellan ignored David's shocked expression and walked with Henry to the enclosed porch, shutting the door behind them.

"What's this about?" Henry asked, standing by the row of windows with his arms folded across his chest.

"You've won," Kellan said. "We're leaving."

"I'm sorry to hear that," Henry said, his voice flat, devoid of emotion. "I pray that God blesses you with a safe trip home."

Kellan shook his head and threw his hands up. "I don't understand you people at all. You claim to be pious Christians, but you're nothing but a hypocrite."

Henry shook his head. "I claim to be nothing. We're all sinners and can only be saved through Christ's grace. We Amish don't think we're better than anyone else. We all are working toward our ultimate salvation. Only God knows what's in your heart and if you've lived a life that's worthy of salvation."

"If you claim that you don't judge others, then why do you treat your sweet Anna Mae like garbage when she comes to visit you?" Kellan demanded, his voice trembling with swelling anger. "How can you consider that a Christian act that will get you salvation?"

Henry glared at him. "You have no right to judge me."

"But you're judging her!" Kellan shook his head. "You've got a lot to learn about what it takes to be a Christian. Your daughter is out in the car nursing a broken heart because of the way *you've* treated her. She thinks you hate her, and from the way you've acted, I'm not certain she's wrong. You need to rethink your role as bishop because I wouldn't go to any service that you led. In fact, I don't know how you sleep at night, Henry Beiler." Kellan turned to leave.

"You're wrong," Henry said, his voice soft. "I don't hate my daughter."

"Really?" Kellan gave a sarcastic snort as he faced him. "You've got a real backward way of showing your love." He paused. "I may not be Amish, but I know what it means to be a Christian," he continued, jamming a finger in his own chest. "I live my life for the glory of God, I love my wife, and I want to raise children who will worship God too. I also know how to show my family that I love them."

Henry stared at him, his expression softening.

"I'll leave you with one thought, Mr. Beiler," Kellan said. "You have a daughter and a future grandchild who may never know you or care to know you. How does that make you feel?"

Turning, Kellan headed back out to the family room, where David stood with an uncomfortable expression. "We're leaving. I'll be in touch." Without waiting for a response, Kellan hurried past the children standing in the family room and out the door to the car. He breathed in a ragged breath hoping to calm his trembling body. A weight had lifted from his shoulders; he'd finally told Henry Beiler what he thought of his hypocritical ways. Now he could focus on what was important: getting his precious Anna Mae home where she belonged.

CHAPTER 11

While she waited in the car, Anna Mae stared out the windshield and took deep breaths. The pain continued to swell, and she bit her bottom lip. She wondered if she should ask Kellan to take her to Lancaster General. However, the pain her father caused in her heart was more overwhelming. She longed to go home and curl up on the sofa in front of the fireplace. Kellan was right: they needed to put this behind them before the baby came. All that mattered was their love, not what her father thought of them.

Coming here was a mistake.

Why did she ever believe her father would accept her?

I'm such a fool to think I can still be considered a part of the family without being Amish.

The door creaked open, and Mary Rose leaned in and hugged her. "I wish you would stay," she whispered. "I hate that you have to leave like this." She held on for several minutes, and Anna Mae hoped she wouldn't cry.

Sniffing, Anna Mae forced a smile. "Maybe we'll come back again someday."

"Or maybe you can come with David and me when we visit in the spring," Kathryn said.

"I would love that," Mary Rose said. "*Ich liebe dich, mei liewe.*"

"I love you too, *Mamm.*" Anna Mae squeezed her hand. "Write me."

Mary Rose stepped back, and Kathryn moved to the car and hugged her. "You be safe. It's snowing pretty badly." Kathryn kissed her head. "Call me. I'll be at the bakery on Monday. Love you."

"Love you too." Anna Mae sucked in a breath as more pain flared in her back.

"*Was iss letz?*" Mary Rose asked, concern flashing in her eyes.

"Nothing." Anna Mae tried to force a smile, but her lips formed a grimace. "You get back inside. It's bitter cold, and the snow is soaking your cloaks." She squeezed their hands. "I love you both. I'll write you as soon as we get home."

Kellan loped over to the car, his expression serious as if he was pondering something.

Kathryn and Mary Rose both hugged Kellan before hurrying back through the snow. Kellan climbed into the driver's seat and jammed the key into the ignition, bringing the SUV to life.

Anna Mae turned her head and watched her mother and Kathryn disappear into the house while fresh tears filled her eyes. She hoped she would see them again soon under better circumstances.

As the truck eased down the driveway toward the road, Anna Mae sucked in a breath. She rubbed her belly with one hand and her back with the other. The sky was pure white, and the large, fluffy flakes kept the windshield wipers working non-stop, *sshhing* back and forth but never making any progress keeping the windshield clear before another batch of snowflakes caked the glass.

Driving in silence, Kellan steered onto the road and the SUV slid sideways. He eased off the gas and slowly continued down the road.

They drove in silence for several miles, and Anna Mae closed her eyes, praying that the pain would subside. However, it increased, and she began to wonder if she was in labor. She opened her mouth to speak, but no words formed. Turning to Kellan, she found his eyes trained on the road, deep in thought.

"When your mom gave me a hug, she whispered in my ear that I should take good care of you," Kellan said, flipping on the defroster. "I find it truly amazing that your mom is so focused on you and so willing to accept you in her life, but your dad is all about the rules. Was he always like that when you were growing up? Was he ever warm to you?"

Anna Mae took short, ragged breaths as more pain surged through her. Suddenly, she felt wetness between her legs, and she gasped.

"Annie?" Kellan jammed on the brakes, and the SUV slid sideways down the road, slamming into a snowbank, throwing Anna Mae forward in the seat.

"Oh no," he said. "This can't be happening. Not now." He put the SUV in reverse, spinning the tires. The vehicle didn't move. Muttering under his breath, he tried again, then he turned to her. "I'm sorry, honey, but we're stuck." He unfastened his seatbelt and leaned over her. "Annie? Are you all right?"

Anna Mae shook her head, tears streaming down her cheeks. "I think my water just broke, and I'm in pain," she whispered. "Horrible pain. You were right. I guess we should've gone to the hospital earlier, but I—" She slammed her eyes shut as another contraction gripped her, stealing her voice.

"Oh, no." Kellan took her hand and she squeezed it with all her might. "Oh, Annie. I'm so sorry. This is a nightmare."

Once the contraction stopped she opened her eyes and breathed in and out slowly. "I need to get to the hospital. Kellan, I think I'm really in labor. I need a doctor now."

He fished his phone from his pocket. Holding it up, he groaned. "No! Not now!" He waved it around, reading the screen. "Stupid cell phone. I thought this company had the best network."

He turned back to her. "You stay in the car. I'm going to see if I can get a signal outside. If not, then I'm going to start banging on doors and get you some help."

"Be careful," she mumbled, sinking back into the seat.

As Kellan climbed from the car, Anna Mae closed her eyes and rubbed her belly, praying that God would grant her a safe delivery for her precious baby.

After they returned to the house, Kathryn followed Mary Rose into the kitchen. "Can I speak with you alone?" she asked.

"*Ya*." Mary Rose wiped her eyes. "Let's go into the pantry."

Once in the pantry, Kathryn shut the door. "I can't believe Anna Mae left."

"I wish she'd stayed." Mary Rose sniffed. "I feel terrible that it ended so quickly. Last night I prayed that I'd get some time to really visit with her. I even dreamed about it."

"Kellan said Henry really upset her." Kathryn shook her head. "I'd hoped for better. I thought that God would open Henry's heart and mind and inspire him to accept Anna Mae and Kellan's life."

Mary Rose sighed. "*Ya*, me too. But Henry is still the same stubborn old man he was yesterday." She wiped her eyes. "It was like a cruel prank that I spent less than a day with her after all this time. We should've had at least a few days."

"I know." Kathryn gave a sad smile.

"But maybe we can go visit her in the spring. I'd love to see my new *kinskind*." Mary Rose smiled.

Kathryn frowned. "I have a bad feeling that they shouldn't have driven out into that blizzard. The snow is blowing very heavily. When I glanced out the window in the living room, I couldn't see the trees down by the road."

Mary Rose nodded, her eyes brimming with fresh tears. "I agree. It's too dangerous to be on the road. I'm going to worry all night about them."

"I think she may be in labor too." Kathryn folded her arms. "She said she was having back pain and that's what I had with Amanda. My back hurt so badly that it was as if our horse had kicked me."

Mary Rose gasped and cupped her hand to her mouth. "Oh no. I never thought of that. This could be bad."

"I didn't mean to upset you." Kathryn took Mary Rose's hand in her hands. "But I can't shake the feeling that she may need to get to a doctor. I feel like we should do something to help them."

"You're right." Mary Rose nodded. "But what can we do?"

Kathryn wracked her brain and then snapped her fingers. "David can take me to the phone shanty. I have Kellan's cell phone number. I can give them a call and make sure they're okay."

"That's a great idea." Mary Rose smiled. "You're always thinking."

Kathryn chuckled. "That's what David says. I think too much." She opened the door to the pantry. "I'll go talk to David."

Kathryn located David looking at a book with Ruthie and Lizzie in the enclosed porch. He met her gaze and smiled, and she motioned for him to join her in the doorway.

"I need to talk to you," she said as he approached.

He looked concerned. *"Was iss letz?"*

"I'm worried about Anna Mae and Kellan traveling in the snow." She nodded toward the window, where the snow blew in waves through the trees. She couldn't see beyond the fence around the pasture. "She was in pain and I'm worried she's in labor. I'm afraid they'll wind up stuck somewhere or get in an accident."

Rubbing his beard, he glanced out the window. "It is bad out there. I'm not sure what you want me to do about it, though."

She gripped his arm. "We need to check on them. I have Kellan's cell phone number. We can go to the phone shanty at the corner and call. Maybe we can convince them to come back here and stay the night. It would be safer to leave after the plows have cleared the road." She gave him a pleading look. "Please, David. It would be terrible if something happened to them. I need to know they're okay or I'll go crazy with worry."

He sighed. "You're right. I'll take Junior and go."

"No." She shook her head. "Take me. I need to hear it for myself."

He raised an eyebrow in question. "Are you certain?"

"*Ya.*" She took his hand and pulled him toward the door. "*Kumm.* Let's go before the storm gets any worse." Kathryn pulled David toward the back door and found Mary Rose and Henry standing near it.

Mary Rose wore a deep frown while Henry gave her a hard expression. She grabbed Kathryn's arm. "Are you going to call them?" Her eyes were full of hope.

"*Ya,*" Kathryn said with a nod. "We're hoping we can reach Kellan in time to stop them from leaving. Maybe they'll come back and wait out the storm. If Anna Mae will agree to come back." She looked at Henry, who quickly cut his eyes toward the window.

David fetched his coat from the hook and pulled it on. "We better go before they get too far from the house." He pulled on his gloves and then handed Kathryn her cloak, helping her wrap it around her body. "Do you have Kellan's number on you?"

Kathryn pulled it from her apron pocket. "I stuck it in there when she sent it to me."

David turned to the door. "Let's go."

"Be careful." Mary Rose hugged David and then wrapped

her arms around Kathryn. "I'll be praying for your safe return as well as that of Anna Mae and Kellan."

Mary Rose sucked in a breath as Kathryn and David rushed through the snow to the barn. Turning to Henry, she narrowed her eyes. "I'm disappointed in you."

He kept his eyes trained on the window. "You've made that perfectly clear, especially by spending the night on the sofa."

"How could you let Kathryn go out in that snow with David?" she asked. "You should be the one heading out into that storm to check on our *dochder*."

To her surprise, Henry's expression softened slightly, but he remained silent. He looked at her, and her bottom lip trembled.

"I'm worried about Anna Mae," Mary Rose said. "I think you're afraid too, but you just won't admit it to me."

Henry turned back to the window, and Mary Rose silently prayed that God would protect Anna Mae and Kellan and also work on Henry's heart.

Anna Mae bit her lip and tried in vain to stop the tears spurting from her eyes while the pain increased. She practiced the breathing techniques her Lamaze teacher had preached during their classes, but nothing stopped the intense cramping from stealing her breath.

When the passenger door flew open, hope swelled within her.

"Did you call the paramedics?" she asked, gripping Kellan's cold hand.

His brown hair had patches of wet peppered with snow, and his teeth chattered beneath his bluish lips.

"No." He shivered. "I can't get a signal out here." He nodded across the street. "I found a house over there. You can't see it beyond the snow. I banged on the front door, but there was no answer." His eyes filled with concern. "How are you?"

"I'm in pain. The contractions are getting harder and closer together." Her tears started again. "I'm scared. What should we do? I may deliver here in the car." She glanced out the back window. "How close are we to my *mamm's* house? Maybe we can walk back there and she can help me. She's had five babies of her own and helped to deliver many more." The pain started again, and she sucked in a breath and gripped Kellan's cold hands. Closing her eyes, she tried concentrating on something else, but the cramps burned through her mind and white-hot pain ran through her entire body.

"Annie," he whispered, pushing sweaty wisps of hair back from her face. "Just hold on to me. You're going to be just fine. I promise. Do you want me to count like we did in class? One ... Two ... Three ... Four ... Five ..."

The pain stopped and she leaned back in the seat.

Kellan kissed her hands and then grimaced. "This is all my fault. We should've stayed at the house and just ignored your father. At least then you would've delivered with your mom and Kathryn there to help you."

"Can we get back to the house?" she asked. "Maybe we can walk."

"No." He shook his head and glanced out the window. "I'm afraid something will happen if we try to walk there. I know I can lift you, but I'm not certain I can carry you that far."

"Then I guess we have to stay here until someone comes by," she said, her voice ragged with exhaustion from the pain. "Do you have that roadside safety kit? Can you put the flares out by the car? Maybe then someone would spot us and stop."

"That's a great idea. I'll be right back." He rushed to the back of the vehicle. The trunk opened with a whoosh, and the vehicle rocked back and forth while he rummaged through it.

After several minutes, the trunk slammed shut, and Kellan appeared by the door. "I set out the flares. Let's pray someone comes by and helps us soon."

"I'm sure most people are not going to venture out into

this blizzard," she whispered. "But I pray someone comes by soon or this baby will be born here."

Kellan's countenance became pale. His eyes then flashed with an idea. "I saw a barn over there." He jerked his thumb in the direction of the house. "We should move you there."

"No." She shook her head. "I don't want to go to a barn. I'd rather stay here. The seat is sort of comfortable."

"I think we need to move you." He took her hand. "I'm worried that someone will come along and crash into our car. Let me get the first-aid kit from the trunk and then we'll move you to the barn."

"But the flares," she said. "Why would you set them up and then leave?"

"They'll alert them that we need help," he said. "Someone will see the abandoned truck and know we need help. I can even leave a note."

He pulled a notepad from the glove compartment, and Anna Mae craned her neck to see what he was writing. He scribbled out a fast note, explaining that he had taken his pregnant wife to the barn nearby. He ended the note by asking them to call nine-one-one as soon as possible and get help. Folding the note, he wrote "HELP" across the front and placed it in the driver's side window.

He kissed her forehead. "Trust me, Annie. This will work. Don't move. I'll go get the first-aid kit and a blanket."

He disappeared for a moment and the trunk opened again. It then slammed shut, rocking the truck and causing the pain in her back to ignite. She sucked in a breath and rubbed her abdomen, praying that the discomfort would subside.

He reappeared with the first-aid kit in his hands and a blanket slung over his shoulder. "Ready?" he asked.

"I guess so." She tried to move, but her legs buckled under her. "I need help getting up."

"Hold this." He handed her the first-aid kit. He then reached down and lifted her into his arms, closing the door with his leg. She held onto him while he carried her through the whipping snow and wind. Closing her eyes, she buried her face in his neck. She held her breath and bit down on her lip when the pain swelled again through her back and abdomen.

After several minutes, they reached the large red barn. Kellan gently placed her on her feet and then yanked the door open, grunting and groaning with the effort. They stepped into the large barn, and Anna Mae breathed in the aroma of wet hay and animals. Stables lined the wall, and a horse whinnied in the distance.

"I think I know how Mary felt," she muttered.

Kellan gave a bark of laughter, his handsome face lighting up. He pulled her into his arms. "You are a trooper, Anna Mae."

"Thanks," she said. She then glanced around the large, open space leading to the stalls. "I guess I should sit here." She took the blanket from his shoulder and placed it on the floor.

Slowly, she gingerly sat down, and the hay beneath the blanket gave her little cushion from the cold ground. She looked up at Kellan and opened her mouth to speak, but a sudden, gripping contraction tore through her, leaving her breathless. She rolled onto her side and gasped.

"Annie!" Kellan dropped to his knees and rubbed her back. "Count with me. One, two, three, four, five—"

"Oh," she groaned, tears flowing down her cheeks as she hugged her arms to her chest. "I need my mother. Please, Kellan, go get her for me. I can't do this alone." She turned to him and pleaded with him. "Please, Kellan. Go get her before it's too late. We're not that far from home. You could be there in less than an hour."

Looking confused, he opened his mouth and then closed it again. "But I can't leave you." He took her hands in his and his eyes filled with uncertainty. "What if something happens and I'm not here? What if you need me?"

She squeezed his hands. "If you hurry, I won't be here alone. Besides, most women are in labor for hours and hours before they deliver, especially when it's their first baby." She pointed toward the door. "Go and hurry back."

He leaned down and brushed his lips across hers. He then stared at her, his eyes full of intensity. "I'll hurry back as quickly as I can."

"Thank you." She gritted her teeth as another pang hit her and Kellan disappeared out the barn door. Closing her eyes, she prayed that she wouldn't be forced to deliver her baby alone.

Kathryn shivered while she ran through the swirling snowflakes to the phone shanty, which was located on the corner between her mother-in-law's home and the neighboring farm. The shanty, which Mary Rose shared with her neighbor, was a small shed containing a phone, stool, and phonebook. Her heart pounded in her chest as she pulled out the phone number scribbled on the piece of paper. She lifted the receiver and punched in the number.

Cradling the receiver between her neck and shoulder, she glanced back at David standing in the doorway. He rubbed his gloved hands together and shivered.

Instead of a ring, a recorded voice sounded through the receiver, saying, "We're sorry. The wireless customer you are trying to reach is not available."

"Oh no," she groaned. "It sounds like Kellan's phone isn't on or it isn't able to find a signal."

"Call the bed and breakfast," David said. "See if they've arrived for their luggage."

"Good idea." Kathryn quickly looked up the number in the phonebook. Sandra Sheppard answered and said no, she hadn't seen Kellan or Anna Mae since they left.

With a sigh, Kathryn replaced the receiver and glanced at David. "No sign of them at the bed and breakfast. If they haven't arrived back there yet, then they're probably in trouble. It's been nearly an hour since they left." She glanced past David toward the falling snow. "Hopefully they've stopped nearby."

David shook her head. "Katie, the snow is coming down like crazy and the roads are slick. We're *narrisch* if we try to venture out too far from the house. We may not be able to get back."

"Please." She tugged at his sleeve. "Let's just go a few miles up the road toward the bed and breakfast and then we'll head home. I just have to see if they need help. I can't stop this feeling I have that we need to search for them."

He sighed, glancing toward the direction of the barn. "Let's go hitch up the horse and buggy."

"*Danki.*" She rushed through the snow, holding onto his arm to avoid slipping on the slick snow on the way to the barn.

Once the horse was hitched, she climbed in and covered her legs with a quilt.

David sat beside her and guided the horse down the road. They headed up the long drive and out to the main road, driving in silence for more than twenty minutes.

Kathryn closed her eyes and prayed with all her might that God would lead Anna Mae and Kellan to safety.

"What color is Kellan's car?" David asked, breaking through her silent prayers.

"I think it's burgundy," Kathryn said. She gasped, cupping her gloved hands to her mouth when her eyes found what had caught David's attention. Flares lined an abandoned burgundy SUV that was nosed into a snowbank, snow covering the roof end and part of the hood.

"Oh no," she said. "Where are they, David? Where are Anna Mae and Kellan?"

CHAPTER 13

While trudging through the snow to the street, Kellan silently prayed Anna Mae and the baby would make it through this ordeal safely. He'd never in his wildest thoughts imagined that he would wind up in a blizzard with Anna Mae in labor. He wished he'd listened to his gut and convinced Anna Mae to stay home and not travel this late in her pregnancy.

When he slipped down a snow-covered hump, he knew he'd hit the pavement. He tented his hand over his eyes in an attempt to shield himself from the raging snow. And then he saw it. A horse and buggy!

He threw his hands in the air, waving frantically. The buggy pulled up next to him, and the door opened, revealing David. "Kellan!" David yelled.

"Thank God you're here!" Kellan climbed up the step.

David leaned over. "Where's Annie? Are you all right?"

"We need your help," Kellan gasped, trying to catch his breath. "Annie's in labor."

"Oh no!" Kathryn pushed past David, her blue eyes full of worry. "Where is she?"

Kellan pointed behind him. "I carried her to a barn

because I was worried a passing vehicle might crash into us if we stayed in the SUV. I told her she'd be safer in the barn. I didn't want to leave her there alone, but she begged me to get her mother. Her water broke, and the contractions are getting stronger."

Kathryn leaped from the buggy and grabbed Kellan's arm. "Let's go quickly. I'll help her."

"Wait a minute." David jumped from the buggy and clasped his hand around Kathryn's arm, stopping her mid-gait. "Who's that?" He nodded toward an oncoming buggy.

Kathryn pulled from his grip. "You wait and see. I'm worried about Anna Mae." She turned to Kellan. "Take me to her."

"All right." Kellan extended his arm, and she took it. He then glanced back at David. "We're going straight toward that red barn, just past that house."

David nodded. "I'll come find you after I see who this is. The buggy looks like someone from our district."

Kellan then led Kathryn to the barn, where they found Anna Mae on her side, sobbing.

"Anna Mae!" Kathryn rushed over to her and dropped to her knees. "How close are the contractions? Do you feel like you need to push?"

The women continued their conversation in Pennsylvania Dutch, and Kellan turned toward the entrance to the barn. He stepped over to the door and leaned on the doorway. Pulling his cell phone from his pocket, he held it up, praying he'd find a bar. However, the phone still displayed: "No service." Closing his eyes, he prayed, begging God to get Anna Mae and the baby through this safely.

Approaching voices caused him to open his eyes. His mouth gaped when he found David flanked by Henry and Mary Rose.

When Henry gave Kellan a worried expression, Kellan's gut swelled with hope. Had Kellan gotten through to him? Had the man finally realized how badly he'd treated his youngest daughter?

"How is she?" Mary Rose asked, worry glistening in her eyes.

"I think she's in labor," Kellan said. "Kathryn's with her."

Mary Rose ran toward the two women and joined in their conversation, barking orders in Pennsylvania Dutch.

"Can we move her?" Henry asked.

Kellan folded his arms across his chest and shivered. "I don't know. I would like to get her out of this barn, but my fear is that I'll do something to hurt her and the baby."

"I think it would be wise to take her to the house," Henry said to David.

David nodded. "At least then it would be warm and sanitary." He looked at Kellan. "We can take her in the buggy and come back for the car when the snow lets up."

"*Ya*, I agree," Henry said. "I'll go see what Mary Rose thinks. We may have to get her out of here fast." He moved past Kellan and joined the women.

"How did he know to come here?" Kellan asked David.

David shook his head with confusion. "I'm not sure. He said my *mamm* was really worried about Anna Mae and insisted he go look for her." He grinned. "I don't know what you said to him at the house, but I get the feeling that you may have gotten his attention."

Kellan nodded. "Good. Maybe we're on the road to an apology."

"Don't get too excited yet. He's a stubborn old man."

"We need to move her now," Henry called, motioning for them to move over to Anna Mae.

"I'll carry her," Kellan said, rushing over. "I carried her in here." He turned to Kathryn. "Is she close?"

"I think so." She nodded with emphasis. "It may be soon, like within the next hour. We're only twenty minutes from home. I think we need to try to get her back."

"Let's go now." Kellan lifted her up. "It'll be all right, Annie," he whispered in her ear. "We're going to take good care of you."

She bit down on her lip and nodded, her eyes full of worry and pain.

Mary Rose looked at David. "Take your buggy and go get Vera, Fannie, and Barbie. Ask them to come to the house to help. I need them to help Kathryn and me."

"I will," David said, nodding.

"Hurry!" Mary Rose called after him.

David and Kathryn rushed off to their buggy, and Kellan carried Anna Mae out to Henry's buggy and placed her in the back seat. He rode with her, holding her hand and talking to her, while Henry steered the buggy back to his house.

During the ride, the snow continued to blow, pelting the buggy windshield. The roads were slick, and Kellan worried that emergency crews wouldn't be able to make it out to the house to help Anna Mae.

When they arrived at Mary Rose's house, Kellan carried Anna Mae into Mary Rose's bedroom and placed her on the bed. He kissed her cheek while she clenched her jaw and moaned in pain. He held her hand and brushed her hair back from her face while whispering words of encouragement and love.

Mary Rose entered the room holding several towels. "Your sisters should be here soon," she said, placing the towels on a chair near the bed. "It shouldn't take long to get down the road to their homes. I'm so thankful they live close by." She stood across from Kellan and gave him a hopeful smile. "She'll be just fine."

He nodded, hoping she was right. He continued to hold Anna Mae's hand while Mary Rose rubbed Anna Mae's lower back and muttered words in Pennsylvania Dutch.

Nearly thirty minutes later, Anna Mae's three sisters and Kathryn burst into the room. The sisters gathered around Anna Mae and hugged her, speaking words he couldn't interpret. Speechless, Kellan watched the scene with his eyes wide, wondering what had moved Fannie and Barbie to finally accept Anna Mae. Was it a miracle?

The women then seemed to call out instructions, because Amanda, her sisters, and cousins rushed through the house, bringing supplies to the bedroom, including pitchers of water, towels, and quilts.

While the women tended to Anna Mae, Kellan moved to the enclosed porch. Sitting in a chair, he clasped his hands, bowed his head, closed his eyes, and sent up a fervent prayer for Anna Mae and their baby, begging God to keep them healthy and safe during the delivery. He then opened his eyes and held up his phone. When two bars appeared, he shouted for joy.

"Is that phone contraption working?" a voice behind him asked.

Turning, he found Henry standing in the doorway.

"Yes, it's finally picking up a signal," Kellan said. "I couldn't get it to work earlier when we were on the road and Annie took a turn for the worse."

Henry stepped onto the porch. "David told me that. I have to commend you on how you took care of Anna Mae while you were stuck in the snow. Putting out flares and taking her to the barn was very wise."

"Thanks," Kellan said with surprise. "I never expected a compliment from you. It means a lot."

Henry pointed toward the phone. "Are you going to call for help? It sounds like Anna Mae is going to deliver that *boppli* soon, and we'll have to get her to a hospital to be sure she and the *boppli* are okay."

"Yes, I'll call right now." Kellan dialed nine-one-one and explained to the dispatcher that his wife was in labor and needed help right away. When she asked for an address, Kellan gave Henry a blank expression. "I'm sorry, but I can't remember the address here."

Henry held out his hand. "I'll take care of it." Taking the phone, he explained the address and even gave detailed directions. He told the dispatcher that it was a dire emergency and to send help as soon as possible. He snapped the phone shut and handed it to Kellan. "She said it may take awhile due to the storm."

Kellan slipped the phone back into his coat pocket. "Yeah, she told me that too."

"Don't worry." Henry patted his shoulder. "My Mary Rose

has delivered many *bopplin* over the years. My other daughters are experienced as well, and I'm certain they can handle it. Anna Mae is in very good hands and the Lord is good. After all, tomorrow is Christmas Day."

Stunned by Henry's sudden compassion, Kellan nodded.

"The Lord will take care of Anna Mae and her *boppli*." Henry sank into a chair. "You look like you have the weight of the world on your shoulders. I'm certain everything will be just fine. Would you like to sit with me while we wait for news of your *boppli*?"

Kellan sat beside him. He stared at Henry. "Why the change of heart? Is it only because the baby is coming?"

Henry's eyes got a faraway look and he tugged at his beard. "I was wrong to be so harsh with you and Anna Mae. You made me see that."

"My words made you realize that?" Kellan asked.

"*Ya*, you made me to see how badly I've treated you and Anna Mae, and I'm very sorry. I hope you can find it in your heart to forgive me."

Kellan shook his head with disbelief. "Of course I can forgive you. Jesus explicitly commands us to love and forgive each other. I may not be Amish, but I believe in the same God you do and I take His teachings seriously."

"I saw you praying out here." Henry held out his hand, and Kellan shook it. "Thank you for taking such good care of my daughter. I can tell she's very happy with you and her life in Baltimore. I should've thanked you a long time ago."

Kellan smiled. "Thank you for welcoming us back into the family."

David stepped out onto the porch. He looked between

Henry and Kellan and raised his eyebrows with surprise. "It's *gut* to see you both talking."

Henry nodded. "I thought I should get to know my English son-in-law."

David smiled. "Anna Mae made a good decision when she picked Kellan."

"I appreciate that," Kellan said. "I feel blessed to have her for my wife." He glanced back toward the doorway. "Do you think she's doing okay in there? Should I go check on her?"

David shook his head. "The women have it under control. They'll call you if they need you."

Kellan ran his lower lip through his teeth and clasped his hands together. While he'd participated in the Lamaze classes, he'd never felt comfortable with the birthing process. He hoped that the women could handle things until the EMTs arrived.

He turned back to Henry, who was in a deep discussion with David about the storm. Glancing out the window, he found the snow still blowing full force. "When do you think the ambulance will get here?"

"I'm sure they'll get here as soon as they can," Henry said.

Kellan moved to the window. "What if they don't get here in time?"

David placed a hand on Kellan's shoulder. "It will be fine. Four of my five children were born at home without any problems. My *mamm* knows what she's doing. Trust me."

❦

"I can't do it," Anna Mae groaned, squeezing her eyes together while lying in bed. "It's too hard."

Mary Rose chuckled while applying a cold compress to Anna Mae's head. "*Ya*, you can and you will. There's only one way to get this *boppli* out, and he's ready to come." She rubbed Anna Mae's arm. "When the next contraction comes, push from the bottom of your toes, *ya*? You're almost there."

Kathryn leaned over. "*Mamm* is right. I think the *boppli* is almost crowning."

The contraction started and Anna Mae pushed as hard as she could, giving it all of the strength she could muster.

"Push again, Anna Mae!" Mary Rose exclaimed. "I can see the head! It's coming fast."

"I need my husband," Anna Mae said. "Please go get him. He needs to be here to see his baby enter the world."

Kathryn rushed to the door and opened it. "Amanda, go get Kellan! We need him now. It's time!" She then stood by Anna Mae and took her hand.

Anna Mae began to push as another contraction hit. Pressure shot through her lower back. "I can't take it." She sobbed. "It hurts too much. I can't do it!"

"Keep going," Mary Rose said. "It's almost here."

The door opened and then slammed shut as Kellan appeared beside her. His face was pale but his eyes were bright.

"Take her hand," Kathryn said. "I'll step back."

"Come on, Anna Mae," Mary Rose said. "One more push."

"Come on, honey," Kellan said, holding her hand. "You can do it." He leaned down and brushed the cool compress over her forehead. "You're strong. Just one more push."

Anna Mae bore down and gave it all she could. Soon she felt the pressure ease and Mary Rose yelped with joy, holding a tiny bundle in her hands. She and Kathryn cleaned the baby, and, with tears streaming down his cheeks, Kellan cut the cord.

"Is the baby okay?" Anna Mae whispered, her strength depleted.

"Yes, he is." Kellan took her hands in his.

"Did you say *he*?" Anna Mae asked.

"I did." He brushed back her hair. "It's a boy, Annie. We have a son."

"A Christmas Eve miracle," Mary Rose said, placing the bundle in Anna Mae's arms.

Anna Mae stared down into the eyes of her newborn child and then glanced up at Kellan. "Merry Christmas, Kellan."

"Merry Christmas to you." He kissed her lips.

Epilogue

Anna Mae hummed while gazing down at her sleeping infant. Leaning back in the hospital bed, she sighed. Life was pretty close to perfect. It was Christmas Day, and she was in Lancaster General Hospital holding her newborn son.

Anna Mae, the baby, and Kellan had arrived at the hospital late last night. Since only immediate family members were allowed to ride in the ambulance, the rest of her family had stayed behind, promising to visit after the plows had come through and cleared the roads.

After reaching the hospital, Anna Mae was admitted, and the baby was whisked away for tests. He passed them all with flying colors and was declared perfectly healthy. The three of them had spent the night in Anna Mae's room. However, Anna Mae had hardly slept. She'd spent most of the night staring at her baby boy, marveling at how perfect he was and how much God had blessed her.

The door squeaked open, revealing Kellan holding a tray containing two large Styrofoam drink cups and some snacks from the cafeteria. "I got you sweet tea and a blueberry muffin."

"Thank you," Anna Mae said with a smile. She nodded

toward the baby. "He's sleeping. Isn't he beautiful? I can't believe he's ours."

Kellan placed the tray on the bedside table and leaned over her. "Believe it because it's true." He brushed his lips across hers. "Merry Christmas, Annie. I love you."

"Merry Christmas," she echoed. "I love you too."

"You gave me the best gift of all, our son." He reached over and ran a fingertip down the baby's cheek.

"No, I didn't. God did." She kissed the baby's forehead. "Now we need to figure out the biggest question of all: What will we name him? We never agreed on a boy's name. You said you didn't like Kellan Junior."

"You're right; I still don't like it. However, the name quandary is going to have to wait." Kellan stood up straight. "There is a group of visitors outside anxious to see you and the baby. Would it be okay if I let them come in?"

"My family? They're here." Anna Mae grimaced. "Oh no. I haven't showered yet. I'm a mess."

"You look beautiful as always." Kellan kissed her forehead. "Should I let them in?"

"I guess so." She took a deep breath. "I'm ready."

Kellan disappeared out the door and then entered followed by Kathryn, David, Amanda, and her parents.

Anna Mae sat up straighter, her eyes trained on her father's smile. Her heart pounded against her ribcage. Had her father had a change of heart? If so, then this was a bigger Christmas miracle than the baby!

"Congratulations!" Amanda rushed over to the bed with Kathryn close behind her. "He's my cutest cousin."

"He's even more beautiful today than last night," Kathryn

touched the blanket wrapped around his tiny body. "Have you chosen a name yet?"

Anna Mae glanced at Kellan. He shrugged while sitting in a chair by the window.

"No, we haven't agreed yet," Anna Mae said.

"You need a good strong name for that handsome fellow," Mary Rose said, standing next to Kathryn. "He's exquisite."

"*Danki*," Anna Mae whispered, staring down at him. "I was just telling Kellan that I can't believe this beautiful little bundle is mine."

"You mean ours," Kellan said with a chuckle.

"Right, that's what I meant." Anna Mae gazed up at David.

"Congratulations, *schweschder*," he said. "He's *schee*. May God bless you with many more."

Anna Mae laughed. "*Danki*, David. I don't think I'm in any hurry, though."

"May I hold him?" Mary Rose held out her hands.

"Of course." Anna Mae lifted the baby, and Mary Rose took him.

Kellan stood and motioned for Mary Rose to sit in his chair. She sank down and began to talk to the baby while rubbing his chin.

Anna Mae looked at her *daed* standing at the end of the bed. "Hi," she said.

"Hello," Henry said, absently fingering the brim of his hat in his hands. "How are you feeling?"

"Fine," she said, smoothing the sheet over her legs. "I'm a little sore, but it's not too bad. I'm taking some good pills." She studied his eyes. "It's good to see you."

He nodded. "*Frehlicher Grischtdaag*."

"*Frehlicher Grischtdaag* to you too." She gave Kellan a sideways glance and found him smiling as if he knew something she didn't. She made a mental note to ask him about that later.

"I wanted to apologize," Henry said. "I'm sorry for treating you so badly. I was very wrong."

Anna Mae sniffed and wiped her eyes that had suddenly filled with tears. "*Danki* for telling me that. You're my *daed* and my son's only *grossdaddi*. We need you, *Dat*."

Moving around the bed, Henry took her hand and kissed it. "Welcome home, *dochder*."

She wiped tears from her cheeks with her free hand. "What caused you to change your mind about Kellan and me?"

Henry nodded toward Kellan, who was still smiling. "Your husband had a talk with me. He told me my actions were not Christian."

Anna Mae gasped. "Kellan told you that?"

"*Ya*, that's right," Henry said, absently turning the brim of his hat in his hands. "Although you didn't pick an Amish man, you chose a man who loves God and takes *gut* care of you."

"*Danki, Daed*." Anna Mae opened her arms, and he gave her a quick, gentle hug. "*Ich liebe dich, Daed*."

"*Ich liebe dich*, Anna Mae," he said, his voice raspy with emotion. Standing up, he wiped tears from his eyes. "I hope you will come often," he said. "I'll want to get to know my grandson."

"I thought we would all go visit Anna Mae and Kellan in the spring," David said, standing by Kathryn.

Her father smiled. "That sounds *gut*." He turned to Kellan. "If you'll welcome us into your home."

Kellan smiled. "Of course we will. You're family."

"Another Christmas miracle," Mary Rose whispered, her voice thick. "First, this beautiful baby, and now our family is back together."

"God is *gut*," David said.

"*Ya*, he is," Kathryn chimed in.

Later that afternoon, Kathryn held David's hand as they crossed the snowy parking lot toward the waiting car. She breathed in the crisp air and smiled.

"It truly feels like *Grischtdaag* when there's snow on the ground," she said, smiling up at him. "Those warm Christmases we had for a few years didn't feel authentic."

He nodded. "You know, I haven't thanked you yet."

"Thanked me?" She stopped and studied his eyes.

"I need to thank you for making this the best *Grischtdaag* ever."

She tilted her head in question. "What do you mean?"

"You managed to bring my family back together," he said. "*Danki*."

"Wait a minute." She took his hand, stopping him in midstride. "So, you're saying that I was right to invite Anna Mae here?"

He grinned. "*Ya*, you were."

She raised her eyebrows. "And I was right that it was a sign from God?"

"Maybe so. I'm sorry for doubting you, Katie. Your best

intentions turned out the way you'd planned. You even changed my father's heart." Leaning down he brushed his lips across hers. "You worked the most *wunderbaar* miracle I've ever seen."

She wrapped her arms around his neck. "I can't take credit for it. It was all God. I just asked Him to use me as He saw fit."

"Then I should say *danki* for listening to God when He inspired you to bring my sister here." He hugged her. "*Iche liebe dich, mei liewe. Frehlicher Grischtdaag.*"

"*Ich liebe dich*, David," she whispered in his ear. "*Frehlicher Grischtdaag* to you too."

Later that evening, Anna Mae held the baby close and ran her fingertip down his warm cheek, causing him to sigh in his sleep. "I think he looks like you."

"How can you tell?" Kellan leaned over her. "He's so tiny."

"Yes, but he has your cute little nose." She grinned up at him. "He's going to be a ladies' man like you."

Kellan laughed. "Right, me a ladies' man." He rubbed her shoulder. "Have you given a name any thought?"

"How about Aidan Beiler McDonough?"

"Hmm," he rubbed his chin. "That's not half bad. I think I like it."

"Aidan in memory of your dad and Beiler in honor of my family and our wonderful trip here." She stared down at the sleeping baby. "What do you think, Aidan? Is it a good name?"

"I think it's perfect." Kellan kissed her cheek. "Aidan Beiler McDonough it is."

Glancing at him, Anna Mae smiled. "Thank you for bringing me here. This has been the most wonderful Christmas ever."

He raised an eyebrow. "You'd rank getting stuck in a snowbank and nearly giving birth in a barn as a good Christmas?"

She nodded. "Yes, because I spent it with you and our baby boy. And I got my family back. Thank you for making my dreams come true."

"You're welcome." He kissed her lips and then grinned. "Can you promise me that next Christmas we'll spend a few quiet days at home in front of a warm fire?"

Anna Mae chuckled. "Yes, I can promise you that."

"Thank you." He brushed his lips against hers. "Merry Christmas, Annie."

"Merry Christmas, Kellan." She glanced down at the baby. "And merry first Christmas, Aidan."

An Amish Christmas Story

Naomi's
GIFT *a novella*

For Lauran

CHAPTER 1

Caleb sucked in a deep breath as the taxi van bounced down Route 340 toward Bird-in-Hand, Pennsylvania. After nearly a decade, he'd returned to the town of his birth. He clasped his hands together. Why was he nervous? This was supposed to be a happy reunion with his family, and yet, his palms were sweaty with anticipation despite the biting December wind.

"*Dat*!" Susie said, grabbing the sleeve of his coat and yanking with one hand while pointing toward the indoor farmers market with the other hand. "*Dat*! Can we stop there? Can we? Please? Please?"

"Why would we stop there?" he asked. "We have a farmers market back home that's much the same."

She blew out an exasperated sigh and glowered with annoyance. "To get a gift for *Aenti* Sadie, of course. Teacher Linda says that you should always bring a nice dessert to dinner. Please, *Dat*? I'll pick something out fast like we do at the market at home." She batted her eyelashes and gave her prettiest and cutest smile. "Pretty please, *Dat*?" She looked like a mirror of her beautiful mother, and his heart turned over in his chest. At the tender age of eight, Caleb Schmucker's daughter already knew how to wrap him around her little finger.

He gave a sigh of defeat, and Susie clapped her hands while grinning with triumph.

"Driver?" Caleb asked. "Could we please make a quick stop at the farmers market?"

The middle-aged man nodded and merged into the parking lot.

"We have to make this quick," Caleb said as the van steered into a parking space. "Your *aenti* and *onkel* are expecting us. They know that our train arrived less than an hour ago and will worry if we don't get to their house soon."

"I'll be quick. I promise." Susie nodded, and the ties to her black winter bonnet bobbed up and down on her black wrap. "We should find a nice pie to bring for *Aenti* Sadie."

"That sounds *gut*." Caleb touched her nose and smiled. Oh how he adored his little girl. There was no greater love in his life.

Except for Barbara.

Pushing the thought from his mind, he took Susie's little hand in his and they climbed from the van. He glanced across the parking lot toward the highway, and his eyes fell on the Kauffman & Yoder Amish Furniture Store, owned by an old family friend, Eli Kauffman. Caleb's elder sister, Sadie, had married Robert, the oldest of the Kauffman sons, while the youngest Kauffman son, Timothy, had been Caleb's best school friend. He wondered how his old friend was doing these days. He would have to stop by and visit him before he and Susie returned to Ohio.

"*Dat*!" Susie yanked Caleb toward the entrance to the farmers market. "Let's go."

Caleb stifled a laugh. The little girl had her mother's impatience too. "I'm coming, *mei liewe*."

They stepped through the double doors and the holiday smells of freshly baked cookies and breads, spices, and pine assaulted Caleb's senses. The market bustled with customers, English and Amish, rushing to the many booths. Scanning the area, Caleb spotted booths for baked goods, jellies and jams, crafts and gifts, and paintings. A sea of shoppers pushed past Caleb and he dropped his hold of Susie's hand as he approached the baked goods counter.

"What kind of pie did you want to get, Susie?" Caleb asked. "Do you think a pumpkin pie or apple?" When his daughter didn't answer, he turned around and found a group of English customers pushing toward the counter.

"Susie?" he called. "Susie?" He glanced through the crowd, finding only unfamiliar faces. "Susan? Susan?" Caleb's heart raced as he pushed through the knot of holiday shoppers, searching for his only child. "Susan!"

Naomi King straightened a king-size Lone Star patterned quilt and glanced at her best friend Lilly Lapp, who was glancing through the order book. "I can't believe Christmas is next week. Where has the year gone?"

Lilly shook her head. "I don't know. That's a very good question." An English customer approached and began asking Lilly questions about custom ordering a queen-size quilt as a gift.

Turning her back to the counter, Naomi hummed to herself while mentally listing all she had to do before Christmas. She still needed to shop for her parents and her eight siblings. And then there was the baking for the cookie exchange. And she had to—

"Excuse me," a little voice asked, interrupting her mental tirade.

Naomi spun to find a little girl leaning over the counter and pointing toward the king-size Lone Star quilt Naomi was draping over a wooden dowel. "May I help you?"

The girl adjusted the black bonnet on her head. "Did you make that?"

Naomi nodded. "*Ya*, I did."

"It's *schee*." The girl studied the quilt, her eyebrows knitting together in concentration. "My *mamm* made a quilt like this once, only she used blues and creams instead of maroons."

Naomi smiled. "I bet that was *schee*."

"Can I touch it?"

"Of course." Naomi held the quilt out, and the girl ran her hand over it.

The girl studied the quilt, her eyes trained on the intricate star pattern. "My *mamm* promised she would teach me how to quilt someday."

"I bet she will. I think I was about your age when my *mamm* started teaching me."

The girl looked up, and Naomi was struck by her deep green eyes. They reminded Naomi of the deep green the pasture turned every spring.

"My *mamm* is gone," the girl said, her expression serious.

"Gone?" Naomi set the dowel in the rack and leaned over the counter. "What do you mean?"

"She's in heaven with Jesus." The girl ran her fingers over the counter.

Naomi gasped, cupping a hand to her mouth. "I'm so sorry. You must miss her."

"I do. I was only—" she began.

"Susan!" A man rushed over, his expression full of fear. He placed his hands on the girl's shoulders and angled her to face him. He crouched down and met her at eye level. "I turned my head for a moment and you took off. Do you know how much you scared me? I thought I'd lost you. What were you thinking?"

"I'm sorry, *Dat*." The girl shook her head, tears filling her striking eyes. "I saw the quilt stand, and I wanted to come see the quilts."

The man sighed and closed his eyes for a split second. Standing, he took her hand in his. "Don't do that ever again." His voice pleaded with her. "Promise me?"

"*Ya*." A tear trickled down her rosy cheek, and she sniffed.

His expression became tender, and Naomi's heart swelled.

"Don't cry, Susie," he said, brushing her tears away with his fingertip. "It's okay, *mei liewe*. You're all right, and that's all that matters." He glanced toward the clock on the wall. "We need to get going. Your *aenti* is expecting us." He turned to Naomi. "I'm sorry for creating such a scene. My *dochder* took off and scared me so."

Naomi opened her mouth to speak, but her voice was stuck in her throat for a moment. Her eyes were lost in his, which were the same deep shade of emerald as the girl's.

"It was no bother," Naomi finally said. "We were having a nice discussion about quilts. I'm sorry she scared you."

"*Danki*." He glanced at his daughter. "We must be going." He turned back to Naomi. "*Frehlicher Grischtdaag*." He smiled, and his handsome face was kind. Yet, there was something sad in his gorgeous eyes. Naomi surmised it was the loss of his wife. Her heart ached for him.

Before she could respond to his Christmas greetings, the man and the girl were gone. He held the girl's hand as they turned the corner. The girl waved at Naomi, and Naomi waved back, her heart touched by the sweet gesture.

The customer who had been chatting with Lilly walked away from the stand.

"What happened?" Lilly asked, leaning over to Naomi.

"What?" Naomi asked, searching the crowd for the man and girl.

"What was all the commotion with the man and the girl?" Lilly closed the order book.

"The girl wandered off from her father, and he was worried about her." Naomi leaned against the counter. "She told me that her mother made quilts."

"Oh, that's sweet."

"*Ya*, it is." Naomi lifted a twin-size quilt from the bag below the counter and began to fold it. "But she also said her mother had died."

Lilly frowned and shook her head. "How *bedauerlich*."

"*Ya*, I know." Naomi glanced toward the door, wishing she could see the girl just one more time. "There was such sadness in her eyes. I saw it in her father's eyes too."

"I can imagine that the sadness was from losing her." Lilly

straightened the pens by the register. "I know how hard it was to lose my *mamm*, and I'm much older than she is."

Naomi touched Lilly's arm. "I know. There was just something . . ." She let her voice trail off and pushed the thought away. She'd been burned more than once by misreading her own thoughts and feelings. It was silly to even consider she'd felt something for the man and the girl, but the feeling was strong, deep in her gut. She'd wanted to hug the girl and ask her how long her mother had been gone, to take away some of the pain in her eyes.

But that wasn't Naomi's business. She didn't even know the girl or her father. She'd never seen them before. She wondered which district they belonged to. Were they from Lancaster County or were they visiting for the holidays? Now she would never know. The moment was gone and so were the girl and her father.

"What is it?" Lilly asked, a grin splitting her pretty face. She jammed a hand on the hip of her purple frock. "You're scheming something, Naomi King."

"Don't be *gegisch*." Naomi draped the quilt over a dowel. "I was just thinking about that poor little girl without a mother. My heart goes out to her."

"Is that it? Or were you thinking about her father who misses his wife?"

Naomi frowned. "Please, Lilly. I don't know his name or even what district he's a member of. There's no such thing as love at first sight. Love is a feeling that grows over time. It can't just appear out of thin air."

Lilly's expression was pensive. "You're different than you were when you were seeing Timothy Kauffman."

Naomi shrugged. "No, I'm not different. I just matured. My *mamm* told me I was boy crazy and made a fool of myself the way I ran after Luke Troyer and then Timothy."

Lilly touched Naomi's shoulder. "That's not true. You were never a fool."

"*Ya*, I was." Naomi cleared her throat to prevent a lump from swelling in her throat as the humiliation rained down on her. She could still feel the sting of her mother's harsh words after she and Timothy broke up. "My *mamm* told me that I need to concentrate on my family and stop worrying about finding a husband. So, my focus now is my siblings. If I'm meant to find love, God will bring it into my life. But honestly, I think God wants me to help my *mamm* raise my eight siblings."

Lilly shook her head. "You don't honestly believe that, Naomi. God wants us to get married and have *kinner*."

Naomi busied herself with hanging the quilt onto the rack in order to avoid Lilly's probing stare. "*Ya*, I do believe it. I tried love twice and failed. That was the sign that I wasn't meant to find true love, if there even is a true love for me."

"Naomi." Lilly took Naomi's hand and gave her a gentle smile. "Listen to me. I didn't think there was a true love for me, but I was wrong."

Naomi raised an eyebrow in surprise. "You found love?"

Lilly's cheeks flushed a bright pink.

"Why haven't you told me?" Naomi asked. "I thought I was your best friend."

"You are." Lilly sighed and sat on a stool. "We were going to keep it a secret until we get published next year."

Naomi gasped. "You're getting married?"

Lilly smiled, and Naomi shrieked and hugged her.

"Is it Zach Fisher?" Naomi asked.

Lilly nodded. "I wanted to tell you, but we're trying to keep it a secret."

Naomi smiled. "That's *wunderbaar*. You deserve to be *froh*."

Lilly touched Naomi's arm. "You do too. God will lead you to the path He wants, and I believe He wants you to find true love. You've been hurt in the past, but that doesn't mean you're meant to be alone." She gave a gentle smile. "Just remember this verse from Corinthians: 'And our hope for you is firm, because we know that just as you share in our sufferings, so also you share in our comfort.'"

Naomi nodded in agreement, but she struggled to believe she was meant to be with someone.

"Excuse me," an English customer said, approaching the counter. "I would like to pick up a couple of quilts for my kids for Christmas. Do you have any queen-size quilts available that are Christmassy?"

"Yes, ma'am, we do," Lilly said, moving to the rack. "Let me show you what I have here."

As Lilly pulled out two quilts, Naomi glanced toward the market exit and wondered where the handsome widower and his daughter were headed when they left.

CHAPTER 2

The van bumped and rattled down the long rock driveway to his sister's large white farmhouse. The dairy farm had been passed down through the Schmucker family for four generations, and Caleb's parents had lived in the apartment at the back of the house until they passed away.

The white clapboard home still looked the same as he remembered from his childhood. The vast three stories sprawled across the front of the property, while one large white barn and three smaller barns sat behind it, housing their livestock and farming supplies. The white split-rail fence outlined the large pasture, and Sadie's gardens—her pride and joy that she replanted every spring—ran the length of the enormous house.

Happy childhood memories swirled through Caleb's mind. He'd spent many hours on the porch with his parents and extended family during the warm months. The back pasture was where he and his cousins would play baseball.

During his teenage years, the pasture became the site for impromptu volleyball courts during youth socials. And it was at one of those socials where he'd met Barbara, who'd been visiting her cousin for the summer. Caleb had taken one look at Barbara's beautiful smile, and he knew he'd met his future bride.

"*Dat?*" Susie's little voice brought him back to the present. "We're here, *ya?*"

Caleb leaned over and touched her chin. "*Ya,* we are." He glanced toward the porch and found his seven nieces and nephews filing out from the front door. "You go ahead and greet your cousins. I'll grab our bags and pay the driver."

"I can't wait to meet them!" Gripping the pumpkin pie in her hands, Susie trotted up the front steps to the circle of cousins.

After grabbing their two bags, Caleb paid the driver and then made his way up the front steps, where he was engulfed in hugs from his nieces and nephews.

"Caleb!" Sadie's voice rang through the crowd. "It's so *gut* to see you!" She pulled him into a tight hug. "How was your trip?"

"*Gut,*" he said.

"We were beginning to worry about you," Sadie said.

"We made a stop on the way," Caleb said, glancing at his daughter, who bit her bottom lip. "Susie wanted to bring you a pie."

"This is for you, *Aenti* Sadie." Susie handed her the pie. "We stopped at the farmers market for it."

"Oh, it smells *appeditlich.*" After hugging Susie, Sadie motioned for them to come into the house. "*Kumm!* Let's eat!"

Caleb sat between his nephews, Samuel and Raymond, at his sister's long kitchen table. Across from him, Susie was engrossed in an animated conversation with her cousins about school.

Robert cleared his throat and Caleb bowed his head in silent prayer. The aroma of baked chicken and freshly baked bread filled his senses and he smiled. Being surrounded by family warmed his soul, and he thanked God for the opportunity to spend Christmas with them.

When Robert's fork scraped the plate, Caleb glanced up at the gaggle of arms resembling an octopus reaching for the dishes and bowls of food in the center of the table. Voices rang out around him as the children discussed the upcoming Christmas plans.

"Caleb," Sadie said, raising her voice above the discussions swirling around them. "It's so *gut* to have you here with us. How does it feel to be home again?"

"*Gut.*" Caleb glanced at his daughter, who was laughing while her cousin Janie shared a story. "Real *gut.*" He loved seeing Susie so happy. He wished they had close relatives back home, but Barbara's cousins lived in a neighboring district and rarely visited.

"How are things in Middlefield?" Robert asked.

"Going well." Caleb grabbed the serving fork for the chicken.

"Is the carriage shop keeping you busy?" Robert asked while cutting up his chicken.

"*Ya*," Caleb said. "The buggy orders have been steady." He filled his plate with chicken and then grabbed a roll. "The Lord is blessing us with plenty of business. How is the dairy business?"

Robert shrugged. "The same. Every time we get ahead,

something happens to set us back, like the rising cost of diesel to run the milkers. There's always something holding us back."

Sadie beamed at her husband. "However, the Lord always provides."

Caleb asked Samuel about the youth gatherings, and soon their plates were clean and the serving dishes were empty.

While Sadie and the girls cleaned up the kitchen, Caleb joined Robert and the boys in the family room. The conversations spanned the hours as Caleb caught up with the latest community news. Susie rushed by, laughing and talking with her cousins as they stomped up the stairs to the bedrooms. Sadie brought in large hunks of pumpkin pie covered in whipped cream, and Caleb ate until his stomach was sore.

"We better get these *kinner* to bed," Sadie said when the clock struck eight. "Service is early in the morning tomorrow."

"*Ya.*" Caleb stood and stretched. "I'll tuck Susie in over in the apartment, *ya*?"

Sadie shook her head. "The girls want Susie to stay with them, but you're welcome to stay in the apartment if you'd like."

"That sounds *gut*." Caleb carried Susie's bag up the steep stairs to the hallway lined with doors. He felt as if he'd been transported back in time since he'd climbed these stairs thousands of times during his childhood.

He found Susie giggling on a double bed with Janie and Linda. When she spotted Caleb in the doorway, they sat up.

"Girls!" Sadie bellowed, joining him in the doorway. "There's no need for all of this noise. You know that your *dat* likes some quiet in the evenings. You don't want him yelling, do you?"

Sadie's daughters silently shook their heads in response.

"*Gut*," Sadie continued. "Have you gotten your baths?"

They shook their heads no.

"It's time." Sadie stepped into the room and yanked night-gowns from the bureau.

The girls moaned their disappointment.

"Church comes early in the morning." Sadie pointed toward the hallway. "Go get your baths and then come to bed." She glanced at Caleb and smiled. "Let me go check on the boys. I'll be back."

Caleb turned to Susie. "Let's find your gown. You can take a bath too." He placed her bag on the bed and rummaged through it.

Susie sighed. "But I took a bath Thursday night."

He tried to suppress his smile. "*Ya*, but you were also cooped up on a smelly train overnight, and we have services tomorrow. Do you want the other *kinner* in the district to call you the stinky girl from Ohio?"

"No!" She laughed.

"Here." He pulled her bed clothes from the bag. "Now remember to keep your voice down. Your *onkel* doesn't like a lot of noise. We don't want to wear out our welcome on the first night. Go wash up."

Susie removed her prayer covering and unwound her long, light brown hair from its tight bun. She started for the door and then faced him, her pretty face pensive. "*Dat*, I'm sorry for scaring you at the market."

Caleb lowered himself on the bed and sighed. "I forgive you, *mei liewe*. I may be a bit overprotective, but it's my job to make sure you're safe." *Like I failed to do with your mother ...*

He pushed the thought away. He needed to suppress that regret and concentrate on enjoying Christmas with his sister's family.

"I know." She bit her lower lip and then smiled. "Did you see that pretty lady at the quilt stand?"

"What pretty lady?" Sadie rounded the corner with her eyes wide with excitement.

Caleb swallowed a groan. While he loved his sister dearly, he'd learned a long time ago that she was a hopeless gossip, who enjoyed sharing the latest community news at her weekly quilting bees. Rumors of his courting Barbara spread like wildfire after Sadie caught Caleb and Barbara chatting on the porch late one night during the summer they met.

"At the farmers market, where we got the pie," Susie said, hugging her nightgown to her chest. "She was at a quilt stand, and she said that her *mamm* taught her how to make quilts when she was about my age."

"Quilt stand?" Sadie tilted her head in question. "That must have been Naomi King or maybe Lilly Lapp. They both work there. Naomi's *mamm* owns the stand. She's had it for years, and it does a good bit of business. I quilt for her sometimes."

"Really?" Susie's eyes were wide with excitement. "Would you teach me how to quilt, *Aenti* Sadie?"

"*Ya*." Sadie touched Susie's nose. "Now you run along and get your bath. We must rise early in the morning."

"Okay." Susie trotted down the long hallway.

"She needs a *mamm*," Sadie said, shooting Caleb a stern look. "It's been two years."

Caleb frowned. He'd expected a lecture with Sadie's unsolicited advice, but he'd hoped she'd wait a day or two before

starting in on him. "She has plenty of female ⸻
our community. She loves her teacher, and ⸻
friends at church."

"That's not the same as a *mamm*." Sadie's exⵧⵧ
ened, and she stepped toward him. "She needs so⸻ⵧⵢe to be
there when she has questions that only a woman can discuss."

Caleb pinched the bridge of his nose in hopes of stopping
the tension headache brewing behind his eyes. "I know you
mean well, but you can't tell me how to run my—"

"Naomi King wouldn't be a good match for you." Sadie
talked over him while shaking her head. "She's a bit too eager
for a husband. You know the type—always mingling with
the men after service and trying to get them to go for rides
with her."

"Sadie," Caleb said, attempting to interrupt her, but she
continued her monologue as if she'd never heard him.

"Naomi ran after Luke Troyer, who married Sarah Rose,
Robert's youngest sister, a couple of months ago," Sadie
frowned. "Then she enticed Timothy Kauffman, but they
broke up." She smiled. "I have just the *maedel* for you. There
haven't been any rumors about her, and she's very sweet."

"Sadie," he repeated, standing.

Her grin widened with excitement. "Her name is Irene,
and her *daed* owns a carriage shop. She'd be a *wunderbaar*
mamm for Susie. You could move back here and go to work
for her *daed* and—"

"Sadie!" His booming voice caused her to jump. "I'm sorry
for startling you, but you're not listening to me. I'm not looking for a *mamm* for Susie just yet. Barbara was the love of my
life, and I'm not ready to try to replace her."

You won't ever replace her, Caleb." Sadie touched his arm. "You'll find a new *liewe*, who will help ease the pain and give Susie the guidance that only a *mamm* can give her. I know it's hard, but it's time to move on."

What do you know about loss? He swallowed the thought and glanced toward the door. "I think I'm going to go get ready for bed. Will you call me when the girls are ready to be tucked in?" He started for the door.

"*Ya*," Sadie said. "Caleb."

He faced her, hoping she wouldn't lecture him again. "*Ya?*"

"Please think about what I said." She stepped toward the door with a hopeful expression. "You and Susie are more than welcome to stay with us. You can move into the apartment, and Susie would love to go to school with her cousins. She needs her family, Caleb. Barbara was an only child, and her parents are gone. Who do you really have in Ohio?"

Caleb folded his arms in defiance. "We have family. Barbara had cousins, and our church district is *wunderbaar*. We're not alone."

"Think about it." She clasped her hands together. "I want you to meet Irene and consider my offer."

He nodded, knowing she wasn't going to let this issue die until he agreed. "Fine. I'll consider it."

"*Gut!*" She hugged him. "I'll call you when it's time to kiss Susie goodnight."

As Caleb descended the stairs, he hoped Sadie wouldn't spend his entire visit trying to play matchmaker. He wasn't ready for another relationship, and he believed Susie was receiving all the female guidance she needed. While Sadie had the best intentions, her meddling was misguided. He was a grown man and capable of making the best decisions for his child; Sadie needed to concentrate on her own family.

Caleb plucked his bag from the family room floor, then stepped through the doorway and into the apartment at the back of the house.

He moved through the small sitting room to the bedroom. As he placed the bag on the bed, he thought of the young woman at the farmers market. While he didn't know her name, he'd noticed her beautiful face and captivating brown eyes. She seemed to have made an impression on Susie. He wondered if he would run into her again during his visit.

Deep in his heart, he hoped he would.

CHAPTER 3

Naomi sat with the other young unmarried women while she sang along with the familiar German hymns in the *Ausbund*. Keeping with tradition, the three-hour service was held in the home of one of the church district families on every other Sunday. With the living room and bedroom moveable walls removed, the downstairs of Eli and Elizabeth Kauffman's home was spacious. Backless benches were lined up for the district members, and later they would be converted to tables for lunch.

The congregation was seated by age and gender, and the service area was plain. There was no altar, no cross, no flowers, nor instruments. They sang the hymns slowly, and a male song leader chosen at the beginning of the service would begin the first syllable of each line.

While the ministers met in another room for thirty minutes to choose who would preach that day, the congregation continued to sing. They returned during the last verse of the second hymn, which was always *"Lob Lied,"* and when the ministers hung their hats on the pegs on the wall, it symbolized that the service was about to begin.

The minister began the first sermon, and Naomi clasped

her hands. Her eyes scanned the congregation, and she tried to concentrate on the minister's words. However, her thoughts kept fluttering to the scene at the farmers market yesterday. She could still visualize the little girl's sweet face when she shared that her mother had died. The fear mixed with relief on the father's face was still fresh in Naomi's mind—along with his expressive eyes.

She was still thinking of him when her stare moved to the married men sitting across the room. She spotted Robert Kauffman, and her gaze stopped when her eyes focused on the man next to him. She blinked, but the figure didn't transform. The man from the market was sitting next to Robert Kauffman.

How can this be?

The man's eyes met hers, and he looked as surprised as she felt. A smile turned up the corners of his mouth, and Naomi felt her cheeks burn with embarrassment.

Why was this stranger causing her to blush? She didn't even know him! She quickly looked away in order to break the trance.

The first sermon ended, and Naomi knelt in silent prayer along with the rest of the congregation. During her prayers, she pushed thoughts of the stranger from her mind and thanked God for the blessings in her life. She also asked for health and happiness for her family during the upcoming holidays.

After the prayers, the deacon read from the Scriptures and then the hour-long main sermon began. Naomi tried in vain to keep her eyes off the stranger during the sermon, but her glance kept moving back to him. He occasionally met her gaze with a pleasant smile, and each time, her heart fluttered and cheeks flushed. She stared at her lap and willed herself to concentrate on the sermon, which was always spoken in High German, keeping with Amish tradition.

She swallowed a sigh of relief when the kneeling prayer was over. The congregation then stood for the benediction, and the closing hymn was sung.

When the service was over, Naomi moved toward the kitchen with the rest of the women to help serve the noon meal. The men converted the benches into tables and then sat and chatted while awaiting their food. As she headed for the kitchen, Naomi averted her eyes from the group of men talking in the corner since she'd spotted the mysterious widower speaking to Timothy Kauffman.

"The service was beautiful, *ya?*" Kathryn Beiler asked Naomi as she moved a tray of pies and cakes over to the counter covered in the desserts.

"*Ya*, it was," Naomi agreed, filling a pitcher of water.

"Are you ready for Christmas?" Kathryn asked.

Naomi laughed. "No. I still need some things to finish my gifts. How about you?"

Kathryn shook her head. "No, I'm not ready either. Perhaps we should go shopping to—"

"Hi!" A little voice screeched. "Hi!"

Naomi glanced over just as Susie came trotting toward her with Robert and Sadie Kauffman's two youngest daughters trailing close behind. "Susie?"

"I remember you from the farmers market!" The little girl beamed. "So this is your church district?"

"*Ya*, it is." Naomi gestured toward Janie and Linda. "I see you know Janie and Linda Kauffman."

Susie took their hands in hers. "They're my cousins. I just met them for the first time yesterday, and we're already best friends."

Naomi plastered a smile on her lips as she inwardly gasped—Susie and her father were related to the Kauffmans! She hoped that meeting Susie wouldn't become awkward. While the Kauffmans had been gracious after her breakups with Luke and Timothy, she still felt uncomfortable. She could only imagine the rumors that were still flying about her and how forward she was with the boys.

"You know Susie?" Kathryn asked, sidling up to Naomi.

"We met at the farmers market yesterday," Naomi said.

Susie beamed. "She makes *schee* quilts like my *mamm* did."

"*Ya*," Kathryn said, smiling. "She does." She turned to Naomi. "Susie and her *dat* are visiting from Ohio for the holidays. Her *dat* is Sadie's *bruder*."

"Oh," Naomi said with a nod while suppressing an inward groan. "That's so nice."

"What's your name?" Susie asked.

"I'm Naomi," she said, shaking the girl's hand. "It's nice to meet you."

"You too," Susie said.

A chorus of voices sounded as a group of women entered the kitchen laughing, including Beth Anne Bontrager, one of Timothy's sisters, and Miriam Lapp, Timothy's fiancée.

Beth Anne's eyes widened as she approached. "Susie!" She hugged the little girl. "I saw your *dat*, and I was looking for you. How are you?"

"*Gut*." Susie gave her a shy smile.

Beth Anne smiled. "You don't know me, do you?"

Susie bit her bottom lip and shook her head. "I'm sorry, but I haven't met you yet."

"She's *Aenti* Beth Anne," Janie said.

"I'm your *Onkel* Robert's sister," Beth Anne said. "And this is Miriam. She's *Onkel* Timothy's fiancée."

Naomi slowly backed up toward the counter. She wanted to sneak away and hide somewhere far away from this uncomfortable moment. Pushing thoughts of Susie and her father out of her mind, she crossed the kitchen and found her mother. She planned to help serve lunch and forget her idea of getting to know Susie.

"Caleb!" A voice bellowed. "Caleb Schmucker!"

Caleb turned just as Timothy Kauffman smacked his back. "Timothy!"

"How are you?" Timothy gave his hand a stiff shake. "It's been what—ten years?"

"It feels that long. I'm *gut*." Caleb examined his face and found it clean shaven. "You're not married yet?"

Timothy smirked. "I'm working on it."

"What are you waiting for?" Caleb asked. "You're thirty now. We're getting old."

Timothy laughed. "*Ya*, we are, but I'm getting there. I think next wedding season I'll be taking my vow with my *liewe*. How's Susie? I believe I saw her running off with Robert's girls."

"She is doing well," Caleb said. He patted Timothy's shoulder. "It's so *gut* to see you. I've missed my family here."

Timothy shrugged. "So move back. You can build buggies here just like you do in Middlefield."

Caleb scanned the room, spotting a host of familiar faces. "It's tempting."

Timothy guided Caleb to a table where they sat with Timothy's brothers and a few other men Caleb recognized. "I think a new start would be *wunderbaar* for you and Susie."

"How are you, Caleb?" Daniel Kauffman asked, leaning over and shaking Caleb's hand.

"It's so *gut* to see you," Eli Kauffman interjected. "I was so sorry to hear about Barbara."

"*Danki*," Caleb said with a nod.

"How are things in Ohio?" Eli asked.

He updated the men on his life, and out of the corner of his eye, he spotted the woman from the farmers market. She approached the table with a tray of potato salad, and he tried to make eye contact.

"*Danki*, Naomi," Daniel said as she filled his plate with potato salad.

Naomi. Her name is Naomi.

Caleb let the name roll through his mind while he tried to remember what Sadie had told him about her. According to Sadie, the woman was too eager for a husband and she had run after Luke Troyer and Timothy. However, she looked very sweet and humble with her pretty face and deep brown eyes. He couldn't imagine her running after any man.

While the conversation at his table continued among the men, Caleb tried again to make eye contact with her. However, she quickly served each of them and then moved on to the adjacent table. He wondered if she'd even seen him. He'd noticed her during the service, and she'd met his gaze. Why was she avoiding it now?

Naomi headed back to the kitchen, and Caleb felt the unfaltering urge to follow her. He set his fork on the table and stood.

"Caleb?" Timothy asked, looking confused.

Caleb nodded toward the kitchen. "I'm going to go check on Susie. I'll be right back." He headed toward the kitchen but was waylaid by David Beiler, who stepped in front of him, blocking the doorway.

"How are you, Caleb?" David shook his hand. "It's so good to see you."

"It's nice to see you too. I spoke to Kathryn earlier." Caleb glanced past him, spotting Naomi chatting with an older woman while filling another pan with potato salad.

"Caleb!" Sadie said, appearing with a tray of rolls. "I've been looking for you. I have someone I want you to meet."

Caleb glanced back toward the kitchen doorway just as Naomi stepped through it. She met his stare and then quickly turned away. Before he could step toward her, Sadie grabbed his arm and yanked him to the other side of the room, causing him to stumble along behind her.

"Sadie, I was going to—" he began.

"Caleb," she said, bringing him to a jolting stop in front of an attractive young blonde, who smiled. "This is Irene Wagler. Irene's *daed* owns Wagler's Buggies in Intercourse."

"*Wie geht's?*" Irene held out her hand.

Caleb gave her hand a quick shake. "It's nice to meet you."

Irene glanced toward the kitchen. "I better get back in and finish serving the drinks."

"Don't be silly," Sadie said, waving off the comment. "You two get acquainted, and I'll bring out the drinks." She winked at Irene, and Caleb wondered if she'd meant to be discreet. However, he was certain his older sister had never been subtle a day in her life.

"Sadie tells me you're visiting for the holidays," Irene said as she leaned against the wall behind her.

"*Ya*." Caleb fingered his beard and glanced across the room where Naomi was scooping potato salad onto a man's plate.

"You should come by and see my *daed's* shop. It's very nice."

"Maybe I will," he said.

Susie raced over, narrowly missing running into a man who was headed in the opposite direction. "*Dat! Dat!*"

"Calm down," he told her, leaning over to take her hand in his. "You almost crashed into that man."

"*Dat!*" Her eyes were wide with excitement. "*Aenti* Sadie told me that I'm going to a cookie exchange tomorrow! Isn't that *wunderbaar?*" She squeezed his hands. "I love it here."

He laughed. "That sounds *wunderbaar gut*. I'm so glad you're having fun." He nodded toward Irene. "This is my new friend, Irene. Can you say hello to her?"

"Hi. I'm Susan Schmucker, but my friends call me Susie."

"Hi, Susie. I'm Irene, and I'll be at the cookie exchange tomorrow too." Although Irene smiled down at his daughter, Caleb couldn't help but notice that the smile didn't reach her eyes.

"I'm going to go back in the kitchen and help with the dishes," Susie said. "Bye!"

Caleb grinned after her. Oh how that little girl warmed his heart.

"So, tell me about Middlefield," Irene said.

He shrugged. "What do you want to know?"

Irene smiled, and this one was real. "Everything."

H ow are you really?" Timothy asked. "You said things are *gut* at work, but how are you really coping?"

Caleb shivered while sitting on the porch at Eli Kauffman's house later that evening. Most everyone had left, except for a few families, the bulk of them related to the Kauffmans. He was disappointed that he hadn't managed to speak with Naomi before she exited with her family. However, he'd shared a brief gaze with her from across the crowded room. She'd given him a shy smile, and he noticed she had an adorable dimple on her right cheek. He hated how cliché the smile across the crowded room felt, and he hoped he'd meet her personally soon.

"Caleb?" Timothy asked. "Did you hear me? I asked how you truly are. You can be honest with me."

Caleb buried his frigid hands in the pockets of his coat. "I'm living, day to day. Susie keeps me going."

Timothy frowned. "How's Susie coping?"

Caleb shrugged. "She seems okay to me. She loves school, and her teacher is *wunderbaar.*" He shook his head. "Sadie told me last night that Susie needs a *mamm*, but it's not that simple. I can't just order one from a catalog."

Timothy gave a bark of laughter. "Mail order *mamm*, eh?"

"Right." Caleb chuckled.

"There's no one special waiting for you back in Ohio?"

"No." Caleb shook his head. "One of Barbara's cousins tried to set me up with a couple of her friends, but we really didn't have anything in common. Her cousin finally gave up on me."

Timothy turned to him, looking intrigued. "Don't you want to find a *mamm* for Susie? I don't mean to sound like your *schweschder*, but why would you want to raise Susie all by yourself?"

"It's not that I choose to be alone, but it sort of feels like I'm supposed to be alone." Caleb paused, gathering his thoughts. He'd never opened up about this subject before and it made him uncomfortable. However, he trusted Timothy and he wanted to get the emotions out in the open. "I feel like I don't deserve to be *froh* after what happened to Barbara. I feel like it's my fault."

Timothy frowned. "It's not your fault, Caleb. It was an accident."

"I know," Caleb said with a sigh. "But it's not fair that I'm still here, and she's not. I feel like I should be punished or suffer somehow." He thought about the nights spent alone in bed, thinking of her and all they lost. "I feel like I'm stuck in this lonely cloud sometimes just floating around all by myself."

"Maybe you and Susie need a new beginning." Timothy brightened. "You can come back here and start over. That would cheer you up a bit and help you move on."

"It's not that easy. I also feel guilty about moving on with my life. How is it fair that I can move on, but Barbara can't?"

Timothy was silent for a moment. "What's keeping you in Ohio? What do you have there?"

"Susie has a few of Barbara's cousins that we see occasionally," Caleb said. "That seems to be the right reason to stay. But to be perfectly honest, I'm not sure why we are stuck in the same old routine. I guess it's easy because I don't have to think about it. I just continue through the daily grind. The reminders of Barbara all over the house are painful, but I try to let go of my emotions and just remain distant. It's the only way I know to cope with it all for Susie's sake."

"So you're the shell of the man you once were?" Timothy shook his head. "That's sad."

Caleb paused, touching his beard while considering Timothy's words. He knew his friend was right, but he didn't want to talk about it anymore. He needed to change the subject. "I'd rather hear about your life, Timothy. When do I get to meet your future *fraa*?"

Timothy jammed a thumb toward the door. "Miriam is here. She was talking with my sisters earlier."

"How'd you meet her?"

Timothy shook his head. "It's a long story. We met at a singing."

"A singing?" Caleb sat up straight on the bench. "Your district has singings for folks our age? I definitely need to move back home."

"Ha, ha," Timothy muttered, his voice seeping sarcasm. "That's not what I meant. We met when we were younger, and then we parted ways. Miriam moved to Indiana for a few years and then came back last year. We worked things out, and now we're finally on the right path. I guess God needed us to grow up a bit before we were ready to get married."

"That may be so." *Is that why God took Barbara from me? Is there a lesson I need to learn before I find happiness again?* Caleb stared out at the small snowflakes beginning to fall from the sky while the thoughts floated through his mind. "We may have a white Christmas," he finally said.

"*Ya*," Timothy said. "It's supposed to snow a few times before Christmas Eve."

Caleb wanted to ask Timothy about Naomi. However, he didn't want to make it sound like he was interested in her. He didn't even know her, but he found her so intriguing. There was something about her, something subtle that he couldn't put into words. She was nothing like the women back in Ohio that Barbara's cousin had tried to push him to get to know.

"You should come by the furniture store," Timothy said, rubbing his hands together. "We rebuilt it after the fire, and it looks a bit different. It's a little bigger. We've been really busy this year. My *daed* hired a few more carpenters."

"I'm glad business is *gut*. I'd heard about the fire," Caleb said. "I'm sorry about Peter."

"*Ya*, that was a tragedy." Timothy frowned. "Much like what happened . . ." His words trailed off, but Caleb knew he was speaking of Barbara.

Caleb didn't want to talk about the accident now and run the risk of getting emotional. "On the way in yesterday, Susie and I stopped at the farmers market, and she spoke to a woman at a quilt stand." He gestured toward the door. "The woman was here today. Her name is Naomi, and Susie has really taken to her. Do you know her?"

Timothy smiled. "*Ya*, you could say I know her."

Curious, Caleb raised an eyebrow. For some reason, he'd hoped the rumors Sadie had shared weren't true.

"I feel bad because I sort of broke her heart." Timothy shook his head. "You won't be proud of me, *bruder*."

"I'm certain it's nothing that you should be ashamed of, Timothy," Caleb said, hoping he wasn't going to regret asking about her.

"I guess you could say I led her on." Timothy stared off toward the falling snow. "We courted for a while, and I guess I sort of used her to get my mind off Miriam when Miriam came back into town. I feel terrible about it. I was going to keep my word and stay with Naomi, but she set me free, saying she knew I loved Miriam and not her. Naomi seems so sad now. I feel bad about it, but I couldn't live a lie either. If I had married Naomi, we would've wound up resenting each other."

Caleb nodded, letting the words sink in. As usual, Sadie had it wrong. From what Timothy had described, Naomi wasn't a desperate woman; she'd simply had her heart broken.

"But Naomi is a real nice *maedel*. We're still friends." Timothy hugged his coat to his chest. "It's cold, *ya*?"

"It is December," Caleb said. "What did you expect—a heat wave?"

Timothy chuckled. "I'm glad to see you're still a wise guy."

The door opened and banged shut, and Robert stepped out. "It's cold out here. How can you sit out here and talk?"

"We can hear our thoughts out here, unlike in there," Timothy said with a smile.

Robert chuckled. "*Ya*, the women and *kinner* are loud."

He looked toward the road. "I guess we better get going. The animals will be hungry." He stepped back toward the door. "I'll gather everyone up."

Timothy stood. "We'll get the buggies hitched."

Caleb followed him to the barn. "It was *gut* visiting with you."

"You should come by the shop and see me this week," Timothy said as he opened the barn door.

"*Ya*, I will." Caleb led Robert's horse from the stall.

"You really should think about moving back here," Timothy repeated, leading his horse out of the barn. "I know you could get a job building buggies here, or you could even start your own business. I'm certain you could get a loan and find some land." Timothy snapped his fingers. "In fact, there's some land with a big shop for sale by the furniture store. If you'd like, I could contact the owner and tell him—"

"Whoa!" Caleb held his hand up to silence his friend. "Slow down, Timothy. I just arrived yesterday, and I didn't come with the intention of moving back."

Timothy grinned. "I know you didn't come with that intention, but you could leave with it."

"Timothy!" a woman's voice called. "Are we leaving? It's getting late."

"Caleb," Timothy said with a sweeping gesture as the brunette approached. "This is Miriam Lapp. Miriam, this is Caleb Schmucker, my best friend from boyhood. He's visiting from Ohio for Christmas."

Caleb shook her hand. "It's nice to meet you."

"You too," she said with a smile. "I met your daughter, Susie. She's a cutie."

"*Danki*." Caleb hitched Robert's horse to the buggy while Timothy hitched his. "I guess I'll see you again," he said, climbing into the buggy seat.

"*Ya*," Timothy said. "I expect to see you."

"You will." Caleb drove the buggy up to the porch, and Robert, Sadie, and the children piled in. As he steered onto the main road and headed toward their house, the children chattered about the upcoming school Christmas program.

He smiled as they talked, their voices filled with excitement, and he watched the snowflakes pelt the windshield. His thoughts turned to Naomi and Timothy's story of how he broke her heart. He longed to talk to Naomi, to get to know her. But why? Why should he think of this woman when he was only going to be in town a short while?

Unless he took Timothy's advice and stayed ...

He pushed the thoughts away as the horse clip-clopped down the road. He would only concentrate on spending time with his family. That was all that mattered. His family would get him through the second anniversary of Barbara's death. He needed them now.

CHAPTER 5

Why do I have to go?" Naomi asked as she placed more cookies into the five-gallon bucket at her feet. "You can take my sisters and then bring them back when it's over."

Lilly tapped her finger on the counter with impatience. "Naomi, we discussed this. You're expected to be at this cookie exchange."

"No, I'm not." Naomi continued to drop cookies into the bucket. "I don't belong there. Sarah Rose and Miriam will both be there for sure. It's going to be at the Kauffmans' bakery, so it's a Kauffman event."

"So?" Lilly threw up her hands. "You're a friend of the Kauffman family."

"But you were invited, not me," Naomi said, dropping the last of the sugar cookies into the bucket, filling it to the brim. "You're Miriam's sister. I'm just an ex-fiancée. You can't get much more awkward than that."

Lilly swiped an extra cookie from the counter. "You're the only one who thinks it's awkward. My sister happens to like you, and all the Kauffman sisters talk to you every time they see you. The only awkwardness is what you perceive in your head." She bit the cookie and moaned. "These cookies are delicious. You really outdid yourself."

"*Danki*," Naomi muttered.

"You really need to get over this idea that the Kauffmans don't like you. It's simply not true," Lilly said, lowering herself into a kitchen chair. "My sister is going to be a Kauffman, so that makes me a Kauffman by default. You're my best friend, so you're going to have to hang out with me and the Kauffmans."

"You could never understand how I feel," Naomi's voice quavered as she swept the crumbs from the counter into the palm of her hand. "Every time I see them, I think of how I made a fool of myself. It's hard to relive it over and over again."

"You didn't make a fool of yourself," Lilly said. "You were just immature."

Naomi nodded. "I know. I pursued Luke in a very unladylike way by running after him and bringing him lunch all the time. I never should've chased after him."

Lilly gave a sad smile. "You didn't realize you were doing that. You thought you were in love with Luke, but it was really a crush. On the other hand, you didn't pursue Timothy. He courted *you*." She pointed to Naomi for emphasis. "He proposed to you and then changed his mind, breaking your heart in the process."

"That's true," Naomi began, "but I think I went about it all the wrong way with both of them. I was so eager, and I was trying to make my future happen instead of waiting for God's plan." She sniffed.

"*Ach*." Lilly stood and touched Naomi's shoulder. "I didn't mean to upset you."

"It's okay." Naomi wiped away her threatening tears and shook her head.

"The Kauffmans are members of your church district," Lilly said softly. "You can't avoid them unless you stop going to church."

Naomi leaned against the counter and swiped a cookie from the bucket. "Sometimes I dream of marrying someone from another district, so I don't have to see them every other Sunday. Is that *gegisch*?"

Lilly snorted. "*Ya*, it's *gegisch*. How can you marry someone from another district if you don't visit other districts? Do you think an eligible bachelor will fall from heaven and transport you into another church district?"

Naomi glowered.

"I'm sorry." Lilly smiled. "Naomi, I'm just trying to tell you that you have every right to go to this cookie exchange. The Kauffmans like you, and they want you there. How will it look if I show up with your sisters and you're absent?"

"Tell them I'm ill." Naomi bit into the cookie. "These cookies aren't half bad."

"It would be a lie if I told them you're ill, and lying is a sin. I'm not going to knowingly sin this close to Christmas." Lilly crossed the kitchen to the doorway heading into the family room. "Lizzie Anne! Levina! Sylvia!" She bellowed each of Naomi's sisters' names.

The girls raced into the kitchen, chattering all at once.

"Lilly!" Lizzie Anne, who was fifteen, hugged her. "*Wie geht's?*"

"Is it time to go yet?" Sylvia, who was eight, whined. "I want cookies!"

"We're going to be late!" Levina, who was ten, pulled on her wrap and bonnet and headed out the door, announcing she was ready to go.

Lilly shot Naomi a smile. "Are you ready?"

"No," Naomi muttered. She snatched her wrap from the peg by the door and moved to the doorway, where she spotted her mother sitting in her favorite chair quilting. "We're leaving," she told her mother.

"Have fun," her mother said with a smile.

"*Ya.*" Naomi crossed the kitchen and grabbed the bucket of cookies. She instructed Lizzie Anne and Sylvia to carry the two covered dishes to the buggy. "Elam should have the buggy waiting for us. *Daed* told him to hook it up earlier."

"Your *mamm's* not coming?" Lilly asked as she tied her bonnet under her chin.

"No," Naomi said, heading for the door. "She has some last-minute quilts to finish. They're Christmas orders that an English customer is going to pick up later in the week. We're going to have a quilting bee at Sadie's on Wednesday to finish them up." She sighed as her sisters rushed out the door. "Let's get this over and done with."

"Naomi," Lilly began with a condescending smile. "It's Christmas. Get in the Christmas spirit."

Naomi rolled her eyes. "I can't wait until this Christmas season is over and we can get back to our normal lives."

Lilly's smile faded. "You don't mean that."

Frowning, Naomi placed the bucket on the counter. "No, I don't mean it, really. The *kinner* are excited." Her eyes filled with tears, and she suddenly felt like a heel. "I'm very blessed. I have a *wunderbaar* family and *freinden* like you.

But sometimes I feel selfish and wish I had someone special to share the holidays with." Clearing her throat, she lifted the bucket. "But that's a selfish and *gegisch* thing to say. Let's go."

"No, it's okay." Lilly touched Naomi's arm. "You'll find your special someone."

"Naomi!" Sylvia's voice shrieked. "It's cold out here!"

Shaking her head, Naomi headed for the door. She hoped the cookie exchange would be quick and painless.

With her sisters laughing and chattering in the back, Naomi guided the horse as the buggy bounced along the road leading to the Kauffman Amish Bakery. The terrain was hilly, and the roads were winding and rural. Soon she spotted the Kauffman farm with a cluster of large houses set back off the road and surrounded by four barns, along with a large pasture dotted with snow.

The property was owned by Elizabeth and Eli Kauffman, Timothy's parents, and included their house, Timothy's house, and Sarah and Luke Troyer's house. The bakery was the fourth house, the one closest to the road. Timothy and his five siblings had grown up in the biggest house, where his parents still lived.

Naomi steered into the parking lot and brought it to a stop by a row of buggies. A tall sign with *Kauffman Amish Bakery* in old-fashioned letters hung above the door of the large, white clapboard farmhouse with the sweeping wrap-around porch.

Out behind the building was a fenced-in play area, and beyond that was an enclosed field. The three other large farmhouses and four barns were set back beyond the pasture. The dirt road leading to the other homes was roped off with a sign declaring: *Private Property—No Trespassing.* A large paved parking lot sat adjacent to the bakery.

"Cookies!" Sylvia yelled, trotting toward the steps.

"Yay!" Levina chimed in.

"Wait!" Lizzie Anne called. "You can carry something." She pulled the covered dishes from the back of the buggy. "Here. Take these."

The girls took the serving platters and hurried toward the bakery.

"Slow down!" Lizzie Anne called. Shaking her head, she hefted the bucket up from the buggy floor.

"*Danki,*" Naomi said while she and Lilly unhitched the horse. "You take the empty buckets, and I'll bring the cookies."

Lizzie Anne started toward the door, carrying the empty buckets that they would fill with cookies. "I'm going to see if Lindsay is here."

While Lilly led the horse to the pasture to join the other horses, Naomi grabbed the bucket of cookies and started toward the stairs. A sign on the door said: *Bakery Closed at 4 p.m. for Private Party.*

Lilly fell in step beside her. "Smile, Naomi," she said as they approached the door. "It's Christmas."

Plastering a smile on her face, Naomi yanked the door open and stepped into the bakery. The room was rearranged with a long line of tables placed in the center of the room with piles of cookies lined up from one end to the other. The counter was filled with a variety of covered dishes, which

Naomi assumed were desserts other than cookies. Women and girls of all ages were gathered around the table chatting. Naomi inhaled the delicious scents of cookies, cakes, breads, and casseroles.

"Naomi!" Susie yelled as she ran over and reached for the bucket. "Can I help you?"

Naomi couldn't stop the smile forming on her lips. "Hello, Susie." She handed the little girl the bucket. "Are you certain you can lift this? It's sort of heavy."

"I got it." Susie huffed and puffed, but she couldn't lift it.

Grinning, Naomi grabbed the handle. "Let me help you."

"That's a good idea. We'll work together." Susie put her little hand on the handle next to Naomi's, and they lifted together. Walking slowly, they moved to the table.

"On three, we'll lift the bucket onto the table," Naomi said. "One, two, three!"

They hefted the bucket onto an empty spot on the table and began to carefully remove the cookies.

"Teamwork," Susie said with a smile.

Elizabeth Kauffman stepped to the center of the room and clapped her hands. "Hello everyone!" she said. "I'm so glad you all could come to our cookie exchange. I'm sure you all remember the rules. We'll file around the table and fill our buckets until all of the cookies are gone." She motioned toward the counter behind her. "And then we'll enjoy our delicious desserts. *Frehlicher Grischtdaag!*"

Chattering and laughing, the women and girls lined up around the table.

Susie looked up at Naomi. "Can I help you get cookies?"

Naomi's heart warmed. "I would love it," she said.

Susie beamed and held up the bucket. "I'll get us the best cookies."

Touching Susie's shoulder, Naomi smiled. "That sounds *wunderbaar gut.*"

As they moved around the table grabbing cookies, Naomi wondered why Susie had latched onto her when there were a host of other women and Susie's cousins in the room. And would Susie's father approve if he saw Susie with her? Her thoughts turned to Susie's father, and she wondered what he was doing while they filled buckets with cookies.

"This is nice," Caleb said. He glanced around the showroom of the Kauffman & Yoder Amish Furniture Store and marveled at the dining room sets, bedroom suites, entertainment centers, hutches, end tables, desks, and coffee tables. All were examples of the finely crafted pieces that Timothy and the other carpenters created.

Timothy's father, Eli, had built the original store with his best friend, Elmer Yoder, before Timothy was born.

"*Danki.*" Timothy looped an arm around Caleb's shoulder. "Let's go in the shop and you can see everyone."

Timothy led Caleb behind the counter and through the doorway to the center of the work area. Caleb scanned the sea of carpenters and waved at Timothy's brother, Daniel. The large, open warehouse was divided into nearly a dozen work areas separated by workbenches cluttered with an array of tools.

The sweet scent of wood and stain filled his nostrils. The men working around him were building beautifully designed pieces that would be favorites among Lancaster County tourists and residents alike. Hammers banged and saw blades whirled beneath the hum of diesel-powered air compressors.

Eli approached and shook Caleb's hand. *"Wie geht's?"*

"I'm doing well," Caleb said. "This is a *wunderbaar* shop you have. It's bigger, and the furniture is still *schee.*"

"Danki." Eli folded his arms and glanced around. "We're pleased with it. Business has been very *gut* this year. The Lord is *gut* to us."

Daniel approached with another man at his side. "Caleb! This is Luke Troyer, my sister Sarah's husband. Luke, this is a dear old friend, Caleb Schmucker. He abandoned us and moved to Ohio several years ago."

Caleb chuckled as he shook Luke's hand. "It's nice to meet you, and I didn't abandon anyone."

Luke laughed. "Nice to meet you too."

"Caleb builds buggies," Timothy said. "He's known in Middlefield as one of the best."

Caleb waved off the comment. "You're exaggerating."

"We could use your talent around here," Timothy said.

"You should have your own shop." Daniel patted Caleb's shoulder. "You need to move back here."

"That's funny," Caleb nodded. "I keep hearing that."

"I'm serious," Daniel continued. "Did you see that shop just down the road?" He pointed in the direction of the showroom. "It's not far from here. An Englisher owns it." He glanced at Eli. "What's his name?"

"Parker," Eli said, rubbing his beard. "Riley Parker."

Daniel snapped his fingers. "Right! He's been trying to sell it for quite a while. I bet you could get a great deal on it."

"That's a great idea," Luke chimed in. "We could help you fix the place up."

"*Ya*, we could," Timothy said with a grin.

"Hold on a minute!" Caleb held his hands up. "Slow down. I have a life in Ohio."

Timothy raised his eyebrows in question, and Caleb glanced away.

"Let's introduce you to the rest of the carpenters," Eli said. "Elmer would enjoy seeing you. It's been a long time."

After meeting all of the carpenters, Caleb sat in the break room with Timothy and Daniel. "Your *dat* has done well for himself."

Timothy passed a bottle of water across the table to Caleb. "*Ya*, he has. It's hard work, but it's paid off."

"Is Susie at the cookie party today?" Daniel asked while opening a bottle of water.

Caleb took a sip and nodded. "She was excited about it this morning. She loves being with her cousins."

Timothy raised his eyebrows.

Caleb shook his head. "Timothy, please don't start nagging me about moving here."

Timothy feigned insult. "I didn't say a word."

"Don't you think it would be good for Susie to be around her cousins and her family?" Daniel asked.

Caleb nodded. "I know it would be. I'm just not certain it will be good for me." He tore at the label on the bottle. "I'm not certain I'm ready to leave the memories."

"*Ach*," Timothy said. "Look at the time. The cookie exchange will be over soon." He stood. "I told Miriam I'd pick her up." He glanced at his brother. "Are you going to get Rebecca and the girls?"

Daniel nodded. "I am."

"Do you want me to get them?" Timothy offered.

"Will you have room for everyone?" Daniel asked. "Rebecca has Lindsay and Daniel Jr."

Timothy shrugged. "I think we'll have plenty of room."

"That would be fine," Daniel said. "I can finish this project I started. *Danki.*"

Caleb stood and shook Daniel's hand. "It was *gut* seeing you again."

"*Ya,*" Daniel said. "Think about what I said about the property nearby. You'd have plenty of business here. I think a new start would be *gut* for your soul."

"I'll consider it," Caleb said.

He followed Timothy through the shop, where he said goodbye to the carpenters. Daniel's words were still fresh in his mind as he climbed into Timothy's buggy. Would moving be good for his soul? Would it be good for Susie, or would uprooting her from all she'd ever known cause her more emotional pain after losing her mother only two years ago? He thought back to the conversation he'd had with Timothy after the church service. While Caleb felt guilty about moving on, he was beginning to wonder if it was time to take the plunge and do it. Perhaps he should consider breaking free of the holding pattern he'd been stuck in since he'd lost Barbara. The questions rolled through his mind as they headed toward the bakery.

Susie sat across from Naomi at a small table and bit into another cookie. "I love chocolate chip cookies. They're my favorite. What's your favorite, Naomi?"

Naomi glanced beside her at Lilly, who grinned in response. "I think peanut butter is my favorite," Naomi said.

"Oh," Susie said. "I love peanut butter too. I guess I have two favorites." She turned to Janie beside her. "You like peanut butter, right?"

Janie nodded. "*Ya*, I love peanut butter. My *mamm* makes the best peanut butter cookies."

Susie glanced back at Naomi. "I like to bake. Do you like to bake?"

Naomi nodded. "I do."

"Do you bake a lot?" Susie asked between bites of cookie.

"*Ya*, I do. I have a big family, and I do a good bit of cooking." Naomi sipped her cup of water.

"How many brothers and sisters do you have?" Susie asked.

"I have five brothers and three sisters," Naomi said.

Susie's eyes widened. "Oh my. That is a big family. You're so lucky. I'm an only child." She frowned. "My *mamm* was going to have another *boppli* when she died."

Naomi dropped her cookie, and Lilly gasped.

Susie nodded. "*Ya*, my *dat* was so sad when my *mamm* died. I was sad too. I cried for my *mamm* and also for the *boppli*."

Naomi was stunned into silence for a moment.

"I'm so sorry," Lilly said softly.

"I am too." Naomi reached over and touched Susie's hand.

"*Danki*. I'm still sad sometimes, but mostly I try to be *froh*. I like to think of the fun my *mamm* and I had. We used to bake cookies and she would read me stories at bedtime." Susie picked up another cookie. "My *dat* said that Jesus needed my *mamm* and the *boppli*, and I'll see them again someday."

"That's right," Naomi said, forcing a smile. "You'll see them, and you can hug them again in heaven."

"Right." Susie's smile widened. "And I can tell them how much I love them." She sipped her water. "I loved watching my *mamm* when she quilted. I used to sit on a stool next to her and she'd teach me how to make the stitches. I loved all of the colors she used. My favorite quilts were the ones that had blues and maroons in them."

Naomi nodded. "I love those colors too. They look very *schee* together."

"I saw those at the farmers market," Susie said. "That's why I ran over to meet you. It reminded me of my *mamm*."

Overwhelmed by emotion, Naomi smiled. *The quilts and memories of her* mamm *are what drew her to me. It makes sense now.* "That's very nice, Susie. I'm so glad that you like my quilts."

"Will you teach me how to make a quilt?" Susie's eyes were filled with hope. "I really want to learn how."

"*Ya*," Naomi said. "If we have time during your visit, I would—"

"Susie!" Sadie yelled from across the room. "Susie, will you come here, please?"

Susie stood. "My *aenti* is calling me. I'll be back." She and Janie ran off to where Sadie stood with Irene Wagler, Miriam, and Sarah Rose.

Naomi turned to Lilly, whose eyes were wide with shock.

"That poor *kind*," Lilly whispered. "She's been through

so much." She wiped her tearing eyes. "And her *mamm* was pregnant. I wonder what happened. How did she die?"

"I don't know," Naomi said. "I was wondering too."

She looked across the room. Sadie gave her a nasty look that seemed to say she should stay away, which sent a cold chill up Naomi's spine. Sadie then said something to Irene who glanced down at Susie and gave her a forced smile. She wondered what Sadie was saying, and for a split second she felt a pang of jealousy. She wanted to spend more time with Susie, but she pushed the thought away. Why should she feel any connection to a child who would soon return to her home in another state?

"What's on your mind, Naomi?" Lilly asked.

"Nothing." Naomi turned her attention back to the plate of cookies in front of her, but her appetite had evaporated after hearing the story of Susie's mother.

"You like her, don't you?" Lilly asked.

"What do you mean?"

"Susie," Lilly said. "You care about her."

"Of course I do," Naomi said simply. "She's a sweet little girl who lost her *mamm*. It's difficult not to care about her. I feel sorry for her."

"But you feel something deep for her," Lilly pressed on. "I can see it in your eyes. And she's attached to you as well."

Naomi avoided Lilly's stare by examining the crumbs on her plate. "Maybe Susie will want to write letters to me. Hopefully she will come to visit again soon."

"Naomi." Lilly touched her arm. "It's okay to say that you care about the *kind* and want to get to know her better. Perhaps you should talk to her *dat*."

"What are you trying to get at?" Naomi asked with suspicion.

"You and the girl get along." Lilly shrugged. "Maybe the *dat* needs some company too after losing his *fraa*."

Naomi sighed. "We've discussed this. I'm not looking for love, and it's wrong to prey on a widower."

"Prey on him?" Lilly laughed. "How is it preying on him if you go and talk to him and tell him that you enjoy spending time with his *dochder*?"

Naomi glowered at her. "I know what you're thinking. You want me to try to court him, and I won't do it. I refuse to be called the *maedel* who runs after every eligible bachelor. My *mamm* called me that, and it didn't feel nice at all. Besides that, he's connected to the Kauffmans. I think it's time I give up on the Kauffman men. If I ever do court again, it will be a man who is in no way related to the Kauffmans. Maybe he won't even know the Kauffmans." She turned back to Susie, who was smiling up at Irene. "Please just drop it."

"Fine," Lilly said with a sigh. "But I have a feeling about this, Naomi. I can't shake the idea that you and Susie's *dat*—"

"Lilly," Naomi seethed. "Stop."

"Fine, fine." Lilly waved off the thought.

Naomi shook her head and wondered if Lilly could somehow be right about the connection Naomi felt toward Susie.

Caleb climbed the steps to the bakery. "It feels like I was just here yesterday," he said, glancing around the wraparound porch. "It looks the same as it did when we were kids."

"*Ya*, my *mamm* loves it and keeps it running with several

of her daughters. We fix it up and repaint every spring." Timothy yanked the door open and they stepped into the bakery, which was bustling with women and girls who were laughing while straightening, sweeping, and cleaning.

"I guess we missed the party," Timothy said.

Caleb chuckled. "*Ya*, it sure looks like—"

"*Dat*!" Susie ran over, interrupting his words. "*Dat*!"

He bent down, and she wrapped her arms around him and kissed his cheek. Holding onto her, he closed his eyes and smiled. Oh, how he cherished his sweet little girl. "Did you have fun?" he asked.

"*Ya*!" She beamed. "I ate so many cookies! And I sat and talked to Naomi, my new *freind*." She pointed across the room to where Naomi stood with another young woman. "She's the one who makes the quilts at the farmers market." Taking his hand, Susie yanked him. "Come meet her."

"Okay," Caleb said. "Slow down."

Holding her hand, he followed her across the room. Naomi's gaze met his, and he was almost certain he glimpsed a flash of panic in her eyes before she glanced away. He wondered what that brief expression meant. Did his presence bother her?

"You'll like my new *freind*," Susie said, pulling Caleb toward Naomi.

"Caleb!" Sadie's voice called as she approached.

Caleb stepped toward Naomi, who looked up at him. As he opened his mouth to speak to Naomi, Sadie stepped in front of him and grabbed his arm.

"I'm so glad you're here," Sadie said, turning him toward her. "Irene is here too. I know she would love to talk to you."

She pushed him toward Irene, who stood with Sarah Rose Troyer and Rebecca Kauffman.

Susie grabbed his hand and tried to pull him backward. "*Dat*," she began with a huff, "I wanted you to meet *mei freind*."

"Susie," Caleb said, looking into her disappointed eyes. "I'll be just a moment."

"Irene was just telling me that her *dat* does have an opening for a new buggy mechanic," Sadie continued. "Right, Irene?"

Irene's smile was almost coy. "*Ya*, that's true, Caleb. I would be *froh* to introduce you."

"She's leaving!" Susie said. She stamped her foot and marched back toward Naomi.

Caleb opened his mouth to correct Susie's disrespectful display, but he didn't get a chance to speak. Instead, Irene continued chatting on about her father's shop, and Caleb wanted to interject. He waited for her to take a breath, but her words were strung together like a buggy wheel: no beginning, no end. He nodded, feigning interest, but his mind was set on a polite escape. He turned in the direction of Susie, and he spotted his daughter waving to Naomi as she headed out the front door with a woman about her age and three younger girls. He gave a sigh of defeat as he looked at Irene, who was still talking.

"I wanted you to meet *mei freind*," Susie said to Caleb while snuggling down in the bed next to her cousin later that evening.

"I know, but you were very disrespectful when you yelled and stamped your foot like a *boppli*." Caleb brushed a lock of brown hair back from Susie's forehead. "I'm certain I will talk to her before we leave."

"I'm sorry I acted like a *boppli*, but I was just disappointed. Naomi is really nice." Susie nodded with emphasis. "She said she's going to teach me to quilt."

Caleb smiled. "Is that so?"

"*Ya*." Susie glanced at Janie, who also nodded. "She's very pretty."

Ya, *she is*. He pushed that thought away.

"Tomorrow is the school program," Susie said. "I hope Naomi is there. Maybe you can meet her then."

He nodded. "Maybe so."

"Naomi will be there. Her sisters, Levina and Sylvia, go to the school. The Christmas program will be fun," Janie chimed in. "Susie is going to help us with the singing."

"That's *gut*." Caleb smiled at his niece. "It's time to get some sleep." Leaning over, he kissed Susie's cheek. "I'm glad you had fun today." He said good night to his nieces and then headed for the door.

As he descended the stairs, he contemplated Naomi. Susie was correct: Naomi was pretty. And he hoped his next encounter with the mysterious woman wasn't hijacked by his elder sister. In fact, he decided at that moment that he would make it a point to speak to the young woman who had his daughter so captivated.

CHAPTER 6

The following afternoon, Naomi shivered and pulled her cloak closer to her body while she trudged through the blowing snow from her family's buggy toward the one-room schoolhouse. Levina stumbled beside her, and Naomi grabbed her arm, steadying her younger sister on her feet as they moved through the swirling snow.

Irma, Naomi's mother, fell in step beside her. "I didn't think this snow was predicted for today. I thought the paper said the snow would start tomorrow."

Shaking her head, Naomi tightened her grip on her bag filled with treats and candies for the children who would perform the Christmas program. Each year, the teacher wrote the program, and the students practiced to get it just right. "No, I didn't think the snow was supposed to start before this evening."

Her brothers ran ahead, laughing and slipping through the snow.

"Slow down, boys," Titus, her father, bellowed. He shook his head. "They have such energy."

"*Ya*," Irma said, taking his hand. "They do. They get it from you." She gave Titus a sweet smile.

Naomi swallowed a sigh at the sweet sign of affection. She'd always admired the relationship her parents shared. She hoped that someday she'd find that kind of love and affection in a husband. She pushed the thought away since she believed in her heart that love wasn't in God's plan for her. Thinking about it too much would put her in a blue mood, and she needed to stay upbeat so she could enjoy the program.

A line of families moved slowly up the road through the snow toward the schoolhouse. Naomi couldn't help but think that the scene looked like a painting. The sky above them was gray, and the snow resembled a beautiful white fog engulfing the families who moved through it like apparitions dressed in dark cloaks and coats, some carrying gas lanterns, which glowed in the dark winter afternoon. The white, one-room schoolhouse was covered in the blowing snow, and buggies peppered with large, white flakes surrounded the little building.

They reached the schoolhouse at the end of the path, and Naomi shivered while stepping into the large room. A coal-burning stove provided warmth from the blustering cold afternoon. Rows of desks, benches, and folding chairs filled the center of the room, which was packed with children and their families. Paper snowflakes hung like mobiles fluttering from the ceiling, and drawings, including nativity scenes, angels, wreaths, and candles decked the walls. Similar drawings filled the blackboard at the front of the room. A makeshift curtain consisting of a few sheets hanging over twine hung at the front of the classroom in front of a raised platform that served as a stage next to the teacher's desk.

Naomi, Lizzie Anne, and her mother sat on an available

bench. Her father and Elam, her eldest brother at the age of nineteen, joined the men at the back of the room. Since Lizzie Anne had completed eighth grade last year, she'd graduated and was no longer a student at the school. Naomi greeted friends and chatted about the cold weather, while scanning the crowd consisting of members of her church district and families she'd known since her family moved to this district when she was sixteen, eight years ago.

Sylvia, Levina, and a group of their schoolmates hurried through the room, passing out handwritten pieces of paper with the schedule of program events, including Christmas-themed poems, songs, and skits. Naomi smiled, remembering her own happy memories of Christmas programs she'd participated in during eight years of school. She'd relished participating in the program with the other children. It was one of the highlights of every school year.

A mutter fell over the crowd and then the voices were silent.

"Good afternoon," Lena, the teacher, said. "*Danki* for coming to our program. The scholars have worked very hard, and we hope you enjoy it." She then glanced around the room. "Okay, *kinner*. Let's begin!"

The students lined up at the front of the classroom, the older children in back and the younger up front. Naomi spotted Susie standing with her cousins. When her gaze met Naomi's, she waved and grinned, and Naomi's heart warmed.

While children sang a round of Christmas carols, Naomi couldn't help but join in, as did many of the adults surrounding her. After the carols, the teacher rang a bell, and the children began acting out their skits and reciting their poems.

When Naomi's youngest brothers and group of friends presented impressions of their favorite animals, Naomi laughed and glanced at her smiling mother. She cut her eyes toward the men in the back of the room and found Caleb watching her, his eyes intense. With her cheeks blazing, Naomi turned back to the front of the room. She wished the sight of the widower didn't turn her insides to mush, but his eyes had mysterious power over her.

After several more skits, the program came to an end with another round of Christmas carols. The children invited the audience to join in, and Naomi tried to concentrate on the songs. However, her thoughts were focused on Caleb's intense green eyes and how they caused her body to warm.

As "Joy to the World" came to a close, the audience clapped and the children beamed.

Lena moved to the front of the room, her young face shining with a smile. "*Danki* for coming to our program," she said. "Please don't forget that Sadie Kauffman has invited us to come to her home for a little party. *Frehlicher Grischtdaag!*"

While conversations broke out around her, Naomi's stomach flip-flopped. She hoped she could convince her mother to skip the party in order to avoid more idle and awkward conversation with the Kauffmans.

Her mother leaned over. "I didn't know that we were going to Sadie's or I would've brought a covered dish."

Naomi shrugged. "Oh well. We can give out the candy and then head home. I'm sure the children are tired and—"

"Naomi." Her mother squeezed her hand. "It's Christmas. I'm certain Sadie will understand that we forgot a covered dish. It's about fellowship. The *kinner* will love being with their *freinden* a while longer."

Naomi shook her head, determined to avoid fellowship at Sadie's home. "*Ach*, I don't—"

"Naomi!" Susie rushed over and grabbed Naomi's sleeve. "I'm so *froh* you're here! I was hoping you'd see the program. Wasn't it great? What's your favorite Christmas carol? Mine is 'O Little Town of Bethlehem.' When I was little, I used to sing it all the time. How about you? Do you like to sing?"

Susie's father approached with a gentle smile. "Susie, you have to give her a chance to answer a question before you spout off six more."

The little girl giggled. "*Ya*, I guess you're right. Let's start with the most important question: What's your favorite Christmas carol?"

Although she was aware of Caleb's stare, Naomi kept her eyes on Susie. "My favorite is 'O Little Town of Bethlehem' too."

"That's *wunderbaar gut*! It was my *mamm's* too!" Susie grabbed Caleb's hand and yanked him closer. "This is my *dat*. His name is Caleb." She glanced up at her father. "*Dat*, this is *mei freind* Naomi I've been telling you about. She likes to quilt, bake, and sing, just like *Mamm* did!"

"It's nice to finally meet you, Naomi." His smile was warm as he held out his hand. "I've heard an awful lot about you."

With her heart in her throat, Naomi hesitated for a split second before taking his hand. The warm feel of his skin caused her breath to pause as her eyes locked with his.

"Are you coming over to my *Aenti* Sadie's house?" Susie asked, breaking the trance.

"Oh," Naomi said, pulling her hand back. "I don't know. I think I—"

"Please?" Susie's eyes were hopeful.

Naomi glanced up at Caleb.

"I think it's going to be a nice time," he said.

Nodding, Naomi finally gave in and smiled. "I'll be there after I help my *mamm* round up my siblings."

Gripping two mugs of Robert's homemade hot cider, Caleb weaved through the crowd in Sadie's family room for a second time and then back into the knot of people in the kitchen. He scanned the faces in search of Naomi's pretty smile. She'd seemed hesitant to join him and Susie at Sadie's house; however, she'd gathered up her siblings and steered them out the schoolhouse door and into the falling snow.

While her parents took their buggy to the house, Naomi and her siblings had walked the short distance from the schoolhouse to Sadie's home. He'd lost track of her amongst the group during the trek down the road toward Sadie's house, but he'd seen her younger sisters running around the house with Susie and a group of children. He hoped Naomi had chosen to stay with them. He was determined to speak to her for longer than that brief introduction they'd shared at the schoolhouse. He'd been captivated by her beautiful brown eyes and dimple while he'd watched her smiling and laughing during the children's program. Her warm handshake stirred something deep in his soul, a feeling he hadn't experienced since he'd lost Barbara.

When he spotted Naomi standing by the back door, his

steps quickened. She was still wearing her cloak, and he hoped she wasn't planning to hurry out the back door before they spoke again.

Moving toward her, he cleared his throat. "Naomi," he said, slipping between two laughing little boys.

"Oh, Caleb," she said. "Hi." Her cheeks flamed a bright pink. It seemed she was always blushing. He couldn't help but wonder if she always blushed in a man's presence. Whatever the reason, he found it adorable, and he was certain Naomi wasn't the temptress his sister had described.

"I hope you aren't planning on leaving." He held out one of the mugs. "I brought you some of Robert's famous hot cider. It's the best I've ever had."

"*Danki*." She sipped from the cup and smiled. "*Ya*, it is *gut*. It's even better than my *dat's*, but I would never tell him that."

Caleb laughed. He opened his mouth to speak, but was interrupted by a group of young girls who ran by screeching through the kitchen on their way to the stairs leading to the second floor. Leaning in close to Naomi, he inhaled her flowery scent that must've been from her soap or shampoo. "Do you mind the cold?" he asked.

She shook her head. "Cold is fine."

"Want to go sit on the porch so we can hear each other speak?" He nodded toward the back door. "Then we don't have to compete with the *kinner*. I'm surprised Robert hasn't yelled for the *kinner* to keep it down, but I guess he knows he can't control the crowd."

"It is loud in here. Sitting outside sounds *gut*," she said.

He held the door open for her and followed her out onto

the sweeping, wraparound porch. She lowered herself onto a bench and shivered.

"Bad idea?" he asked.

She shook her head. "It's nice out here. The house was getting stuffy." She gestured toward the snowflakes dancing across the white pasture. "From the looks of those clouds, this snow may not stop any time soon."

"I think you're right." He sank onto the bench beside her and swallowed a shiver. He should've grabbed his coat from the peg by the door, but he was more focused on having an uninterrupted conversation with her than how he would weather the crisp December air. "We'll definitely have a white Christmas this year."

"Do you prefer white Christmases?" she asked before sipping from the mug.

"*Ya*." He shrugged. He hadn't thought much about Christmas since he'd lost Barbara. "How about you?"

She mirrored his shrug. "*Ya*. I figure if it's going to be so cold, it might as well snow and make the scenery *schee* as a celebration of God's glory and our Savior's birth."

"I have to agree with that." He drank the hot cider and watched the snowflakes for a moment while trying to find a way to keep the conversation going. "What are your family Christmas traditions?"

"*Ach*, you know, nothing out of the ordinary." She set the mug down on the bench beside her. "We have the Christmas table with a place set for each of my siblings. I'm the oldest, and I love helping my mother set it up the night before. We put out little toys and candies for each of the *kinner*. I love seeing their faces Christmas morning. We have a big breakfast and then my *dat* sits in his favorite chair and tells the Christmas story from the book of Luke. It's *wunderbaar*. I look forward to it every year. How about you?"

Caleb studied the flakes that fluttered down onto the snow lining the wooden porch railing while he considered his answer. In all honesty, he and Susie hadn't really practiced any traditions since they'd lost Barbara. Last year, he gave her little gifts Christmas morning, and they'd placed a poinsettia on the mantle. But they didn't sing Christmas carols or share the Christmas story like they'd done when Barbara was alive. Beyond the Christmas program at school and a dinner shared with a neighbor, it seemed like just another day without Barbara.

"Susie and I don't really have any traditions anymore," he finally said. "We seem to just take things day by day with God's help."

Naomi's expression was sad. "I'm sorry for your loss." Her sweet voice was a mere whisper.

"I appreciate how nice you've been to my Susie," he said, placing his mug on the seat beside him. "You've taken a lot of time to talk with her, and not many adults seem to care enough to do that. *Danki*."

Her smile and dimple were back. "Oh, it's nothing." She waved off the comment. "She's an easy girl to love."

"She's quite taken with you," he said, studying her eyes. "You seem to have a gift with *kinner*."

Her cheeks were pink again, and he was certain it was more than just the cool breeze that colored them. "I've had a lot of experience with my siblings. My *mamm* once said I should've been a school teacher, but I thought quilting was the talent God wanted me to share." She paused as if gathering her thoughts. "Susie is a very special little girl. I've enjoyed spending time with her."

He nodded. "I believe she feels the same way about you. She's talked about you constantly since we met at the farmers market." He shook his head, embarrassed. "I'm sorry we made a scene that day."

"You didn't make a scene. It's scary when you think you've lost a *kind*. I took my siblings to the park one day last spring. My littlest brother, Joseph, was only four and wandered off while I was tying Leroy's shoe." She frowned. "I was scared to death with worry. There's a little stream that runs through the park, and I was certain he'd drowned." She laughed. "It turned out he was hiding behind a nearby tree, pretending to be a squirrel." Her expression was serious again. "But I understand how you felt at the farmers market. When you've lost sight of a child, your mind runs away with the most horrible possibilities of what could've happened to them."

The understanding in her pretty eyes touched him. "I feel like I've become even more protective of her since I lost Barbara," he said. "I guess it's because she's all I have left."

Naomi hugged her cloak closer to her body. "You must miss her so."

He nodded. "Every day."

"May I ask ...?" Her voice trailed off.

"What?" He rubbed his arms as the frosty air seeped into his skin. He wished he could run in and snatch his coat without losing a moment of conversation with Naomi.

"Nothing." She cleared her throat and glanced back toward the pasture. "The snow is beautiful, *ya*? I could watch it all night." She looked at his arms. "You should go get your coat. You don't want to spend your Christmas visit in bed or at the hospital with pneumonia, do you?"

"Naomi, you don't have to change the subject," he said with a smile. "You can ask me anything."

Standing, she pursed her lips. "You're going to catch a cold." She slipped in the door and returned a few moments later with a coat. "I grabbed one from off the peg by the door. It's my father's, but I don't think he'd mind if you borrowed it during our visit."

"*Danki.*" He pulled it on. Although the coat was a little large in the shoulders, it was warm. "What were you going to ask me?"

She bit her lower lip as if choosing her words. "I was wondering what happened to Barbara." She held a hand up, palm out. "But if it's too painful to share, I understand. I don't mean to pry into your life."

"It was Christmas Eve two years ago," he began, staring across the pasture. "We were so *froh* and excited back then. She was pregnant with our second *kind* and due at the end of January. Although she was feeling tired, she insisted that we celebrate with her cousins who lived on the other side of town. She'd baked a torte . . . Susie had helped her while they talked and laughed."

The memories flooded his mind like a rushing waterfall, with every detail bubbling forth, from the smell of her baked raspberry dream torte to the sight of her honey blonde hair sticking out from under her prayer *kapp*.

"I'd wanted to stay home because Barbara said that she had some back pain, but she'd insisted we go," he continued, lifting the mug of cider. "She'd even invited our neighbors to join us, and looking back, I'm certain she did to give herself an excuse to go no matter what." He chuckled to himself. "Barbara was good at that—finding ways to get what she wanted. Not that she was deceitful. She had a heart of gold. She knew our neighbors were celebrating Christmas alone that year, and she wanted to give them *froh* memories."

"She was very caring," Naomi said softly.

"*Ya*, she was." He glanced over at her, and her lip twitched as her eyes filled with tears. He hoped she didn't cry. He didn't want to cause her any sadness while they visited together. He also didn't want to cry and show too much emotion in front of her and seem as if he were weak.

"We'd spent all afternoon with her cousins and had a *gut* time," he said. "We ate too much, and the *kinner* played well together while sharing their Christmas candy and toys. We stayed much later than we should've, but Susie was having so much fun with her cousins."

He sipped the cider and looked back over the pasture as the memories of that tragic night gripped him.

"On the way home, I was riding in a buggy behind her and witnessed the whole thing." His voice quavered. He cleared his throat before continuing. "Barbara had wanted to ride back to our house with our neighbor and her family. For some reason, Susie insisted on riding with me. She said she was afraid I would get lost if I rode home alone." He snorted at the irony.

"She's such a thoughtful *kind*," Naomi whispered, wiping a tear.

"A pickup truck ran a red light and . . ." His voice trailed off as the graphic images of the crash flooded his mind. He shook the memories away. "My neighbor and her family suffered bruises and scrapes. But my Barbara and our unborn baby took the brunt of the impact." His voice fell to a whisper. "They were killed instantly."

"I'm so sorry." Tears glistened in Naomi's brown eyes. "I can't imagine how difficult it was for you and Susie."

He wiped his eyes, hoping to prevent any threatening tears from splashing down his cheeks. "The month that followed her death was a blur. Of course, God was with me the whole time, and I believe He still is." He paused and pulled at his beard while gathering his thoughts. "To be honest, the most difficult part has been the day-to-day routine, the things we do without thinking twice. You know, getting Susie ready for school, making her lunch, combing her hair, going to bed alone at night. That's when I miss Barbara the most."

Naomi wiped her eyes again. "That would make sense. You miss her the most when you're alone with Susie or just plain alone."

He nodded, impressed by her understanding of his loss. "That's it exactly. It's funny how your life can change in a split second. One minute I was riding down a road thinking about how much fun I'd had at the little party and listening to my little girl chatter endlessly about Christmas. Then the next moment I was trying to hold my emotions together while I held my little girl at the scene of the accident."

"Life does have a tendency to change on us in a split second," Naomi said, holding her mug in her hands.

He raised his eyebrow. "You sound like you speak from experience."

She shrugged while studying the contents of the mug. "I've made plans that haven't turned out the way I'd thought. Of course, it's nothing like you've experienced. My heartaches have been on a much smaller scale."

"Your heartaches?" he asked, his curiosity piqued. "Do you want to share?"

Naomi shook her head. "I'd rather not. It's just silliness." She sipped more of her drink. "This is the best cider I've ever tasted. Makes me thirsty for Robert's summer root beer. It's especially tasty with some vanilla ice cream."

"*Ya*, it is good. We'll have to do that next time we come visit," he said. "Susie and I will be sure to have the floats ready."

She gave him a surprised expression. "Okay."

He studied her eyes, wishing he could read her thoughts. "I've talked your ear off," he said. "Tell me about your life here in Bird-in-Hand."

She shrugged and cleared her throat. "It's nothing out of the ordinary. You already know that I work at the quilt stand in the farmers market and I help care for my siblings."

"What do you like to do for fun?" he asked, crossing his ankle onto his knee.

She laughed. "For fun?"

"That's right." He nodded. "You have fun, right?"

"Hmm." She gnawed her bottom lip and hugged her cloak closer to her body. "I enjoy reading with my youngest siblings. Leroy and Joseph are learning quickly how to sound out words." Her fingers moved to the ties of her black bonnet, and she absently moved them on her chin. "I love to quilt, and we sometimes have quilting bees." She turned to him, her eyes full of excitement. "In fact, we're having one here tomorrow, and I hope Susie will attend. She's asked me to teach her to quilt, and I'd love to give her some instructions."

He grinned. "She'd love that."

"*Gut*." She smiled. "I guess that's about it."

"So everything you enjoy is for someone else?"

She laughed. "I guess so. But isn't that what God has instructed us to do—to give of ourselves?"

"*Ya*, He has." Caleb wondered why she wasn't married yet. He surmised she was in her mid-twenties. Why hadn't some eligible bachelor swooped her up?

She gestured toward the front door. "You grew up here, *ya*?"

"I did."

"What took you to Ohio?"

"Love." He folded his arms across his chest. "I met Barbara while she was visiting her cousin here one summer. We courted through letters and the phone for a while, and I made a couple of trips up to visit her. She didn't want to leave her *mamm*, who was alive when we first met, so I moved there."

"Are many of Barbara's relatives still there?"

He shook his head. "No, just a handful of cousins in neighboring church districts."

"What do you do for a living?" she asked.

"I'm a buggy maker."

"Do you ever miss living here?"

He nodded. "Sometimes I do. Sometimes I wish I'd convinced Barbara to come live here, but when I think about that too much, I make myself *narrisch*, wondering if she'd still be alive. Then again, it's not our place to question God's will, is it?"

Naomi shook her head. "No, it's not." She then tilted her

head in question, her eyes thoughtful. "Do you believe that God only gives us one chance at true love? Or do you think He provides us the opportunity to love more than once during a lifetime?"

"That is a very *gut* question." He idly rubbed his beard while considering his answer. "I would say that God gives us second chances. I think Timothy's youngest sister is a great example of that." He was almost certain he saw her flinch at the mention of his best friend's name.

"*Ya*," she said softly. "That is a *gut* point."

Her eyes were full of something that seemed to resemble regret or possibly grief. He wanted to ask her what had happened to her to make her so sad, but the back door opened with a whoosh, revealing Sadie. Did his sister have a sixth sense when it came to ruining perfect moments?

"Caleb!" Sadie exclaimed, her face full of shock. "What are you doing out here in the cold?" She turned to Naomi and her eyes narrowed slightly, looking annoyed. "Oh, Naomi. *Wie geht's?*"

"I'm fine, *danki*." Naomi rose and stepped toward the door. "How are you?"

"Fine, fine. You must come in out of this cold before you both get sick." Sadie motioned for Naomi to enter the house. As Naomi stepped through the doorway, she shot Caleb a quizzical expression as if to ask what he'd been doing on the porch with Naomi. "That's not your coat, is it?" she asked.

Caleb stood and shook his head. "No, this coat belongs to Naomi's *dat*. She grabbed it for me when I started shivering."

Once Naomi was through the door, Sadie stepped back

onto the porch and closed the door. "What are you doing out here, Caleb?"

"Just talking with my new *freind*." He moved past her. "We were discussing the snow and Christmas." He shrugged. "That was all."

She took his arm and pulled him toward the door. "I have plenty of families I want you to meet, so you must come back inside."

"Yes, *schweschder*." He forced a smile and she steered him through the door. As he walked by Naomi and her mother, Caleb rolled his eyes and then smiled. Naomi laughed, and he gave her a little wave.

Sadie guided Caleb toward Irene Wagler who stood with her father and another couple. Caleb nodded a greeting and then glanced back at Naomi, who blushed and looked away.

"Caleb," Sadie said with a sweeping gesture, "this is Hezekiah Wagler, Irene's father."

Caleb shook the middle-aged gentleman's hand. "It's nice to meet you."

"You too," Hezekiah said. "I hear you are a buggy maker. I've owned my own shop for thirty years."

While the man began to describe his shop, Caleb glanced toward Naomi standing with her mother, and his mind wandered back to their conversation on the porch. He wished he could've sat with Naomi for much longer, perhaps hours, while they continued their conversation. She was so beautiful and so easy to talk to and he felt a connection to her, as if she could be a kindred spirit.

While he missed Barbara so much his heart ached some days, he felt something new when he looked at Naomi. She ignited a glimmer of hope that he might somehow find love again. Although he could never replace Barbara, he suddenly wondered if he could find happiness and build a life with a woman as special as Naomi. He had the suspicion he could love again, and Naomi King could possibly hold that key.

A smile turned up the corner of Caleb's lips. The possibility of finding a life mate again filled him with a joy he hadn't felt in years. He looked forward to exploring that future, but he knew he had to move slowly and make sure it was right. He didn't want to do anything to hurt Susie or Naomi.

Caleb turned back to the Waglers, and Sadie shot him a curious look.

Ignoring his sister, Caleb continued to smile and nod while Hezekiah discussed his booming business. He tried his best to look interested and engaged in the discussion, even though his thoughts were on the other side of the room with Naomi.

Caleb would keep his excitement about his evolving feelings for Naomi King to himself and let God lead him. He believed that with God, all things were possible, even the potential of a widower finding love again.

CHAPTER 7

The word *quilting* refers to the hand stitching of three layers: a pieced top, a layer of batting, and a bottom fabric layered together, then stitched together in a pattern to hold the layers together," Naomi began while holding up a quilt and showing it to Susie the following morning while they stood together in Sadie's kitchen.

Deep in thought, Susie scrunched her nose and swiped her hand over the cream, blue, and maroon quilt created in a log cabin pattern.

"See here?" Naomi ran her hand over the pattern. "The top layers were pieced together on the treadle sewing machine I have at my house in my room. The quilting is always done by hand. Then a binding is sewn onto the bottom layer by the machine and hand stitched to the top layer." She smiled at Susie's little tongue, sticking out of her mouth as if she were contemplating the meaning of life. "I'm sure you already know that we use what the Englishers consider an old-fashioned sewing machine powered by a pedal and no electricity." She felt her admiration for the little girl growing by the minute.

Naomi had arrived at Sadie's that morning along with

her sisters, mother, and Lilly. As soon as Naomi stepped in the door, Susie ran over and began chatting without taking a breath—asking question after question about Naomi's quilt, which she held in her hands. Naomi brought it in order to explain how a quilt was created.

While Naomi was excited to spend time with Susie, she couldn't help but be disappointed that Caleb had already left for a day of visiting his friends and acquaintances in town. She'd spent all evening thinking about their conversation on the porch.

Throughout the night, she'd tossed and turned, analyzing his words and remembering the sadness in his eyes while he'd discussed his beloved wife. She knew that she was developing feelings for the man, and she wished she could suppress them. However, her stomach fluttered at the thought of seeing him and speaking to him again.

Susie ran her hand over the stitching. "You sewed the top layer and then you hand stitched it all together?"

"That's right." Naomi nodded toward the family room where the women sat around a frame that held Sadie's latest creation. "See how all the women are stitching that quilt your *aenti* made? My *mamm* and I stitched this one. Since it's only a twin size, we didn't need a whole group to help us."

Susie studied the creation in her hands. "Who did you make this one for?"

Naomi shrugged. "This one was really just for fun. I was experimenting with the colors. Do you like it?"

Susie's eyes were bright. "I love it."

Naomi smiled. Perhaps the quilt could be a surprise Christmas gift for her little friend. She gestured toward the family room. "Did you want to go help the women with that quilt your *aenti* is finishing for the English customer?"

"No. Let's talk instead." Susie sat on a kitchen chair. "Did you have any of my *onkel's* cider last night?"

Naomi sat across from her. "I did. It was *appeditlich*."

The little girl nodded. "*Ya*, it was *wunderbaar*. I told my *dat* he needs to learn how to make cider like that."

Naomi laughed while standing. "That would be nice, wouldn't it?"

Susie tilted her head in question. "Do you believe in Christmas miracles, Naomi?"

Naomi's smile faded as she crossed the kitchen, grabbed two cups of water, and brought them over to the table. "Sure, Susie. Why do you ask?"

"*Danki*," Susie said, taking the cup. "Janie and Linda said that one of their cows was born on Christmas Eve last year, and their *dat* said it was a miracle because it was so cold." She sipped her water.

"I imagine it was a miracle." Naomi sipped the water, wondering where this conversation was headed.

Susie glanced toward the women in the family room next to the kitchen and then moved closer to Naomi. "May I tell you a secret?" she whispered.

"Of course," Naomi said softly, leaning closer to her.

"There's a Christmas miracle I've been praying for." Susie wiggled her chair closer to Naomi. "My dream is for my *dat* to be *froh* again on Christmas. I want to see him smile. I mean really smile. He smiles now, but I don't think he's truly *froh* since *Mamm* is gone. I want him to be really and truly *froh*."

Naomi smiled as tears filled her eyes. "That's very sweet, Susie."

"Do you think it's possible?" Susie asked, still whispering. "Do you think God will grant me that one miracle?"

Naomi pushed a lock of hair that had escaped Susie's prayer covering away from her face. "With God, all things are possible," she whispered.

"What are you two scheming?" Sadie asked, stepping into the kitchen and shooting Naomi a suspicious expression.

"We're just talking, *Aenti* Sadie," Susie said. "Naomi was telling me all about quilts."

Sadie grabbed a stack of dishes from the cabinet. "I thought you wanted to learn how to make them. If you want to learn how, then you need to come join us in the *schtupp* and not sit out here gabbing with Naomi."

Naomi bit her bottom lip to hold back the stinging retort she wanted to throw back at Sadie. Why did Sadie have to nag Susie when they were having a nice time together?

"Let's serve lunch, Susie," Sadie said.

Naomi and Susie helped Sadie spread out the food for lunch, including chicken salad, homemade bread, pickles, and meadow tea. The women gathered around the table. After a silent prayer, they discussed their upcoming Christmas plans while eating.

Naomi was filling the sink with soapy water for the dirty dishes when the back door opened and shut with a bang. She spotted Caleb following Robert into the family room, and her stomach flip-flopped. She was glad that Irene Wagler hadn't come to the quilting bee. Although she knew it was a sin, she couldn't ignore the jealousy she'd felt when Caleb had spoken to Irene and Irene's father last night. She'd felt a special connection with Caleb during their conversation on the porch. She knew that she had no future with the widower since he and his daughter would soon return to Ohio. However, she couldn't stop the growing attraction that bubbled up in her every time she saw him.

"*Dat*!" Susie rushed over and hugged Caleb, nearly knocking him over. "We've had such fun!" She began rattling off details of her new knowledge of quilt-making.

Grinning, Caleb shucked his coat and hung it on the peg by the door. Turning, he met Naomi's stare, and her pulse skittered. She looked back toward the sink and began scrubbing the dirty utensils as a diversion from his captivating eyes.

Conversations swirled around her while she continued washing the dirty serving platters and bowls. A tug on her apron caused her to jump with a start. She glanced down at Susie smiling up at her.

"Naomi?" Susie asked, her big green eyes hopeful. "My *dat* and I were wondering if you would go shopping with us."

"Shopping?" Naomi wiped her hands on a dish towel as she faced Susie and Caleb.

Sadie stepped behind Caleb and studied her brother. "Shopping?" she echoed. "Where are you going shopping?"

He shrugged. "Susie wants to go Christmas shopping, and it sounds like fun to fight the crowds. I don't care where we go. I'll leave the location up to Susie and Naomi."

"Will you come with us?" Susie grabbed Naomi's arm and tugged. "There are some things I want to get for my cousins."

Sadie gave Naomi a hard look, and Naomi paused. She

knew how Sadie relished sharing gossip at her quilting bees, and that was the reason why Naomi had enjoyed staying in the kitchen with Susie instead of listening to Sadie's latest news.

Naomi met Susie's hopeful eyes and silently debated what to do. She didn't want to hurt the little girl's feelings, but she also knew the possible consequences. Going shopping alone with Caleb and his daughter could start rumors that would upset Naomi's mother.

"Well, I don't know." Naomi turned back to the sink. "There are an awful lot of dishes to be cleaned up, and then I need to help finish the quilt. Sadie has a customer who is going to pick it up tomorrow since it's a Christmas gift for her daughter."

"I'll help finish the dishes," Caleb said, grabbing a dish towel.

Stunned, Naomi stared at him. "You will?"

He chuckled. "Believe it or not, I cook and do dishes back home."

"I just don't know." Naomi felt Sadie's scrutinizing stare. "I think I need to stay and help with the quilt."

Susie frowned. "Are you certain?"

Once Sadie had walked away, Caleb sidled up to Naomi and began to dry a serving platter. "Would you feel more comfortable if one of your sisters or perhaps one of my nieces came along with us?" he asked her under his breath.

Naomi studied him, wondering how this man could read her mind. "How did you know?"

He gave a small smile. "I know how *mei schweschder* works."

Naomi leaned closer to him. She couldn't help but inhale his manly scent, like earth mixed with a spicy deodorant. "What do you mean?" she asked.

He placed the dry platter on the counter. "She had spread the news about my proposal to Barbara before I had even decided to propose. She should've been an editor for the local paper instead of a quilt maker." He snatched a handful of clean utensils from the sink. "I'll finish the dishes, and Susie can help me put them away. Why don't you see if one of your sisters or my nieces wants to join us? That will quell any rumors about our shopping expedition."

"Are you certain?" Naomi placed the dish towel on the counter.

"I'm drying the dishes, aren't I?" he asked with a grin.

She couldn't help but smile. His handsome face was nearly intoxicating. "*Danki*."

"No need to thank me," he said, opening the utensil drawer. "You're going to help me more than you know. Shopping is not one of my strengths."

CHAPTER 8

Caleb walked through the flea market with Naomi by his side while Susie, her cousin Janie, and Naomi's sisters, Levina and Sylvia, skipped ahead toward a candy concession stand.

The ride over to the indoor flea market in Robert's borrowed buggy had been noisy, with the four girls chatting all at once in the back seat. Caleb had stolen several glances at Naomi and found her fingering the ties on her black bonnet and the hem of her cloak. He wondered what she was thinking and if she was enjoying her time with him as much as he enjoyed his time with her.

"How come we haven't met before now?" he asked, falling into step with her while holding the bags containing a few small gifts he'd picked up for Sadie and Robert.

She gave him a confused expression. "Excuse me?"

"You didn't go to school with the Kauffmans, right?" he asked.

She shook her head. "No. I grew up in a district that's a few miles away. My *dat* decided to move to a larger farm when I was sixteen." She paused, gathering her thoughts. "You're close to the Kauffmans, *ya*?"

He nodded. "Timothy's been my best *freind* for as long as I can remember."

"Oh." She frowned.

"You don't like the Kauffmans much, do you?" He felt like a liar for asking the question. He knew part of the answer since Timothy had shared that he'd broken Naomi's heart. However, he wanted to hear her version of her past with Timothy and Luke. He knew in his gut that Sadie was wrong about Naomi. She seemed like a quiet, honest young woman, not a woman who was too eager to find a husband.

"It's not that." Her cheeks were pink again. "I just. *Ach.* I sort of—"

"Naomi!" Levina's loud voice interrupted Naomi. "Can I have some money? I want to get some licorice."

"Oh." Naomi pulled out her small black handbag.

"I got it." Caleb touched her warm hand and then pulled out his wallet.

"Oh no." Naomi shook her head. "That's not necessary. I don't expect you to buy candy for my sisters."

"It's my pleasure." He handed Levina a ten. "Please buy for all of the girls."

"*Danki*, Caleb." Levina smiled and trotted off to the candy counter.

"*Danki*," Naomi said.

"*Gern gshehne.*" He motioned toward a bench near the candy stand. "Let's sit for a moment. What were you saying about the Kauffmans?"

She smoothed her skirt. "It's rather embarrassing."

"I'm certain it can't be that bad."

She frowned and placed her plain, black handbag on her lap. "I'd rather not talk about it."

"That's fine," he said, glancing toward the girls, who were busy ordering candy at the stand. "What do you want for Christmas?"

"Me?" Naomi laughed. "*Ach*, I don't need anything."

He studied her deep brown eyes. "There must be something you'd like. There's always something we don't need that we'd like to have, even if it's considered unnecessary or frivolous."

"Well." She tapped her chin and glanced toward a bookstand. "There's a pretty Bible that I looked at a few weeks ago. I'm still waiting for it to go on sale. The binding on my Bible is falling apart, but I don't necessarily need a new one. However, every night when I open it for my devotional time, I feel the fraying binding and think about how nice it would be to have a new one."

"Interesting." He smiled. "You'll have to show it to me before we leave."

Naomi shrugged. "Alright. So what about you? What do you want for Christmas?"

At first he waved off the question because he couldn't think of anything he wanted. But then the answer hit him like a speeding, oncoming freight train. The truth was that he did want something, and it was as if a light bulb went off in his head and in his heart. The feeling was overwhelming and it was brand new, something he hadn't felt in a long, long time. What he wanted for Christmas was something he'd probably never experience again. He wanted a companion. Someone to share his life with. Someone to tell his hopes and dreams to and to help him through the tough times. Someone to help him raise Susie in a faithful Christian home.

He wanted a life partner.

He wanted a wife and a mother for Susie.

But finding that wasn't as easy as Sadie had made it sound.

Besides, worrying about his own needs was selfish and self-serving, since he knew his focus had to be on being the best parent he could for Susie. Aside from God, she was the center of his life now. Concentrating on finding a new wife would only take his focus away from Susie, which would be wrong.

Therefore, he couldn't tell Naomi the truth about what he wanted for Christmas because it was too embarrassing.

"I don't need anything." Grinning, he raised an eyebrow. "Sound familiar?"

She mirrored his grin, and she was adorable. "There must be *something* you want, no matter how unnecessary and frivolous it may sound, Caleb. Isn't that what you told me?"

He glanced across the large flea market toward a booth with antique tools they'd passed earlier. "There was a tool I spotted over there that would be a great one to add to my collection, but it's nothing I necessarily need."

She touched his hand. "I'll make a deal with you. I'll show you my dream Bible if you show me that tool you want but don't need."

He shook her hand. "It's a deal."

Her smile was bright, revealing her dimple. "*Wunderbaar.*"

"*Dat,*" Susie asked, approaching them. "Can we get some fudge?"

Caleb glanced at Naomi, and she shrugged while pulling

out her wallet. "Let me pay this time. You paid for the licorice."

He leaned close to her and inhaled her flowery scent, wondering briefly if it was her shampoo. "Put your money away," he whispered. He then turned to Susie. "That's a *gut* idea. Let's all get some fudge."

Stepping over to a fudge stand, he ordered a slab for the girls and then some for himself and Naomi.

"You're much too generous," Naomi said before breaking off a piece from the small block. "I could've paid for my sisters and me."

He shook his head. "Don't be *gegisch*. It was just fudge."

"*Danki*," she said.

He wished he could get her to open up to him, but he didn't want to push her. He and Susie would head back to Ohio soon, so any thoughts of a relationship would be preposterous. Yet, he was captivated by her.

She smiled and then nodded toward the girls, who were disappearing in the crowd. "We'd better catch up to them."

He nodded. "You're right."

They weaved through a knot of shoppers and caught up with the girls at a toy stand.

"Did you have a nice day in town today?" she asked.

"*Ya*," he said. "I ran some errands with Robert and visited some old *freinden*."

"I bet your friends were *froh* to see you," she said, wiping her mouth with a napkin.

"I think so." He shrugged while biting into the chocolate. "We stopped by the Kauffman Furniture store so Robert could talk to his *dat* and brothers." He shook his head as he recalled the conversations. "Timothy and his brothers are mounting a campaign to get me to move back here. They were trying to get me to go visit a shop that's for sale near the furniture store."

"Oh?" Her eyes rounded with interest. "Did you go visit it?"

He shook his head. "Not yet. But I might."

The girls sat on a bench outside the toy stand and giggled while eating their fudge, and Caleb wondered if he should go visit the shop owner. Would moving Susie closer to his family be a way to help her heal after losing her mother?

He motioned toward a bench near the girls. "Should we sit and finish our chocolate?"

"That's a *gut* idea." Naomi sat down. "I didn't mean to be rude before."

"Rude?" He sank down next to her. "What do you mean?"

"When you asked me what I thought of the Kauffmans." She studied her remaining square of fudge, and he wondered if she was avoiding his eyes. "It's just that I've made some mistakes that I regret, and they aren't easy to talk about."

Guilt rained down on him for pushing her to discuss it. He didn't want to make her uncomfortable. "You don't have to tell me. It's none of my business."

"No," she said, frowning as she looked up at him. "You've been honest with me, so I need to be honest with you. Timothy and I courted for a short while, but we broke up when we realized that we weren't right for each other. I also courted Luke Troyer for a short time. *Mei mamm* said I was too eager with them, and I know she's right." Her cheeks blazed a bright pink, and he wished he could ease her embarrassment. "But I was young then. I'm almost twenty-five and I know better now. I won't rush into another relationship. In fact, I think God would prefer I help *mei mamm* raise my siblings rather than court."

He raised an eyebrow in surprise. "Don't you think you're being a bit too hard on yourself? We've all had our hearts broken at one time or another, but God still wants us to get married and have a family. You said yourself that God can give us a second chance at love."

She shook her head. "That's not what I said. I asked you if *you* believe God gives us a second chance, but I never said I believe it."

"But you agreed that God gave Sarah Rose a second chance with Luke."

"*Ya*, I did," she said softly. "But I'm not so sure he'd be willing to give me a third chance."

"What makes you think God puts a cap on how many chances we can have to find love?"

Naomi looked away from his stare. "I don't know. It's just a feeling I have."

"You're young," Caleb said. "Don't give up on love so quickly. Barbara had an *onkel* who didn't marry until he was almost fifty. He never gave up on love."

She gasped. "Really? He was almost fifty?"

"I'm not saying you'll have to wait that long," he added, wiping his beard with a napkin. "I would imagine you'll be snatched up quickly with that *schee* smile of yours."

Looking embarrassed, she bit into the fudge. He wondered what on earth Timothy did to shatter her heart into pieces. Timothy had hinted that he wasn't proud of how their relationship had ended. He must not have let her down too easily.

They ate in silence for a few moments. The girls finished their fudge, and Susie came over and got money from Caleb in order to purchase a few small toys. While the girls shopped, Caleb and Naomi finished their chocolate.

"How about we go into that antique place?" she asked, wiping her mouth. "I want to see that tool you need."

He took her used napkin from her and tossed it into the trash along with his. "You forgot what I said. I don't *need* it. I would like to have it."

She grinned as she stood. "I meant to say, show me the tool that you *would like* to have."

"That's right." They walked over to the toy shop together, and he approached the girls. "We'll be right next door looking at the antiques. When you're finished shopping, come over and join us."

The girls agreed, and he and Naomi entered the antique shop, where he led her over to the tools. Her eyes widened as she glanced over the assortment of gadgets.

"Wow," she said. "Are these the tools you use for your buggy projects?"

He grinned. "No, I actually use modern tools, but I like to collect antiques. I can use them, and sometimes I do. But mostly, I collect them for fun."

She picked up an antique saw and studied it as if it were a precious piece of glass. "How did you start your collection?"

He picked up a hand drill. "My *grossdaddi* started the collection. Actually, he used the tools in his carriage shop. I like to add to it every now and then. It's not really a frivolous expense because I can actually use them." He turned the drill over in his hand, examining the craftsmanship.

"Is that the one you want?" she asked as she stepped over to him.

Caleb nodded. "*Ya*. Like I said, I don't need it, but it would be nice to have." He placed it back on the counter. "I guess we should go find the girls and see if my *dochder* is finished spending my money yet."

"Are women ever finished spending a man's money?" Naomi's smile was coy.

He grinned. "If I answer that question truthfully, will I get smacked?"

She tapped her chin, feigning deep thought. "I don't know. I suppose it depends on the answer."

He laughed and suppressed the urge to put his arm around her shoulders and pull her in to his arms for a hug. He enjoyed her easy sense of humor. Spending time with her was akin to relaxing, a feeling he hadn't enjoyed in months — no, more like years.

"*Dat*!" Susie rushed over, her three shopping bags rustling against her cloak. "I think I'm finished. I got some candy and toys. Want to see?" She held open one of the bags and found a plethora of lollipops, chocolate coins, ring pops, candy canes, marbles, small rubber balls, and little toy cars.

"Very nice, Susie." He touched her cheek. "I think you're going to make your *freinden* and cousins very happy on Christmas."

"Are we heading home now?" Janie asked. "I think I have to help my *mamm* start supper."

"*Ya*," Caleb said, placing his hand on Susie's shoulder. "I believe your *dat* may send out a search party if we don't head home soon." He glanced at Naomi. "You need to show me that Bible you were talking about earlier before we head out."

"*Ach*, it's not something I need." Naomi waved it off as they weaved through the crowd.

Levina sidled up to Naomi and took her hand. "That pretty Bible you always visit when you come in here?"

Naomi swung her sister's hand and smiled down at her. "It's not something I need. I can still enjoy God's Word with the Bible I have."

Caleb smiled at the tenderness between the sisters and he took Susie's hand. "We'll stop at the book store on the way out."

They entered the little book stand, and he followed her over to a display of Bibles.

Sylvia pointed to a plain but elegant black Bible. "This is the one she wants."

Naomi's cheeks were pink again. "But I really don't need it."

Caleb glanced at the price tag. "Would you want your name engraved on the front?"

Naomi shook her head. "Oh, it's just too much. I couldn't expect you to—"

"*Ya*, she does," Levina chimed in. "*Mamm* and *Dat* have one that was engraved for them on their wedding day, and Naomi has always thought that was a nice gift. She said she wants one with her name on it too."

"Levina," Naomi gently scolded. "You need to mind your own business."

Janie glanced toward the clock on the wall. "We better go," she said, starting toward the door. "I don't want my *dat* angry with me. You know how he gets."

Caleb nodded, knowing how short his brother-in-law's temper could be. He distinctly remembered the early years of Sadie's marriage to Robert, when he'd yell at her for things as simple as supper not being ready at his requested time.

Once the girls were loaded into the back of the buggy, Caleb climbed into the buggy seat next to Naomi. "Do you want me to drop you and your sisters off at home?"

She nodded. "That would be *wunderbaar.*"

While the girls chatted about snow and Christmas, Caleb and Naomi rode in silence. He wondered if she'd had as much fun as he'd had today. He wished the afternoon didn't have to end. The idea of moving back to Bird-in-Hand swirled through his mind. Should he go look at that shop? Should he make an offer on the place if it was a good deal? Did he want to uproot Susie? Was he entitled to the happiness he could possibly have here in Lancaster County?

Out the corner of his eye, he spotted his daughter laughing with her cousin and Naomi's sisters. If he moved her here, he wouldn't so much as uproot her as give her a sense of family. Surely, she would miss her friends back in Ohio, but she would also make new friends, including Naomi's sisters and Naomi herself.

"Turn here," Naomi said, breaking through his thoughts. "Then go about half a mile and turn right."

"Oh," Caleb said with a smile. "You're not far at all from Sadie's house."

Naomi shook her head. "Just a little ways, really."

"Close enough to walk," he said, steering around a corner.

"*Ya,*" she said, lifting her purse from the floorboard. "I think Susie got all that she wanted today."

"I think so," he said.

She pointed toward a large, white farmhouse. "That's it."

"*Danki* for coming," he said as he steered toward her driveway.

"*Danki* for the invitation," she said, turning toward him. "I had a nice time."

"I did too." And he hoped that they could get together again sometime soon.

"Let's go, girls," Naomi said, facing her sisters. "We have to get started on supper." She opened the door, hopped down from the buggy, and helped her sisters down. After saying good-bye to the girls in the back, Naomi turned to Caleb. "Have a nice evening."

"You too," he said. "I hope to see you again soon."

She smiled. "*Ya*, I do too." She said good-bye to the girls and then hurried toward the house with her sisters in tow.

As Caleb steered toward Sadie's house, he decided he needed to check into that shop that Timothy had recommended, and an unfamiliar excitement filled him.

CHAPTER 9

"Go wash up," Naomi told her siblings as she set the table later that evening. "Supper is almost ready."

The children filed out of the kitchen, and Naomi lined the plates up on the long table.

Her mother placed a large bowl of mashed potatoes at the center of the table. "Did you have fun today?"

"*Ya*," Naomi said, snatching a handful of utensils from the drawer. "Susie wanted to shop for Christmas gifts for her cousins and friends. She, Janie, Sylvia, and Levina had a *gut* time shopping, and Caleb and I just walked around and talked."

"What did you and Caleb discuss?" Irma began to fill a platter with homemade rolls.

"Oh, nothing much." Naomi lined the utensils up by the place settings. "We talked about Christmas and things like that. He's very easy to talk to. We had a nice time together." She didn't want to admit they'd talked about her doomed relationships.

Irma gave Naomi a hard look, and Naomi wished she hadn't even mentioned Caleb's name.

Rather than argue about Naomi's track record with

dating, Naomi decided to change the subject. "How did the quilt turn out? Did you get it finished before the customer arrived?"

Irma placed the platter next to the rolls and glowered. "I hope you're not getting any ideas about this widower, Naomi. You know he's going back to Ohio after the holidays and you're just going to get your heart broken if you get too attached."

Naomi breathed out a deep sigh. "*Mamm*, I know that. He's just a *freind*."

Her mother continued to frown. "Don't make a fool of yourself again. You never should've gone out with him today. You know how that will look to the rest of the community."

"He invited me," Naomi said, pointing to her chest. "It wasn't my idea. In fact, I think it was Susie's idea. She really likes me, and I enjoy spending time with her too. You know she lost her *mamm* only two years ago. For some reason, she's latched on to me, and how can I turn her away?"

Irma wagged a finger at Naomi. "You can't be her *mamm*. That's not your place."

"I never said I wanted to be her mother. I just want to be her *freind*. Is that so wrong?"

"*Ach*, no." Irma shook her head. "But I know you, Naomi. You get too attached, and that will only lead to trouble."

Naomi shook her head. "I can't do anything right in your eyes, can I, *Mamm*? The way you see it, I mess up completely when it comes to love, and I'm destined to be alone."

"I wasn't speaking of love," Irma said, pulling the broccoli and rice casserole from the oven. "I was talking about perceptions. It just didn't look right for you to go out shopping with that widower and his *dochder*. It looked very inappropriate, and you know how people talk."

"I don't see how any of my behavior was inappropriate, *Mamm*." Naomi wished her voice wouldn't quaver with her frustration. She grabbed a handful of napkins and began adding them to the place settings in order to keep busy and stop her threatening tears. She was tired of her mother's constant criticism. "It was Susie's idea, and I didn't want to disappoint her. I even invited Levina, Sylvia, and Janie to join us in order to quell any rumors that Sadie Kauffman might feel the need to start about me."

Irma set the casserole dish on the table and pursed her lips. "I know you're not trying to give people the wrong impression, but I know how they think. If you even go for a walk alone with a man, some women assume things they shouldn't about you."

"Why should I care what people think of me?"

"It reflects on this family, Naomi." Irma set the potholders on the counter and then lowered her voice. "How do you think your *dat* will feel if he hears people call you too eager?"

Naomi shook her head. "He would know that I'm not those things, and he would defend me."

Irma touched Naomi's shoulder. "I know you. I know your heart and how you get too attached too soon."

"I'm not attached," Naomi insisted, even though she knew it wasn't the whole truth. "He's *mei freind, Mamm*. What's wrong with being *freinden* with him?"

Irma gave her a sympathetic expression. "I've seen the way you look at him and the way you blush when he's around.

Your feelings for him are written all over your *schee* face, Naomi."

Naomi cupped a hand to her mouth. "They are?"

"*Ya.*" Irma touched Naomi's cheek. "I don't want to see you get hurt again. I remember clearly the pain you suffered when you had your heart broken by Luke Troyer and then Timothy Kauffman. I don't want to see you suffer that again, and I don't want you to get a reputation."

"Caleb and I are just *freinden, Mamm*," she repeated, her voice quavering.

Irma raised an eyebrow in disbelief. "Is that what you're trying to convince yourself?"

A lump swelled in Naomi's throat as tears filled her eyes. "It's the truth, *Mamm.*"

"He's a widower, Naomi," she said. "He's not ready to give his heart away."

"I know," Naomi whispered. "I've already considered that, and I respect his feelings for his *fraa.*"

Her siblings returned to the kitchen with a roar of footsteps, chatter, and giggles, and Naomi breathed a sigh of relief. She longed for her mother's focus to turn to someone other than her.

"Lizzie Anne," Naomi called over the noise. "Would you please grab the glasses from the cabinet?" She glanced at her younger sisters. "You can put the glasses out by the dishes."

Lizzie Anne instructed Amos to go out to the barn and call Elam and their father to come in for supper. She then gave Naomi a concerned expression, but Naomi quickly looked away and turned toward the refrigerator.

Irma grabbed Naomi's arm and pulled her back. "Caleb will

go home to Ohio soon," she whispered in Naomi's ear. "Don't let him take your heart with him. You've been hurt enough."

Naomi sighed with defeat. "Yes, *Mamm*," she said before grabbing the pitcher of ice water and the tub of butter. She took a deep, cleansing breath, pushing away the emotions rioting within her. She knew her mother was right about Caleb's plans to return to Ohio. However, Naomi also couldn't squelch the notion that the feelings she had for Caleb were different from anything she'd ever felt for Luke Troyer or Timothy Kauffman. What she felt for Caleb was deeper, something that touched her soul.

Lizzie Anne sidled up to Naomi. "Are you okay?" she whispered.

Naomi nodded. "*Ya*. I'm *gut*."

Lizzie Anne frowned. "You look upset."

"*Wie geht's?*" Titus's voice boomed as he entered the kitchen. "It smells *appeditlich*."

Naomi forced a smile and touched her sister's arm. "*Danki*," she whispered, "but I'm fine."

Lizzie Anne gave her a look of disbelief.

"It's all ready," Irma said. "*Kinner*, please take your seats."

Naomi delivered the pitcher of water and the butter, placing them near her father's seat, and then sat in her usual place, which was between Lizzie Anne and Elam. As she bowed her head in silent prayer, she asked God to guide her in her confusing feelings for Caleb Schmucker.

"Did you have a *gut* day?" Caleb asked Susie as he sat on the edge of her bed and tucked her in.

"Of course I did, *gegisch*." Susie grinned, hugging her favorite doll to her white nightgown.

He smirked and rubbed her brunette head. Glancing toward the hallway, he wondered how much time he'd have alone with Susie before her cousins came clambering in from the bathroom down the hall. He leaned in close. "Susie, how would you feel about selling our house in Ohio and moving here?"

She gasped, her big, green eyes rounding with excitement. "You mean, like live here forever, *Dat*?"

"*Ya*." He touched the tip of her little nose. "Forever."

She screeched, and he pressed a finger to her lips shushing her.

"Your *onkel* will get very upset if he hears you yell like that," he said.

"Are we going to live here?" she asked, sitting up and gesturing around the room. "Then I can stay in this room with Janie, Nancy, and Linda, and I could go to school with them." Her smile widened. "And maybe I could learn to quilt with *Aenti* Sadie and Naomi. And we could go shopping again with Naomi, and I could play with her sisters. Right, *Dat*?"

He brushed his fingers through her long, brown hair. "*Ya*, maybe so." *And I could spend more time with Naomi as well.*

She leaned forward and wrapped her arms around his neck, hugging him. "*Ich liebe dich, Dat.*"

"I love you too, *boppli*," he whispered before he kissed the top of her head.

Closing his eyes, he sent up a prayer to God, asking Him for help with this decision. While he felt in his heart it was time to move back home, a small part of his mind was apprehensive.

It seemed all the signs were there leading him back home: his family, his friends, the welcoming of the church district members, and the possible opportunity of a job. But was he moving for the right reasons? Would this be a new start or would he be trying to outrun the loneliness that had overtaken his soul when Barbara died? Was he doing this for selfish reasons or did he have his daughter's best interests in mind?

"*Dat?*"

Opening his eyes, he found Susie studying him. "*Ya?*"

Wrinkling her nose, she gave him a confused expression. "Were you sleeping or praying?"

He touched her cheek. "I was praying."

"What were you praying about?"

"I was asking God if He thought we should move back here."

"Oh." She nodded, her expression serious. "And what do you think God's answer was?"

He smiled. "I'm not certain yet, but I'll tell you when He gives me a sign."

"Do you think He'll give me a sign too?"

"Maybe."

She leaned closer and lowered her voice. "You know what Naomi told me?"

"What?"

"She told me that she believes in Christmas miracles," Susie whispered. "Do you believe in them?"

Sighing, he gave her a gentle smile. "Sure I do, Susie."

Muted giggles and loud thumping footsteps echoed down the hallway, announcing the arrival of Susie's cousins. Caleb stood as the girls entered the room and jumped into the beds.

Sadie appeared in the doorway. "It's time to settle down." Crossing the room, she kissed them all on their foreheads.

Caleb wished them each a good night and then followed Sadie down the stairs to the family room.

"Would you like some cocoa?" she asked.

"*Ya. Danki*," Caleb said.

"Have a seat. I'll be right back." She disappeared into the kitchen.

Caleb sat in a chair in front of the fire, which crackled, popped, and hissed.

Across the room, Robert sat in his favorite chair, reading the paper. Fingering his beard, Caleb wondered what to say to his brother-in-law. Although he'd known Robert since he was a teenager, Caleb never felt much of a connection to him. Not like he did with Timothy and Daniel, anyway. Robert was the least friendly of the Kauffman men. Caleb used to wonder why Robert was so different from his brothers, but he'd finally decided Robert was just stoic. He was more focused on work and running a smooth household and farm than on fun and games.

"I was thinking about going to see that house and workshop that are for sale," Caleb blurted out. "Daniel and Timothy mentioned it was near the furniture store."

Robert peeked at Caleb over the paper. "Really?"

Caleb nodded. "Timothy mentioned that the owner wanted a fair price, and I have some money I've been saving up to rebuild my barn."

Looking intrigued, Robert folded his paper and placed it on the table beside him. "You're considering moving back here, *ya*?"

"I think so." Caleb shifted in the chair. "I mentioned it to Susie, and she's very excited. I think it would be good for her to be with her cousins."

Robert was silent for a moment, fingering his beard and considering Caleb's words. "That makes a lot of sense. It would be *gut* for you and Susie to have a new start, and we would love for you to join our church district."

"*Danki.*" Caleb glanced around the room as memories of his childhood cluttered his mind.

It seemed as if only yesterday he was sitting in this same wing chair and looking at the mantle. The same old, plain cherry clock sat in the center and ticked over the crackle of the fire. The Christmas decorations consisted of a large poinsettia and some greenery, just as when he was a child. For a moment, he expected his father to flop into the armchair across from him, open his Bible, and begin to read aloud while his mother knitted in the love seat next to him.

"Did you have a nice time at the flea market?" Sadie asked, returning from the kitchen holding a tray with three mugs of hot cocoa.

"*Ya*, I did." Caleb lifted a mug from the tray. "*Danki.*"

"*Gern gschehne.*" She handed a mug and napkin to Robert and then sat across from Caleb in their *daed's* favorite chair.

Caleb sipped the mug and felt the whipped cream in his beard. "*Appeditlich.*" He swiped the napkin across his whiskers.

Sadie cradled a mug in her hands. "Susie seemed like she had fun today."

Caleb nodded, sipping more cocoa. "I think she had a *wunderbaar gut* time with her cousin and friends."

"And Naomi." Sadie tapped the side of her mug, a frown turning the corners of her mouth downward.

"*Ya*," he said, ignoring her tone and her expression. "Susie loves spending time with Naomi."

She wagged a finger at him. "You remember what I told you about her."

"Sadie," Robert snapped. "Gossiping is a sin."

Caleb drank from his mug in an effort to suppress the grin threatening to curl his lips. This was one instance in which he appreciated his gruff brother-in-law.

With an indignant frown, Sadie sipped her cocoa.

An awkward silence fell among them as they enjoyed their drinks. Caleb searched for something to say, but found himself only thinking of Naomi and wondering if she'd enjoyed their day together.

After a few sips of cocoa, Robert cleared his throat and glanced at his wife. "Caleb was telling me he wants to go look at the shop that's for sale near my father's store."

"What?" Sadie gasped and grinned. "You're going to consider buying a shop here?"

"Maybe." Caleb held up a hand as if to calm her from across the room. "Don't get your hopes up yet. I'm thinking about moving back, and Timothy and Daniel told me about the shop. Apparently it has a house on the property as well."

Placing her mug on the table beside her, Sadie clapped her hands together. "*Ach*, that's *wunderbaar*. We would love to have you and Susie here."

"Don't get too excited," Caleb repeated. "I discussed it with Susie tonight, and she likes the idea. But I need to do some research and some careful consideration. I have a little bit of money I've been saving to refurbish my barn, but it's only enough for a small down payment. I can't do anything until I get a buyer for my farm. And with today's economy—"

She waved off the thought as she interrupted him. "Your farm would sell easily, Caleb. From what you've told me, you have prime land that an investor would love."

"I'd be glad to take you over to see the shop tomorrow," Robert said. "The owner is Riley Parker, an Englisher who grew up here. He's a *gut* man, and he'll give you a fair price."

Caleb nodded and studied the plain white mug while mulling over the notion of buying a place and setting up business after being gone from Lancaster County for so long. It seemed like such a hasty decision to look at a shop. Would it be prudent to put in an offer? But he wasn't necessarily going to buy it. He was only going to research it and weigh options.

"You know, Caleb," Sadie began, "you don't need to invest in a business quite yet. You could simply take a job working at Wagler's Buggies."

Meeting her probing gaze, Caleb swallowed a sigh, hoping his sister wasn't trying to play matchmaker again. Would she ever listen and respect his decisions? "It's a thought, but I'm not sure I want to be an apprentice anymore. I think I'm ready to open my own shop." His words surprised himself. He hadn't realized he'd wanted to branch out on his own until he said it out loud.

Sadie's eyes widened. "Really?"

Caleb nodded. "I've been working for Jonas since I moved to Middlefield, and as much as I admire him, I think I'm ready to run my own business. As a bonus, he taught me how to make Lancaster-style buggies, in addition to our Ohio ones. So I'd be well prepared to take on business here."

Sadie glanced at Robert, who looked equally shocked.

Robert stood. "I'll take you by there tomorrow. I think I'm going to head up to bed. It's getting late."

Sadie glanced at the clock and popped out of her chair. "Oh my. It's after nine. I best head to bed too." She stepped over to Caleb and glanced at his mug. "Are you finished?"

He shook his head. "No, I've been savoring it." He smiled up at her. "I think I'll sit here for a few minutes and enjoy the fire. I'll clean up after myself."

She patted his shoulder. "*Gut nacht, bruder.* I do hope you decide to stay."

"*Danki.*" He frowned. "Don't start any rumors about my moving here, Sadie. Right now I'm trying to figure out God's plan for Susie and me."

She gasped. "I'll do no such thing, Caleb. I'll keep it to myself."

He raised an eyebrow with suspicion.

She made a motion as if to zip her lips and then headed into the kitchen.

Sighing, Caleb leaned his head back on the chair and closed his eyes. Opening his heart to God, Caleb silently asked Him to reveal the right path for him and his precious daughter.

CHAPTER 10

Caleb steered the horse toward the For Sale sign sitting at the edge of the property. Since Robert had to tend to business at the farm, Caleb had borrowed the horse and buggy and ventured out to find the place on his own.

Guiding the horse into a rock driveway, Caleb spotted a large cinderblock building containing three bay doors and an office off to the right. He stopped the horse by the office door, and his boots crunched across the snow as he walked around to the front of the building. Caleb climbed the stairs, and the door opened with a loud squeak, revealing a stocky middle-aged English man with dark hair and eyes.

"Good morning," the man said. "May I help you?"

"Yes," Caleb said. "My name is Caleb Schmucker, and I wanted to speak with the owner regarding the price of this property."

"I'm the owner, and it's nice to meet you." The man shook Caleb's hand. "I'm Riley Parker. Please come in." He gestured for Caleb to enter the shop. "I'm glad you came by. Do you live around here?"

"No. I'm visiting from Ohio. My sister lives in Bird-in-Hand." Caleb glanced around the office, which was a small room that led to the large work bays. "My daughter and I are here for the holidays, and I'm considering moving back."

"Oh." Riley rubbed the stubble on his chin. "You're from around here originally?"

Caleb nodded. "That's right. I moved to Ohio about ten years ago after I got married. My wife passed away two years ago, and I don't have any family there, except for a few of her cousins."

Riley frowned. "I'm sorry for your loss."

"*Danki*." Caleb smiled. "I'm thinking that I want to come back here so that my daughter has some family around her while she grows up."

"Yes, family is important." Riley leaned on the counter behind him. "I know quite a few Amish families around here. Who is your sister?"

"Sadie Kauffman." He jammed his thumb toward the door as if in the direction of the road. "Her husband's family owns the furniture store a few blocks down."

"Oh!" Riley nodded. "I know Eli Kauffman quite well. Nice family."

"Yes." Caleb stepped over to the door and looked toward the bays, imagining his toolboxes and supplies lining the walls while he built buggies. He could see himself coming here every day and working to make a living. "This is a nice place you have here. Have you owned it long?"

"Oh yeah." Riley limped toward the bays and motioned for Caleb to follow. "This land has been in my family for years. My father built this shop about fifty years ago, and I added on twenty years ago. I ran a towing company and did some minor car repairs on the side." He patted his thigh.

"I've got a bum leg, so I can't work much anymore. My kids have all married and moved away, and my wife and I decided it was time to retire and move to Florida. But we need to unload this place before I can buy my condo."

Riley gestured toward the row of toolboxes and work-benches. "I'll have all of this cleared out soon. My youngest son is supposed to come and get the tools at some point. I don't want to take any of them to Florida." He smiled. "Well, just a little box with the basics for the honey-do lists my wife likes to make to keep me off the sofa."

Caleb walked the length of the shop, imagining how he would set it up if it were his. The building was bigger than the shop he worked in back in Ohio. "This is quite spacious."

Riley moved the curtain and pointed toward a brick home behind the shop. "The house is out back if you'd like to see that too."

"*Danki.*" Caleb followed Riley out a side door and down the driveway.

"We have a barn out back too," Riley said, pointing toward a small fenced pasture. "It's not big, but it's functional if you have a few animals."

"How many acres are here?"

"Six," Riley said as they approached the brick ranch house. "The house has three bedrooms and two bathrooms. The rooms are fairly big. We raised four boys without any problems. Would you like to come in? My wife is at the market right now, but I would be happy to show you around."

"That would be great," Caleb said.

While Riley led him around the house, Caleb imagined making a home for him and Susie. The bedrooms were a good size, and the woodwork on the trim in the little house was also nice. The house was nothing fancy, but Caleb didn't need fancy.

Before he could move in, he would have to have the electricity removed from the house in order to keep with his Amish traditions. He would also need to convert to gas appliances, but that wouldn't be a problem.

Caleb glanced around the kitchen, trying to imagine his table and chairs in the center of the room. His heart warmed at the idea of being home in Lancaster County, celebrating holidays and milestones with his sister and her family, worshipping with her church district and his old friends. He would also make new friends, and he would possibly get to know a very special friend better: Naomi King.

His last thought caused him to smile to himself. He would definitely enjoy spending time with Naomi, as would Susie.

Caleb turned to Riley, standing in the doorway to the family room. "May I see the barn?"

"Sure." Riley led him out through the small one-car garage toward the pasture.

Stepping into the barn, an overwhelming calmness enveloped Caleb. He glanced around at the horse stalls, and he knew—this was the house. This was meant to be for him and Susie.

This was the sign from God he'd been waiting for.

Smiling, Caleb faced Riley in the doorway. "What's your final price, Mr. Parker?"

❧

Later that afternoon, Caleb steered the buggy into Sadie's

driveway. After putting up the horse and buggy, he grabbed his armload of bags from his shopping trip and headed up the back steps. Entering the kitchen, he found Susie sitting at the table eating cookies with her cousins.

"*Dat*!" she called when she spotted him. "Look at the cookies we made at Naomi's today." She held up a plate with assorted Christmas cookies. "Levina and Sylvia invited us over after school. We had fun."

"Oh my." Dropping his bags on the floor, Caleb swiped a chocolate chip cookie from the plate and took a bite. "*Appeditlich*!" He finished the cookie in two big bites and then hung his coat on the peg by the door before kicking off his boots.

Susie leaned over and examined the pile of bags. "What's in there?"

He picked up the bags and held them close to his body. "Nothing for you to be concerned about." He backed out of the kitchen. "Enjoy your cookies, girls."

Caleb crossed the family room and into his parents' former apartment where he'd been staying. He walked through the small sitting room to the bedroom and dropped the bags onto the bed. He then opened the closet to make room for the gifts. He was placing the bag from the bookstore onto the top shelf of the closet when a knock sounded on the door frame.

Sadie stepped into the room with a curious expression. "How was your visit to the Parker place?"

"*Gut*." Caleb lowered himself onto the bed, and it creaked beneath his weight.

"Oh?" She raised her eyebrows with curiosity.

He crossed his arms over his wide chest. "I made an offer."

She gasped and clasped her hands together. "My *bruder* is moving back home!"

He nodded and smiled. "I think so."

"*Ach*! This is *wunderbaar gut*!" Sadie gestured widely with an equally wide grin. "Our *kinner* will go to school together. We'll worship together and also celebrate birthdays and holidays together! This is a dream come true. I'm so *froh*!"

"Don't get too excited just yet," he said, standing. "I have to try to sell my farm and then it will take some time to get my business going here. I'm hoping I can make a smooth transition from Jonas's shop to my own."

"Wait." She held a hand up. "You shouldn't open your own business just yet. You should work for Hezekiah Wagler until you have enough money to open your own business. That way you could—"

"Sadie," he began, his voice firm. "Stop trying to set me up with Irene Wagler."

"What are you implying, Caleb?" Her surprised expression was forced. "I'm not trying to set you up. I'm just looking after your finances."

He glowered at his older sister. "I can look after my own finances just fine, *danki*. I'm a grown man. I also will decide if and when I'm ready to court women."

She frowned, looking hurt by his words. "Caleb, I only have your best interests in mind. I want you to make the right decisions for you and Susie."

"I can make my own decisions, *danki*." He spotted Susie crossing the sitting room and heading for the door, and he bit back the angry words that were bubbling forth from his throat.

"*Dat!*" Susie bounded into the room. "Where did you go today? I thought you'd be home sooner."

"I told you," he said, forcing a smile for his daughter's sake. "I ran a few errands."

"Errands?" Sadie asked.

He nodded at Sadie and then glanced at Susie. "I just had a few things I needed to pick up at the store while I was out."

Susie looked curious. "Oh. Did you have a *gut* day?"

"I did," Caleb said. "Did you have a *gut* day?"

Susie nodded. "I had lots of fun with my cousins."

"I'm going to go start supper." Sadie stepped toward the door. "Did you tell Susie the exciting news?"

Susie's eyes rounded. "What news?"

"It looks like we're going to move here," he said slowly. "I talked to a man about a house today."

"Yeah!" Susie wrapped her arms around Caleb's neck, and he hugged her.

Caleb glanced toward the doorway. Seeing that Sadie was gone, he breathed a sigh of relief. While he loved his sister, he grew weary of her constant interference. He hoped that moving closer to her wouldn't be a mistake. However, in his heart, he knew this was the best plan for him and Susie. Besides, he could get to know Naomi better and see if his growing feelings for her would turn into something more permanent.

And that was when Caleb realized the truth: he was planning this move for himself as much as for Susie. God wanted him to break free of the loneliness that had hung over him like a black cloud since Barbara's death. Caleb believed he was entitled to find happiness again even though Barbara was gone.

"I can't believe Christmas Eve is tomorrow," Naomi said as she walked through the indoor flea market on Friday.

"I know." Lilly stopped and glanced at the candy concession stand. "I should get some candy for Hannah's *kinner*." She smiled at the clerk and began rattling off a list of candy.

Lizzie Anne sidled up to Naomi and tapped her shoulder. "Are you okay?" she whispered. "You've been sort of quiet since Wednesday. Is everything all right?"

Naomi held back a sigh. Her younger sister was quite intuitive. Naomi had been quiet since her discussion with her mother Wednesday night, after her shopping excursion with Caleb and the girls. And Naomi's reticence was caused by the conflicting thoughts swirling through her head. Her mother had warned her not to allow Caleb to return to Ohio with her heart. While Naomi knew that the advice was sound, she feared that Caleb Schmucker already had possession of it.

Naomi tried to smile, but her lips formed a grimace. "I have some things on my mind."

"Is something wrong?" Lizzie Anne asked, her brown eyes full of worry.

"No," Naomi said, glancing toward the counter, where

Lilly stood talking to the candy clerk. "Everything is fine. I just have a lot to get done. I still have to make a batch of butterscotch cookies for *Dat* and then get all of the gifts together for the little ones."

Lizzie Anne tilted her chin in question. "Are you certain that's it?"

"*Ya.*" Naomi pulled her list from the pocket of her apron. "I need to pick up a few gifts for *Mamm*. She wants me to get some little gifts in case we go visiting tomorrow."

"For the Kauffmans, *ya*?"

Naomi's eyes snapped to her sister's face. "The Kauffmans?"

"*Ya*. We were invited to Sadie's tomorrow night for the Kauffman Christmas Eve get-together," Lizzie Anne said with a smile. "I have to pick up something special for Lindsay," she said, referring to Rebecca Kauffman's niece who lived with her. "You know she's my best *freind.*"

Nodding, Naomi had wondered when she would see Caleb again. Although the thought of seeing him again sent her stomach into a knot, she also couldn't wait. She'd enjoyed the time spent baking and laughing with Susie and her sisters yesterday afternoon. She felt her attachment to the girl growing, but she also knew the attachment wasn't limited to just the girl. She had deep, growing feelings for Susie's father, and it both scared and excited her at the same time. And this feeling was nothing compared to what she'd believed she felt for Luke Troyer and Timothy Kauffman once. This attachment was more meaningful. The risk of heartbreak was high, but for some inexplicable reason, Naomi felt a willingness to take the risk.

"Naomi?" a voice asked.

Naomi turned and found Lilly studying her.

"You okay?" her friend asked.

"Funny," Lizzie Anne began with a grin. "I just asked her the same question."

Naomi blew out a defeated sigh. "I feel like I'm on trial here."

Lilly took Naomi's arm and pulled her through the knot of shoppers. "Let's go get some fudge and talk."

"Fine." Naomi gave in with a grimace. Getting fudge would bring back memories of her shopping day with Caleb. How ironic.

After ordering the chocolate, they sat at a small table. Naomi felt her sister's and her friend's eyes studying her as she broke off a piece of milk chocolate fudge.

"What's going on?" Lilly asked between bites of her dark chocolate fudge. "You're very distracted and quiet."

"That's what I said," Lizzie Anne said while wiping a piece of milk chocolate off her sleeve and balancing her slab of remaining fudge in her other hand.

"I have a lot on my mind," Naomi said with a shrug.

"Such as?" Lilly prodded.

Naomi knew neither of them would back down until she spilled her heart to them. It was time to confess her feelings, and she wasn't certain she could put them into coherent words.

"On Wednesday, I went shopping with Caleb Schmucker, Susie, Janie Kauffman, and my younger sisters," Naomi said, keeping her eyes on her block of fudge. "In fact, we came here, so Susie could do some Christmas shopping for little gifts for her cousins and new friends."

"What?" Lilly's voice nearly squeaked with shock. "Why didn't you tell me this yesterday?"

"I didn't think to tell you." Naomi felt wretched for telling a fib, but she continued, despite Lilly's hurt expression. "That night, my *mamm* gave me a lecture on not giving my heart to Caleb because he's a widower and also because he's going to go back to Ohio. She said I'm just setting myself up to get hurt."

"Why would *Mamm* say that?" Lizzie Anne asked while wiping more stray crumbs off her sleeve. "Why does *Mamm* think you like Caleb?"

"I don't know." Naomi's cheeks heated. She wasn't very good at lying.

"Oh," Lizzie Anne said with a wide smile. "You do like Caleb."

"*Mamms* have a way of knowing these things," Lilly said, patting Lizzie Anne's arm. "Sometimes they know before we do. It's their job." She then turned her gaze to Naomi. "How did shopping go? Did you have a *gut* time?"

Naomi nodded. "We had a *wunderbaar* time. He's so easy to talk to, and he's so very sweet and thoughtful." She frowned and shook her head. "I'm doomed. I never should've gone out with him."

"Why do you say that?" Lizzie Anne asked. She bit into the fudge, and the crumbs were finally under control. "It sounds like you're *gut freinden*. Why can't you be *freinden* with him? Susie obviously likes you. I've seen how she talks to you and follows you around."

"It's more complicated than that," Naomi said with a gentle smile. She ate more fudge and wished she could turn off her feelings for Caleb. But did she really want to turn them off? When she was with him, she felt a true happiness that she'd never felt before.

"You're not going to listen to your *mamm* are you?" Lilly asked before popping a final piece of fudge into her mouth.

"I don't know." Naomi shrugged. "I don't know what to do. My *mamm* is right about him leaving. He's going to go back to Ohio, and where will that leave me? I'll be right back where I was when Timothy and I broke up—alone and nursing a broken heart."

"Maybe not," Lizzie Anne said. "Maybe he'll want to court you, and he and Susie can move here." She shrugged. "He may like you too, and he may want to be back by his family since Susie's *mamm* is gone." She looked between Lilly and Naomi. "It's a possibility, right?"

Lilly nodded. "You could be right."

Naomi shook her head. "That would be a big move for him."

"Or you could move to Ohio," Lizzie Anne said. "I would hate to see you go, but we could visit."

Naomi shook her head. "I don't know if I could leave *Mamm*, *Dat*, and all of you."

"It would be difficult, but my cousin did it," Lilly said. "She misses her family, but she keeps in touch with letters and occasional phone calls."

"Lilly is right." Lizzie Anne wiped her mouth. "If it feels right for you to go with him to Ohio, then you should think about it. You need to follow your heart, Naomi. That's what you used to say."

"I was wrong," Naomi whispered, thinking back on her failed relationships.

"No, you were never wrong about following your heart," Lilly chimed in with a knowing smile. "You simply did it at the wrong time. Don't judge your future by your past. Things happen in God's time."

"*Ya!*" Lizzie Anne snapped her fingers. "It's like the verse *Dat* read last night during devotions. Remember? I think it went something like: 'I wait for the Lord, my soul waits, and in his word I put my hope.'"

Lilly grinned at Lizzie Anne. "You are one smart *maedel*."

Lizzie Anne smoothed the tie of her prayer covering. "Sometimes I have a *gut* thought or two."

Naomi smiled while finishing her fudge.

"It's like what you told me the other day," Lilly said. "You said that in the past you were too eager and you didn't wait for God's time for love. Maybe now it's God's time."

Naomi nodded slowly while considering the words. "Maybe it is." *I hope you're right, Lilly.*

Lilly wiped her hands and stood. "Let's shop, *ya*?"

Naomi tossed her dirty napkins in the trash can. "I have a store I want to go into."

Lizzie Anne chatted about the weather report and threat of more snow as they weaved through the crowd toward the antique store.

"What are we doing here?" Lizzie Anne asked as they stepped through the doorway.

"I'll be fast," Naomi said and then rushed toward the tool section, holding her breath and hoping that the antique drill was still there. She picked up the contraption and smiled.

After paying for it, she hurried over to Lizzie Anne and Lilly, who were in a deep discussion about a desk and whether or not it was an antique or just an overpriced piece of furniture.

"Did you get what you needed?" Lilly asked as they headed back out into the flea market crowd.

"*Ya*," Naomi hugged the bag to her cloak. "I'm all set. I just need to go to the toy store and find some little things for the *kinner*."

"What's in the bag?" Lizzie Anne reached for the bag.

Naomi swatted her hand away. "Nothing."

Her sister's eyes widened with curiosity. "*Ach*, then it must be *gut*. Is it for Caleb?"

Naomi nodded.

"What is it?" Lilly asked, looking intrigued.

"It's something he told me he wanted but would never buy himself," Naomi said, loosening her grip on the bag.

"What is it?" Lizzie Anne asked again. "Just tell us. We'll keep it a secret, right, Lilly?"

Lilly nodded. "You have my word."

Naomi moved out of the crowd and stood outside the toy store. She pulled out the drill, and Lilly and Lizzie Anne stared at the tool as if it were from another world.

"What is it?" Lizzie Anne asked.

"It looks sort of like a drill my *grossdaddi* had in his barn," Lilly said.

"That's exactly what it is, Lilly," Naomi said. "Caleb collects antique tools, and he uses them too."

"Wow," Lizzie Anne said, touching the handle. "He'll love it."

Naomi smiled. "I hope so."

CHAPTER 12

Caleb was reading his Bible when a knock sounded on his bedroom door later that evening. He opened the door and found Susie glowering. "*Wie geht's?*"

"Irene is here." She spat out the words. "I don't think I like her."

He raised an eyebrow. "Susan. What's gotten into you?"

"She doesn't even say hello to me," Susie said, her frown deepening. "She looked at me and said, 'Where's your *dat?*' It's like I don't exist."

Caleb touched her prayer covering. "I'm certain she didn't mean it. Remember your manners."

"Why?" Susie asked as they headed through the sitting room. "She doesn't remember hers, so why should I remember mine?"

He suppressed a smile. "You must always be respectful of adults, even when it seems as if they don't have any manners. Maybe she will learn by your example."

"Yes, *Dat*." She stopped at the doorway leading to the large family room. "But I'm certain she doesn't like me," she whispered, her pretty face twisted with a deep scowl.

He touched her nose. "Anyone who doesn't like you is misled, *mei liewe.*"

She scrunched her nose, and he laughed. Taking her hand, he steered her to the kitchen where Irene sat talking with Sadie. Sadie's younger children were seated at the table coloring on construction paper.

"*Wie geht's?*" Caleb said.

"Oh, Caleb," Sadie said, popping up from her chair. "I'll let you two chat." She shooed her children into the family room and then looked at Susie. "You come too, Susie. Let your *dat* and Irene chat."

Susie frowned up at Sadie. "I'm staying with my *dat.*"

Sadie lifted a finger in preparation to scold her.

"She's fine," Caleb said, his voice booming a little louder than he'd intended.

"Oh," Sadie said, looking surprised. She disappeared into the family room.

"*Wie geht's?*" Caleb repeated, sinking into a chair across the table from Irene.

"I'm *gut.* How are you?" Irene smiled sweetly at Caleb and then glanced past him, her smile fading.

Caleb turned to find Susie leaning in the doorway, looking unhappy. "Join us, Susie." He motioned for her to come to the table, but she shook her head. He could feel her uneasiness from across the room, and his heart ached for his usually happy-go-lucky daughter.

He turned back to Irene, and her sugary sweet smile returned. "What brings you out this way?" he inquired, hoping to ease the tension.

"I was going to ask you what you were planning for

supper," she said, leaning across the table just slightly as if to share a secret. "Do you like Hamburg goulash?"

"*Ach*," he said, fingering his beard. "I'd have to count that as one of my most favorite meals."

"*Gut!*" She grinned. "Why don't you grab your coat, and we'll head out to my parents' house. I made a special dessert too."

"Sounds *appeditlich*." He turned to Susie, who was still in the doorway, twisting one of the ties from her prayer covering in her little finger. "Grab your cloak, Susie. We're going to dinner at Irene's."

"Oh," Irene said quickly. She leaned toward him and lowered her voice. "I thought maybe Susie could stay here with Sadie so that you and my *dat* could talk about the shop."

"See, *Dat*," Susie exclaimed, stomping into the room. "She doesn't like me!"

"Susan." Caleb stood. He gestured for her to calm down while working to keep his voice composed. "We just talked about this. Remember your manners." He turned to Irene. "I'd rather not have dinner without my *dochder*."

Irene bristled. "Oh. I thought you might like to discuss the buggy business without the interruption of a *kind*."

"I don't see my *dochder* as an interruption." He walked over to Susie and placed a hand on her shoulder.

Irene looked stunned. "But don't you want to discuss working at my *daed's* shop?"

Caleb shook his head. "If she's not welcome, then I'll politely turn down your supper invitation." He glanced down at Susie, and she smiled. Her eyes were so full of love that his heart felt as if it would melt.

Popping up, Irene crossed to the door and snatched her cloak from the peg on the wall. "I suppose I'll see you later." Scowling, she pulled on her cloak. "Please tell Sadie I said *gut nacht*."

"I will," Caleb said, gently squeezing Susie's shoulder.

Irene rushed through the door, which slammed behind her.

"*Dat*!" Susie beamed up at him. "You didn't want to go without me?"

He shook his head. "How could I go without you? You're *mei liewe*. We're in this together, remember?"

She wrapped her arms around his waist and hugged him. "*Ich liebe dich*."

"I love you too," he said. "But you must remember not to talk back to adults, Susie. You can get your point across without being rude."

She grinned up at him. "Like you did."

He chuckled and rubbed her shoulder. "*Ya*, I guess I did."

She headed for the door. "I'm going to go tell Janie!"

"Susie!" He hoped to stop her from telling the family about his conversation with Irene, but she was gone. He heard her shoes clunking up the stairs to the bedrooms.

Stepping over to the window, Caleb glanced out at the sky, seeing snowflakes floating down to the porch railing and dotting the rock driveway.

"Did I hear a door slam?" Sadie asked behind him.

"*Ya*," he said, facing her quizzical stare. "Irene left."

Sadie stepped through the doorway. "Didn't she invite you for supper?"

He nodded. "She did."

"And what happened?" Her eyes searched his face.

"I declined her invitation."

"Why would you do that?" She stepped toward him. "I don't understand. Irene is young and attractive, and her father has a successful carriage shop. You don't need to invest in a new business." She gestured with her hands. "You could simply work for him, and you and Irene could get to know each other better."

He frowned, running his hand through his hair. Would his sister ever stop her interfering? "I'm going for a walk." He gripped the doorknob and wrenched the back door open with a squeak.

"Caleb?" Sadie called after him.

Stepping out onto the porch, the cold, moist air seeped through his shirt and into his skin. He took a deep, cleansing breath and walked over to the railing. Closing his eyes, he let the cool snowflakes kiss his warm cheeks while breathing out the frustration boiling in his soul.

He knew that allowing his sister's interference to upset him wouldn't help the situation. He remembered clearly how she tried to run his life when he lived with his parents. She was interested in all of Caleb's comings and goings, suggesting how he should spend his social life and even giving her unsolicited opinions of his friends. While he loved his sister, she was a hopeless meddler.

Opening his eyes, he stared up at the sky, wondering how he would handle her when he moved back. How could he keep the lines of communication open with his sister without losing his temper?

He glanced toward the driveway, and his thoughts turned

to Irene. He'd hoped that Susie was wrong when she'd proclaimed Irene's dislike for her. However, Irene's facial expressions and her blatant disregard for Susie's feelings were apparent. He'd never understand how someone could disregard a child the way that Irene did. Even if Caleb had wanted to discuss business with Hezekiah Wagler, he would've done it in front of Susie. She was old enough to be quiet while the adults were having a serious conversation.

He turned back toward the pasture. If he cut across the pasture and continued about a half mile, he would wind up on Naomi's road. He wondered if she was home. And if so, would she want to visit with him? He hadn't seen her since Wednesday, and he missed her. He wondered if she missed him too.

Caleb snickered to himself. He sounded like a lovesick teenage boy.

"*Dat?*" Susie's voice sounded behind him.

He faced her and swallowed a shiver. "Susie?" he asked with a smile.

She jammed a hand on her little hip. "You know you're going to catch a cold, *ya?*"

He nodded. "*Ya.* I know."

She smiled. "Janie says you're a *wunderbaar gut dat* for what you said to Irene Wagler."

He grinned. "I'm *froh* she approves."

"I like Naomi more than I like Irene," she said.

"*Ya*, I know," he said. "I can't blame you."

"Are you going to come inside or do I need to get you your coat?" She frowned, and her face reminded him of Barbara's when she disapproved of something Caleb had done.

"I'll be in shortly," he said, rubbing his arms.

She gave him a confused expression, shrugged, and closed the door.

He looked back up at the sky and prayed for strength and help for dealing with both his sister and the uncertainties of the upcoming move from Ohio to Pennsylvania.

CHAPTER 13

"It's a regular blizzard out here," Naomi commented, climbing from Lilly's buggy. She helped her siblings out of the back and then grabbed her bag of gifts. "Lizzie Anne and Levina, grab those platters of cookies and carry them in please. Sylvia, please take the bag with the gifts for the *kinner.*"

"I can't believe the snow." Lilly tented her hand over her eyes to block the raging flurries. "I don't know how we're going to find our way home."

Stepping on the sidewalk, Sylvia slipped and then righted herself. "Maybe we'll have to stay the night."

Naomi chuckled. "I don't think Sadie has enough room for all of us."

Naomi, her younger siblings, and Lilly made their way up the steps to the porch. A buggy bounced up the drive, leaving tracks revealing its path, and Naomi spotted her parents and Elam emerging from the buggy into the snow. Elam stowed her parents' horse and Lilly's horse, and her parents began their trek through the blowing snow to the stairs. Naomi waited for her parents while Lilly and Naomi's siblings disappeared into the house, carrying the food and gifts.

"Naomi, you should go inside," Titus said on his way up the stairs. Moving past her, he held the door open. "Go on. You'll catch a cold."

"*Danki, Dat,*" Naomi said with a smile. She gestured for her mother to go in first. "After you, *Mamm.*"

"*Danki.*" Her mother smiled as she stepped into the foyer. "I assume the *kinner* brought in the food and gifts?"

"*Ya.*" Naomi followed Irma into the family room and then helped her remove her cloak.

They hung their cloaks on the pegs on the wall, jamming them on top of the pile and then stepped into the family room, clogged with people talking and laughing. Irma disappeared into the crowd, shaking hands and greeting friends while smiling.

Naomi scanned the group, her stomach fluttering as she searched for one certain face: Caleb's.

"Naomi!" A little voice yelled as a hand pulled on the skirt of her frock. "*Frehlicher Grischtdaag!*"

Naomi glanced down into Susie's smiling face. "Oh, Susie." She hugged the little girl. "*Frehlicher Grischtdaag* to you too! I have something for you." She perused the crowd, looking for one of her siblings and her bag of gifts.

"I have something for you!" Taking her hand, Susie yanked Naomi toward the far side of the family room. "I'll have to find my gifts."

They crossed the family room, and Naomi glanced through another doorway into a smaller sitting room, where she spotted Caleb standing with Timothy Kauffman and Hezekiah Wagler. The three men were talking and laughing while holding mugs, which she assumed were full of Robert's famous hot cider.

Susie dug through a large shopping bag and then pulled out a small doll. "This is for you."

Naomi held the doll up and examined it. The tiny, cloth doll wore a blue dress, black apron, and black winter bonnet, and held a little sign that said "Friends." Tears filled Naomi's eyes as she looked at Susie. "It's *schee*."

Susie beamed. "I got it for you because you're *mei freind*."

"It's perfect." Leaning down, Naomi engulfed Susie into a hug and squeezed her tight.

When she stood, she felt someone's stare focused on her. Glancing over, she spotted Caleb watching her. He nodded and smiled, and she returned the gesture before turning back to Susie.

"Now, I hope you don't think this is *gegisch*, but I got you something too." Naomi put the doll into the pocket of her apron and then reached into her bag and pulled out the quilt she'd shown Susie during the quilting bee. "This is for you."

"For me?" Susie gasped as she hugged the quilt to her chest. "I love this so much! I will sleep with it on my bed every night. *Danki*, Naomi."

"*Gern gschehne.* That's not all." Naomi then pulled out a flat box. "This was my favorite game when I was your age." She held her breath, hoping Susie would like it.

"Scrabble!" Susie's green eyes rounded with excitement as she draped the quilt over her arm. "Oh, Naomi! *Danki*!" She hugged Naomi again, and Naomi chuckled. "Will you play with me?"

"Of course," Naomi said. "I think it's too crowded to play here now, but I promise we'll get in at least one game before you and your *dat* head back to Ohio."

Susie examined the box. "Then you'll play more when we get back, right?"

"*Ya*," Naomi said. "If you bring it each time you visit, we'll play it. I don't think my game at home has all of the pieces anymore." She gripped the handles of her shopping bag, wondering when to give Caleb his special gift.

"Not when we visit." Susie looked up. "I mean when we move here."

Naomi gasped. "What did you say?"

Susie grinned. "We're moving here. My *dat* said he found a house."

Stunned, Naomi was speechless. She looked toward Caleb and found him nodding while listening to Hezekiah. Her heart filled with warmth and hope of a possible future with Caleb and Susie. Maybe they could be a family? Was this what Lizzie Anne had been talking about with her verse about waiting for the Lord and putting hope in Him? Was it God's time for her like Lilly had said?

She glanced back at Susie. "Are you certain?"

Susie nodded. "*Ya*. I heard my *Aenti* Sadie say something about *Dat* working for Irene's *daed*." She frowned. "I hope that isn't true. Irene doesn't like me. She doesn't smile at me. She invited my *dat* over for supper and said I wasn't invited. She's not very nice."

Naomi swallowed a groan as her hopes evaporated. Caleb's plans included Irene, not Naomi. "Oh," she said, her voice barely a whisper over the conversations floating around them.

"Irene is always smiling around my *dat*," Susie continued, looking disgusted. "She always wants to be with him alone. She acts nice around him, but she's not really nice at all."

Speechless, Naomi listened as her frown deepened.

"She acts like I don't exist," Susie said, gripping the box and the quilt in her arms. "She doesn't even want me in the room with her and my *dat*." She glowered. "My *dat* says I have to respect adults and use my manners, but I don't want to use my manners around her." Her expression softened. "But you're always so nice to me. You're *mei freind* and I could never be friends with Irene. I know it's not Christian to say that, but it's the truth."

Naomi nodded again. She couldn't form the words to express the emotions that were weighing down on her shoulders. She felt her spirit wilting, like a thirsty flower in desperate need of water.

"I want my *dat* to be with you, not Irene. I don't understand why he even talks to her. Irene would never bake with me or quilt with me. She would never even play a game with me." Susie placed the flat box and the quilt on the bench next to her and began to open the box. "Can we play now?"

"I don't think that would be a *gut* idea," Naomi said, hoping her anxiety didn't show on her face. "There are too many people here, and I'm afraid the pieces will get lost."

"Oh." Susie looked disappointed. "I can't wait to play. Maybe we can go up to my room." She nodded toward the sitting room behind them. "Or maybe my *dat's* room on the coffee table? We could spread the game out and play."

Naomi glanced toward the sitting room and spotted Irene standing next to Caleb while her father chatted. Caleb and Timothy both laughed at something Hezekiah said, and Naomi's heart sank. She'd been so wrong about Caleb. And now that he was going to move here, she'd have to see him and endure the sting of her heartache just as she had to endure seeing Luke Troyer and Timothy Kauffman. She felt herself falling into a pit of despair, as if her heart were being smashed into a million pieces right before her eyes.

Her stomach twisted, and she glanced at Susie. "I'm not feeling well. I think I need to go get something to drink."

Susie hoisted her game and quilt. "I'll come with you. Let me just run these upstairs." She trotted through the knot of people toward the stairs.

Naomi moved past familiar faces, nodding and shaking hands on her way to the kitchen. She reached the kitchen doorway and stopped when she spotted Sadie speaking to one of her quilting friends.

"Oh, *ya*," Sadie said. "Caleb and Susie love it here. In fact, he put a bid in on Riley Parker's place. You know, the one by the furniture store."

"Oh, right," her friend said. "The one with the little workshop."

"That's right," Sadie said. "But I told him not to open a shop. He can work for Hezekiah Wagler." She smiled. "Caleb and Irene would make such a *wunderbaar* couple. As we all know, Susie needs the guidance that only a *mamm* can supply."

Naomi's stomach clenched and bile rose in her throat. She had to make a quick getaway before she became physically ill. She spun on her heel and rushed through the crowd toward the front door.

"Naomi!" a voice called.

Naomi forged ahead, ignoring the voice.

"Wait!" A hand grabbed Naomi's arm and pulled her off balance, causing her to stumble.

Naomi turned to find Lilly studying her.

"Where are you going?" Lilly asked.

"I don't feel well," Naomi said. And it wasn't a lie. She felt as if she were going to be sick, and she couldn't allow herself to be sick in public, especially in Sadie Kauffman's home.

Susie rushed over to them. "Naomi! Let's go get a drink." She took Naomi's hand.

"I'm sorry, Susie." Naomi touched the girl's cheek. "I'm not feeling well, so I'm going to head home. *Danki* for the gift."

Susie frowned. "But I thought we were going to spend time together."

"Not tonight." Naomi glanced down at the bag containing Caleb's gift. She held it out. "Would you please make sure your *dat* gets this? Tell him that it's from me, *ya*?"

Looking disappointed, Susie took the bag. "Okay."

"Good night." Naomi leaned down and kissed Susie's cheek. She then hugged Lilly. "I'll talk to you soon."

Lilly shook her head. "You shouldn't go out into that blizzard alone. Let me find Elam for you."

Naomi touched Lilly's shoulder. "I'll be fine. When I was seventeen, I left the house alone to get some medicine for Amos because he was really sick. On the way back from the store, my buggy broke down in the snow not too far from here. I had to leave the horse and buggy and walk home in a blizzard. I found my way, and everything was okay." She pulled on her cloak. "I know I can do this."

Before Lilly could respond, Naomi slipped out the door. She almost slipped twice on her way down the porch steps. The snow swirled around her, blinding her vision and soaking her cloak as she slowly moved down the driveway.

I can do this. I have to do it. I can't fall to pieces in front of Caleb, the Kauffmans, and the rest of the community.

Stopping at the pasture fence, she considered which route to take home. Although she couldn't see much beyond the fence, she knew that if she crossed the pasture, she could then cut through two farms and find her way to her road. It looked similar to the route she'd taken when her buggy had broken down years ago.

Heaving a deep breath, she began to trudge through the snow, shivering and gritting her teeth. The further she moved, the less she could see in front of her.

What was I thinking? This is a bad idea.

Naomi glanced back in the direction of what she thought was Sadie's home, but she couldn't see the outline of the house, not even the pitch of the roof.

She turned completely around in a circle and couldn't see anything except for snow. Her teeth chattered, and her eyes filled with frustrated tears.

I'm lost.

She looked straight up toward the white sky, and large, moist flakes blinded her.

Naomi gazed in the direction that she thought was the road and then trudged ahead two steps. She then moved forward, and her foot landed in a hole, causing her ankle to twist in an awkward direction. Screaming out loud, she wobbled, fell, and rolled down a hill. The sting of pain shot like lightning from her ankle up her leg.

She tried to lift her leg, but she couldn't move it. Taking a deep breath, she attempted to sit up, but the sting in her ankle forced her to stop.

Sobbing, Naomi rolled to her side and prayed that someone would come and find her while the bitter cold air closed in around her, prickling her skin like thousands of tiny icicles.

CHAPTER 14

Caleb smiled and nodded, wondering if Hezekiah Wagler would ever take a breath. Irene stood across from her father and chimed in frequently, adding details to the man's endless stories about his business, mechanical techniques, old friends, and family memories. Caleb was surprised Irene was even speaking to him, but she acted as if nothing had happened the previous day.

Glancing toward the door, Caleb noticed that the crowd in the main family room was dissipating. Timothy had left the conversation to join his fiancée and her family quite a while ago. Caleb had hoped Timothy would return and rescue him from the Waglers, but Timothy was a smart man and had stayed away. Caleb wondered how long it had been since his best friend had abandoned him. Had it been more than an hour? Had Caleb missed the entire Christmas party?

Susie, Janie, Nancy, and Linda scampered into the sitting room and gathered around the coffee table where Susie opened a Scrabble board game box. Taking out the contents of the box, the girls giggled while setting up their letters. Caleb swallowed a sigh of relief. This was his chance to break away and try to find Naomi. He couldn't wait to give her the special Christmas gift he'd picked up for her.

"It's been nice talking to you, Hezekiah. I'm going to go see what my *dochder* is doing," Caleb said, stepping toward the group of girls. He glanced at Irene and nodded. "*Frehlicher Grischtdaag.*" He then stepped over to Susie. "What are you girls up to?"

Susie gestured toward the game. "It's Scrabble, *Dat*. Naomi gave it to me for Christmas."

"Want to play, *Onkel* Caleb?" Janie asked while putting letters on the letter stand.

"No, *danki*." Caleb nodded toward the door. "Have you seen Naomi?"

"No." Linda shook her head.

"She left a long time ago," Susie said.

"She left?" he asked.

"*Ya*, that's right," Susie said.

"A long time ago?" Caleb asked, glancing at the clock on the bookshelf. Could it really be close to seven? Disappointment coursed through him. How had he managed to miss Naomi? She was the one person he was truly looking forward to seeing tonight.

"*Ya*," Susie said. "She wasn't feeling well." She stood. "But she left me something to give you." Taking his hand, Susie pulled him toward the door. "Come upstairs with me." She glanced at her cousins. "Don't start the game without me. I'll be right back."

Susie and Caleb walked through the family room, and Caleb was surprised to see that nearly everyone had left. As he started up the stairs behind Susie, Lilly approached him.

"*Frehlicher Grischtdaag,*" she said with a smile.

"Same to you," Caleb said with a nod. "Susie told me Naomi wasn't feeling well. I'm sorry that she left."

Lilly frowned. "*Ya.* It came on suddenly, and she said she had to leave. I tried to encourage her to stay, but she was determined to go."

Caleb pursed his lips. A feeling of suspicion rained down on him. Why would Naomi leave without speaking with him? Could she have been upset with him, and if so, why?

"Lilly," Miriam called, stepping into the family room. "Are you ready to go? Timothy said the snow looks pretty bad out there. We should get on the road." She looked toward the stairs. "Hi, Caleb. *Frehlicher Grischtdaag.*"

"Merry Christmas to you too, Miriam," Caleb said with a nod before trotting up the stairs after Susie. He found her in her room sitting on the bed while holding a large bag.

"This is for you from Naomi." She held it up. "Open it! It's very heavy. I can't wait to see what it is."

He opened the bag and his eyes rounded as he pulled out the antique drill he'd shown her at the flea market on Wednesday.

"Oh, Naomi," he whispered. She'd gone back and bought him exactly what he'd wanted. He examined the antique drill, and his heart filled with warmth for the beautiful, soft-spoken young woman. A small piece of paper fell into his lap, and he read the words written with a flourish:

Dear Caleb,

Please accept this small gift as a token of our new friendship. I'm so glad that God saw fit to bring you and

Susie into my life. I look forward to sharing the holidays with you and Susie, and I pray that with God's blessings we'll share many more together.

Frehlicher Grischtdaag!

Your new friend,
Naomi

Caleb stared at the note, reading it over and over again, committing it to memory. The note touched him deep in his soul, awakening feelings he thought he'd never feel again. He wondered why Naomi hadn't given this gift to him in person. Why would she write such a sweet, loving note and then give it to Susie to deliver?

Leaning over, Susie gave him a confused expression. *"Was iss letz?"*

"What did Naomi say when she gave you this bag?" he asked.

Susie shrugged. "She said she didn't feel well, and she asked me to give it to you."

"How was she acting when she gave you the bag?"

Susie shook her head. "I don't know. Upset, I guess."

"Upset?" He let the word roll through his mind as he tried to remember when he saw her. He'd been trapped in the sitting room listening to Hezekiah's monologue when he spotted Naomi chatting with and hugging Susie. He remembered thinking that Naomi looked like an angel as she smiled and spoke to his daughter. His heart had swelled when he observed the two of them talking together. Naomi was like no woman he'd met since he'd lost Barbara. He could tell that Naomi truly loved Susie, and Susie loved her as well.

And Caleb loved Naomi.

He shook his head at the realization. Yes, he did love her, and he needed to know why she'd left in such a rush. If she'd been ill, he would've been happy to take her home. Why did she rush out without even saying hello to him? Maybe there was something that had upset her. If Susie had been the last person to see her, maybe she would hold the key to finding out what had upset Naomi.

He turned to his daughter. "Did you say anything to Naomi before she left?"

Susie looked at him like he was crazy. "*Ya*. I said good-bye."

He shook his head. "No, that's not what I meant. Did you say anything that might have upset her?"

She shook her head. "I don't think so."

"Please, Susie." He placed his hand on her shoulder. "Can you try to think about everything you and Naomi discussed before she left?"

Deep in thought, she tapped her chin and looked up at the ceiling. "We talked about Christmas gifts. I gave her the little doll I bought her, and she gave me the game and a *schee* quilt that I love." She tapped a pretty quilt on her bed. "Then I asked her to play the game with me, and she said that she would play it with me every time I came to visit. So I told her we were moving here, and she was really surprised."

"You told her?" He'd hoped that he could get a chance to speak with her alone and tell Naomi the news, but he wasn't surprised that Susie was excited to share it, especially with Naomi.

However, Caleb had hoped that the news would be something he and Naomi could celebrate. Why would that news cause her to leave without speaking to him? Had he been wrong about her feelings for him?

He studied his daughter's eyes, praying she held the key to what had upset Naomi. "What exactly did you tell her?"

Susie shrugged again. "I don't know. I said that you'd found us a house and that *Aenti* Sadie said you might work for Irene's *dat*."

"You told her that I'd be working with Hezekiah?"

"No, I said I didn't know." Looking confused, she hugged the blanket to her chest. "I said that *Aenti* Sadie said you might. I mentioned that I didn't think Irene liked me because she's not nice to me and she didn't want me to come to dinner with you and her. I also told her that I have a hard time using my manners when she's around and that Irene acted like she only wanted to be alone with you. I said that I could never be friends with Irene, but I was friends with Naomi." She paused, blushing a little. "And I also said that I wanted you to be with Naomi and not with Irene."

Caleb frowned. *This is not good.* "What did Naomi say?"

"She kind of looked sad," Susie said.

Caleb stood and placed the drill on the bureau while he considered Susie's story. It didn't make sense. Was Naomi upset that Caleb might be working with Hezekiah? But why would that upset her—unless it had something to do with Irene? Was she jealous of Irene? Did she feel the same strong attraction to Caleb that he felt for her? If so, then being jealous of Irene might make sense—except that nothing was going on between him and Irene.

"Oh, there you are," Sadie said, stepping into the room.

"The girls are cleaning up the kitchen, Susie." Her eyes moved to the bureau. "What's that?"

"It's a Christmas gift from a friend," Caleb said, lifting up the drill and stepping toward the door. "Susan, please go down and help your cousins in the kitchen."

"Okay." Susie hopped down from the bed and skipped out of the room.

"What is it?" Sadie asked, her nose scrunched as she studied the drill.

"It's an antique drill," he said, holding the note from Naomi in his hand. He stuck it in his pocket for safe keeping.

"Oh." She smiled and clasped her hands together. "I saw you talking to Hezekiah and Irene. Have you decided to go into business with him?"

Caleb frowned. "No, I haven't. I've already told you what my plans are, and I need you to respect them. I'm tired of repeating myself over and over again, Sadie."

She blanched. "Well, it was *gut* to see you talking to Irene again. I think she would be a good *maedel* for you. I think she likes you."

He ran a hand down his chin and considered his response as his blood boiled with frustration. "I don't know how else to say this to you since you refuse to listen. Therefore, I'm going to say it the only way I know how. Sadie, I need you to mind your own business. I'm going to make the best decisions I can make for my *dochder* and me, and I need you to worry about your own family."

She winced. "Caleb, I only want what's best for you. It's my job to watch out for you since *Mamm* and *Dat* are gone."

He shook his head. "I'm a grown man, Sadie. Let me live my life the way I choose to live it." He held up the drill. "This gift is from a very special friend."

She raised her eyebrows, looking curious. "Who is this special friend?"

"Naomi King," he said with a smile. "That's who I—"

"Caleb!" A voice shouted from downstairs. "Caleb, come quick!"

Dropping the drill on the bed, Caleb rushed down the stairs, taking them two at a time, to where Robert stood next to Elam and Titus King, who were both frowning while holding their snowy hats.

"*Was iss letz?*" Caleb asked, his heart pounding in his chest as he looked between Elam and Robert.

"Naomi's missing," Elam said.

"What?" Caleb asked. "What do you mean?"

"She never made it home." Titus shook his head. "Lilly told Elam that Naomi didn't feel well and walked home alone, but she wasn't there when we arrived. We've searched our road and the surrounding area, but we haven't seen any sign of her."

"We need to look for her," Robert said, grabbing his coat from the peg by the door. "I'll get my horse hitched to my buggy."

"What's going on?" Sadie asked.

"Naomi's missing," Caleb said, putting on his hat and gloves. "We're going to go look for her." He grabbed a flashlight from the table by the door.

Sadie gasped. "Oh, no."

Caleb followed Elam and Robert to the door. He turned around one last time and faced Sadie. "Tell Susie I'll be home soon."

CHAPTER 15

"Which way do you think she went?" Caleb asked Elam as they stood by Elam's buggy in the driveway. The snow blew so hard that Caleb shivered and wiped the flakes from his face.

Elam shook his head. "I don't know. I thought she would've taken the main roads, but maybe she didn't."

Caleb turned in the direction of the pasture and remembered how he'd stood on the porch the night before and thought about how he could walk to her house. "Maybe she thought she'd take a shortcut?"

"Maybe," Elam said.

"I'll walk around the pasture, and you two go in the buggy and check the main roads again," Caleb said, holding up the flashlight, which gave a soft yellow glow reflecting off the snow. "Tell Robert to take his buggy further up the road past your house in case she made a wrong turn."

"Sounds *gut*." Titus walked up to them. "I remember one time when Naomi was a teenager, she was out in a blizzard getting medicine and the buggy broke down not far from here. One of the wheels came clear off the hub." He gestured in the direction of the pasture. "She walked home and she may have gone through this pasture."

"Oh no," Caleb said. "She's done this before?"

Titus nodded. "*Ya*. She made it home okay that time, but I'm not certain the wind was blowing like it is tonight."

Caleb shook his head as dread pooled in his gut. "I pray she's not hurt."

"I know." Titus looked grim. "Maybe you can find her footprints in the snow. Be careful."

"You too." Caleb set out across the pasture, his boots crunching as he trudged through the deep snow. He silently sent up prayers, begging God to lead him to Naomi. He hoped and prayed she was okay.

While he walked, he thought about her note in his pocket. Naomi had to be okay. They could have a future together, as a family, with Susie.

He couldn't imagine losing her. He'd just met her, and she already meant so much to him.

Losing another person he cared about would simply be too much . . .

As he moved through the snow, he lost his footing and nearly slipped. He righted himself again and then moved forward.

As he crossed the pasture the visibility worsened, and he couldn't see the house behind him or the fence in front of him. Lifting the flashlight, he searched the surrounding snow, looking for footprints. He thought again of Titus's story about Naomi walking home in a blizzard and he wondered if she'd taken this path. Was that why she thought she could make it home alone in this fierce storm?

Caleb spotted faint tracks that he thought might be her

footprints, and he followed them, moving slowly despite the frigid wind. "Naomi?" he called. "Naomi, are you out there?"

He trudged forward, following the tracks and shouting her name. Holding the flashlight up higher, he silently begged God to lead him to her. He needed to find her. He needed her in his life. Caleb continued on, marching through the snow and praying while he moved the flashlight back and forth and searched for any sign of her.

Suddenly, off in the distance, he thought he spotted something in the snow. Tenting his hand over his eyes, he tried to focus his eyes against the blowing flakes. The object looked like a black blanket peppered with snow.

Could that be her cloak?

His heart pounded against his rib cage as he quickened his steps.

"Naomi!" he shouted. "Naomi! Are you there?" As he approached, the black blanket came into view, resembling a person lying in the snow.

"Naomi?" he called, nearly running through the snow. "Is that you, Naomi?"

His heart beat faster when she didn't respond. Anxiety shot through him. *She's hurt!*

Caleb broke into a run, slipping and sliding over to the person. "Naomi?" he called. "Is that you?"

He found Naomi lying on her back with her eyes closed. Her cheeks were bright red, and her lips were a light shade of blue.

"Oh no," he moaned, praying softly. "Lord, please don't let it be too late. Don't take her from me now. Please, don't!"

Placing the flashlight in the snow, he pulled her into his

arms. "Naomi. Please answer me." When she didn't respond, panic gripped him, stealing his words for a moment. "I can't lose you, Naomi. Please answer me. Please, Naomi. I need you. Susie and I both need you." He sucked in a breath and silently prayed with all of the emotional strength he had left in him.

She moaned and stirred, causing him to release the breath he'd been holding.

"You hear me," he said. "It's okay if you can't answer. I'm going to get you home, and I'm going to take care of you." He liked the sound of that. He wanted to take care of her on a more permanent basis starting right now.

Slowly, he grabbed the flashlight and then lifted her into his arms. He heard the hum of a car and the clip-clop of hooves in the distance and he knew that he would locate the road if he followed those sounds.

Holding Naomi close to his chest, Caleb managed to balance the flashlight in one of his hands. In a hurry to get her to safety, he moved as quickly as he could while trying his best to not lose his footing in the snow. He slipped twice and slowed his pace down slightly.

He marched through the snow, praying that he would find his way to the road and Naomi would be okay. The sounds of the cars and hooves grew louder, and he knew he was heading in the right direction.

"We're almost there, Naomi," he said. "I can hear road noise up ahead of us." When she stirred again, he hoped she'd answer him. "Naomi? Are you awake? You're going to be just fine. I promise I'll take *gut* care of you."

"Caleb?" she asked, her voice tired and hoarse. "Caleb?" She looked up at him. "Where am I?"

"I found you in the pasture," he said, still trudging through the snow. "I'm so thankful I located you in this horrendous storm. Are you hurt?"

"*Ya*. I think so." She sucked in a deep breath with her face red and tears spilling from her brown eyes. "It's my ankle. I fell, and it twisted. It hurts so much." She wrapped her arms around his neck, and he relished the feeling of holding her so close.

"Don't worry," he said. "We're almost there. I promise I'll get you home safe."

"*Danki*." She rested her head on his shoulder.

Caleb felt a weight lift from his shoulders. He was thankful that she was awake and talking. Now he just had to get her home into the warmth and then have someone look at her ankle. She was lucky that only her ankle was hurt. A twinge of frustration nipped at him as he considered how much worse this situation could've turned out.

"What were you thinking trying to walk home alone in these conditions?" he asked.

"I thought I'd be okay," she said, holding tight to his neck. "I thought I could find my way. I've done it once before, and I found my house despite the snow."

"I don't think that would be possible in this blizzard." He spotted the fence in front of them. Relief flooded him. If they were close to the fence that meant they were almost to the road! "You're lucky I found you. You could've been out there all night and wound up with pneumonia or worse."

"I know," she said with a sigh. "It wasn't very smart."

Although the questions of why she left were still haunting him, Caleb carried her in silence while he concentrated on balancing her and the flashlight in his arms and continuing their trek through the blowing snow. She shivered against him, and he wished he had a blanket to shield her against the frigid weather.

When he stepped onto the road he spotted a buggy bouncing toward them with lanterns blazing like a beacon. "I hope this is Elam," he said, picking up his pace.

The buggy approached, and Titus jumped out. "Naomi!" he called. "You found her!" He trotted over and took Naomi from his arms. "What were you thinking, *dochder*? You scared us to death."

"I'm sorry, *Dat*," she said, her voice breaking into a sob.

Caleb hugged his arms to his chest. He could only imagine the fear Titus and Irma had felt for their daughter. He'd felt the same terror when he thought he'd lost Susie at the farmers market.

Titus looked at Caleb. "*Danki*."

Caleb nodded. "*Gern gschehne*."

Titus looked down at Naomi. "Let's get you home where it's warm and dry."

Caleb sat in Naomi's family room while he awaited the news on her injuries. Titus had carried her into her bedroom where her mother was going to examine her ankle and help her change into dry clothes. He'd spent the time drinking cocoa and talking with her siblings, but his mind had been focused on her, worrying and thinking of what he'd say when he finally got to talk to her again.

"Caleb," Irma called. "Naomi would like to see you."

He made his way to the bedroom located behind the kitchen and stood in the doorway.

Naomi gave a forced smile while she lay propped up on the bed with pillows. A quilt covered the length of her, and only her foot, wrapped in bandages, and the white sleeves of her nightgown were visible. Her cheeks and nose were still pink from the cold. She sipped from a mug of cocoa and then motioned for him to come in.

"I'll be right outside the door," Irma said as she stepped past Caleb.

"How are you feeling?" Caleb asked, moving to the end of the bed.

"I've been better," Naomi said. "The *gut* news is it's not broken." She nodded toward her foot. "It's a few pretty shades of red, but my *mamm* thinks it's just a real bad sprain. I was really cold, but there's no sign of frostbite. Cocoa helped warm me up right away."

"You're very lucky," Caleb said, sinking into a chair. "Everyone was worried about you. Robert was out looking in his buggy too. I'm glad I found you."

"I am too." She nodded. "*Danki.*"

"You're welcome." He smiled and then wagged a finger at her with feigned anger. "Don't you ever scare me like that again."

She laughed, revealing her adorable dimple. "I'll try not to."

"Now, tell me," he began, leaning against the bedpost, "why did you rush out of the party after you gave Susie her gifts?" He was certain her cheeks turned a deeper shade of pink.

"I didn't feel well," she said, fingering the ties on her prayer covering.

He raised an eyebrow with disbelief. "Then why didn't you ask Elam or me to take you home?"

She shrugged. "I didn't want to take anyone away from the party."

He snorted. "I would've been *froh* for you to steal me away from Hezekiah Wagler. That man held me captive with his boring stories for hours."

Naomi chuckled. "Did he?"

"I thought he would never stop talking." He raked his hand through his hair. "Why didn't you look for me?"

She frowned. "I'd thought you were busy with Hezekiah and Irene."

"Busy?"

"Talking business." She lifted her mug and took another sip.

He shook his head. "No, we weren't."

She gave him a thoughtful expression.

"*Danki* for the gift," he said. "It's perfect."

She cleared her throat. "*Gern gschehne.*"

He took a deep breath. It was time for him to be honest about his feelings. He pulled her note from his pocket. "I was touched to get this. It meant a lot to me."

Her cheeks flushed a deeper pink. "I'm glad to hear that."

"I wanted to tell you that I—" he began.

"I think it's time for you to get some rest, Naomi," Irma interrupted, stepping into the room. "It's very late and tomorrow is Christmas." She tapped Caleb's shoulder. "Robert is here. He stopped by to see if we'd found you. He's ready to take you home."

"Okay." Caleb stood. "Let me just say good-bye."

Irma gave him a stern expression. "Keep it short."

Feeling like a teenager, Caleb nodded and suppressed a grin. Did Irma truly think he was planning on misbehaving with her injured daughter?

Caleb waited until Irma stepped out to the kitchen and then walked around the bed to Naomi. Taking her hand in his, he looked deep into her eyes, which rounded with surprise.

"I'm glad you're okay," he said softly. "I was very worried about you."

She nodded, looking speechless.

"*Danki* again for the note you gave me with the drill," he said, holding the note up before putting it back into his pocket. "Your words touched me deeply. I, too, am looking forward to where our friendship takes us." He shook her hand. "*Frehlicher Grischtdaag, mei freind.*"

"*Frehlicher Grischtdaag,*" she echoed, her eyes still wide.

He then stepped out into the kitchen. "*Gut nacht,*" he said to Irma.

"*Danki,* Caleb," Irma said, shaking his hand. "We're so glad you rescued her."

Naomi adjusted herself in the bed. The pain from her ankle radiated up her leg in waves, stealing her breath.

However, the buzz in her mind affected her more deeply than the pain from her foot as she watched Caleb walk out into the kitchen. Her heart pounded and a smile spread on her lips as she remembered the look on his face as he'd held her hand. His words had left her both dizzy and speechless.

The note she'd written to him had touched him, and he looked forward to a future with her.

A future?

But what did that mean exactly? Did he only want to be friends or did he want something more?

"You're a very blessed *maedel*," Irma said, stepping back into the bedroom. "You could've been lost out there all night."

Naomi sighed. "I know." She tried to move her leg and sucked in a ragged breath when the discomfort shot through her ankle.

"*Ach*," her mother rushed over and took her hand. "Are you okay?"

Naomi nodded as the pain subsided a bit. "I think so."

"Do you want more painkiller?" Her mother's eyes were wide with worry.

"No, *danki*." Naomi forced a smile. "I'll be okay in a moment. The pain comes and goes."

Her mother pulled a chair up next to her. "Caleb is a *gut* man."

Naomi blinked, stunned by how direct her mother was.

Irma smiled. "I believe he may have feelings for you."

Naomi cleared her throat. "I'm not certain about that, but I hope so."

Irma raised an eyebrow. "I believe you know the answer to that."

Shaking her head, Naomi smoothed the quilt over her nightgown. "Susie told me that Caleb found a house and they're moving here, but I'm not certain of what that will mean for him and me. All I know is that I do care for him and Susie, and I hope to get to know them better."

"He cares for you too, Naomi," Irma said with a knowing smile. "I believe he cares quite deeply for you. I wish you could've seen his face when your *dat* carried you in."

Naomi rubbed the back of her neck, which was stiff from the fall. "I don't understand."

Irma rubbed Naomi's arm. "He was worried sick about you. I was wrong to tell you not to consider him because he's a widower." She smiled. "My mother's favorite verse was from Romans. It went something like this: 'But if we hope for what we do not yet have, we wait for it patiently.'"

Naomi shook her head. "What are you trying to say, *Mamm?*"

"You've waited for your true love," Irma said, still smiling. "Now let God lead you and Caleb down the road."

"My true love?" Naomi whispered.

"I think so, but only time will tell. See where God leads you and Caleb. I think you're off to a *gut* start." Irma stood. "You need to get some sleep."

"What about the Christmas table?"

Irma kissed Naomi's head. "I'll take care of it."

"*Danki*," Naomi said, trying to find a comfortable position on the bed despite the discomfort in her ankle.

"You get better." Irma wagged a finger at her. "And don't you ever take off alone in the snow again. You hear me?"

Naomi smiled. "Yes, *Mamm*. I definitely learned my lesson. *Gut nacht*."

"*Gut nacht*." Her mother left, gently closing the door behind her.

Naomi stared up at the ceiling, ignoring her injury and

thinking of Caleb. She fell asleep with a smile on her face, dreaming of her possible future with Caleb and Susie.

Epilogue

Naomi smiled despite the pain in her ankle while sitting at the kitchen table the following afternoon. Around her, all of her siblings laughed, ate candy, and played with their new toys.

"Naomi," her father said, tapping her on the shoulder. "You have visitors."

"I do?" She looked up at him, hoping that her prayers had come true. She'd been thinking of Caleb and Susie all morning.

"Let me help you into the *schtupp*." Taking her arm, Titus helped Naomi while she half hopped, half limped.

Moving to the doorway, she found Caleb and Susie standing in the room, and tears filled Naomi's eyes. Her prayers had been answered. She was going to spend Christmas with her new friends.

Caleb rushed over and took Naomi's other arm. "Let me help you."

"*Danki*," Naomi said, her cheeks burning with embarrassment.

"Are you in much pain?" he asked, his green eyes filling with concern.

"I'll be fine," she said.

They helped her to the sofa, and she sank onto the end cushion.

Susie rushed over and hugged Naomi. "*Frehlicher Grischtdaag!*"

"*Frehlicher Grischtdaag, mei liewe,*" Naomi said before kissing the little girl's head.

"Can I go see Levina and Sylvia?" Susie asked.

"Of course," Naomi said, gesturing toward the adjacent room. "Have fun."

Susie ran off toward the kitchen.

The sofa shifted beside Naomi as Caleb lowered himself down next to her. "*Frehlicher Grischtdaag.*" He handed her a bag.

"Oh, Caleb," Naomi said, taking the bag. "You didn't have to."

He laughed. "Of course I did. Please open it."

Naomi's heart fluttered as she opened the bag and pulled out the black Bible she'd longed to buy for herself. She ran her fingers over the cover. "Caleb," she whispered, meeting his intense stare. "You spent too much."

"No, I didn't." He nodded toward the Bible. "Please open it. There's something inside."

She opened the cover and found a note in neat handwriting:

Naomi,

I thought it was only fitting to give you this Bible for Christmas. I know how much it would mean to you to have a new Bible for your nightly devotions. I hope that you realize how much you mean to both Susie and me.

*Your friendship is precious to us, just like the precious
verses contained in this holy book.*

*I'm so thankful that God led Susie and me back to
my hometown for Christmas and I'm even more thankful
that He led me to you. You've taught me so much about
finding joy in life again despite past heartaches. You've
helped me remember what it means to be happy. I look
forward to where God leads us on this journey together.*

Frehlicher Grischtdaag!
Caleb

She read the words over and over again, and she was both
stunned and confused by the sentiment they contained.
Questions swirled in her mind. She needed to know what
the inscription truly meant, but she couldn't form the words
to ask him.

Finally, with tears pooling in her eyes, Naomi looked up.
"*Danki.* It's *schee.*"

He touched her hand, and her pulse skittered. "I need to
know something. What did you mean last night when you
said you thought I was discussing business with Hezekiah
and Irene?"

"Susie said you were going into business with Hezekiah,"
Naomi said.

Caleb shook his head. "No, I'm not. I found a house that
has a shop, and I'm going to open my own carriage shop."

Naomi smiled. "That's *wunderbaar!*"

"Hezekiah and Irene were talking my ear off last night,
but it was nothing but idle conversation."

Naomi took a deep breath and glanced down at the Bible.

She needed to know the truth about him and Irene. "Are you courting Irene?" she asked while running her fingers over the cover of the Bible.

He snorted. "No. Why do you ask?"

She met his expression, not finding any sign of a lie. "I heard Sadie talking."

He frowned. "What did *mei schweschder* say now?"

"She was telling someone that you and Irene would be a *gut* couple. She made a point of saying that Susie needed a *mamm*, implying that Irene could be a *gut* candidate for that role."

Caleb rolled his eyes. "Sadie tries too hard to run my life. She means well, but she does more damage than good." His frown deepened. "And the last role that Irene would be *gut* for would be a *mamm*. She's terrible with Susie, and she's been nothing but rude to my precious *dochder*."

Naomi shook her head. "I can't imagine ever being rude or nasty to Susie. She's such a special girl. I'm sorry that Irene isn't nice to Susie, but I'm so glad Sadie was wrong."

"Sadie has been wrong about a lot of things," Caleb said. "Most of all, she was wrong about who I belong with. I definitely don't belong with Irene."

"Is that so?" Naomi's smile reappeared.

He nodded, his own smile growing. "She's not any fun to go shopping with."

"And I would imagine she doesn't like root beer." Naomi coyly tapped her chin. "I seem to remember that you promised me a root beer float."

He grinned. "I did. And I intend to keep that promise." His smile faded. "But I must ask you one question first."

"What's that?"

He took her hands in his, and the feel of his warm skin caused her heart to beat at hyper speed. "Naomi, that time we sat on the porch together, you asked me if I believed God gave second chances at true love. I told you yes, but I honestly wasn't sure." His eyes sparkled. "Since I've met you, I know that answer for certain. I think God has given me a second chance when he brought me to you. We would be a *gut* couple, and I would be honored to court you."

Tears filled her eyes. "After I had my heart broken twice, I was certain I'd never find love. Now I see that God had a plan all along for me. I think this is the Christmas miracle Susie wanted for you. It's also a miracle for me."

"She told me that she'd asked you if you believed in miracles," he said, running his finger down her jaw line.

She nodded, butterflies fluttering in her belly at the feel of his gentle touch.

"She also asked me if I believe in miracles, and I do believe in them," he said. "And, *ya*, my little girl was right because you're my miracle. No, actually, you're a miracle for Susie and me. We both love you." He nodded toward the Bible. "There's a reason why I didn't have your name engraved on the Bible. I thought that you might change your name someday and I wanted to be certain that I put the correct name on the cover."

Before she could respond, he leaned over and gently pressed his lips against hers, sending the pit of her stomach into a wild swirl.

"*Frehlicher Grischtdaag*, Naomi," he whispered against her lips.

"*Frehlicher Grischtdaag*," she whispered, leaning her head against his shoulder and closing her eyes.

Kauffman Amish Bakery Fruit Cake

1½ cups sugar
2 eggs
2 cups applesauce or
    2 cups fruit (any kind)
½ cup oil
2 cups flour
¼ tsp salt
2 tsp baking soda

Mix together all ingredients and pour into a greased 9 x 13 pan. Bake at 350 degrees for 45 minutes.

Icing

1 stick butter
½ cup evaporated milk
¾ cup brown sugar
1 tsp vanilla

Stir together in a saucepan, then boil 5 minutes. Cool cake and cover with icing.

RASPBERRY DREAM TORTE

1-10 oz. pkg. frozen raspberries
1¼ cup vanilla wafer crumbs
¼ cup melted butter
½ cup butter
1½ cups 10x (confectioner's) sugar
¼ t. vanilla
¼ t. almond extract
¼ cup sugar
2 T. cornstarch
Whipped cream for garnish
2 eggs

Defrost raspberries. Combine vanilla wafer crumbs and ¼ cup melted butter. Press into bottom of 7 ½-inch spring form pan. Cream ½ cup butter and 10x sugar. Add eggs, beating well after each. Blend in extracts. Spread over crumb layer. Chill until firm. Combine sugar, cornstarch, and raspberries in a pan. Cook on stovetop at medium heat, stirring constantly until clear and thick. Pour raspberry filling over torte. Refrigerate several hours. Garnish with whipped cream.

Acknowledgments

I'm thankful to my loving and supportive family, including my mother, Lola Goebelbecker; my husband, Joe; my sons, Zac and Matt; my mother-in-law, Sharon Clipston; and my wonderful aunts, Trudy Janitz and Debbie Floyd.

I'm more grateful than words can express for my amazing friends who critique and edit for me: Jean Love, Sue McKlveen, and Lauran Rodriguez. Special thanks to Lauran for admiring the character of Naomi King and inspiring this book.

Thank you also to Ruth Meily for her continued help with Lancaster County research and recipes. I'm also grateful to Cathy Zimmermann for her help and quick answers to my Amish and Lancaster County questions. Thank you also to Stacey Barbalace for her help with the Amish details and accuracy.

As always, thank you to my special Amish friend who patiently answers my endless stream of questions.

Thank you to my awesome agent, Mary Sue Seymour, for her professional expertise and her friendship.

I'm grateful for the fabulous team at Zondervan, especially Sue Brower, Becky Philpott, and Alicia Mey.

Thank you also to my faithful readers for your love and friendship.

Thank you most of all, God, for giving me the opportunity to glorify You. I'm so thankful and humbled You've chosen this path for me.

Special thanks to Cathy and Dennis Zimmermann for their hospitality and research assistance in Lancaster County, Pennsylvania.

Cathy & Dennis Zimmermann, Innkeepers
The Creekside Inn
44 Leacock Road—PO Box 435
Paradise, PA 17562
Toll Free: (866) 604–2574
Local Phone: (717) 687–0333

The author and publisher gratefully acknowledge the following resources that were used to research information for this book:

C. Richard Beam, *Revised Pennsylvania German Dictionary: English to Pennsylvania Dutch* (Brookshire Publications, 1991).

Rose Heiberger, *Buggy Seat Bare Feet*, rev. ed. (Gordonville, Pennsylvania Print Shop, 1994).

A sample from Amy Clipston's

A GIFT *of* GRACE

Rebecca Kauffman's pulse fluttered as the large SUV she was riding in rumbled down the narrow road past the rolling farmland and green pastures dotted by heifers. The cows chewed their cud and nodded their greeting as if welcoming her back. The serenity of the lush, open fields intersected only by clusters of white farmhouses filled her soul with a peace she hadn't felt since she'd left last month.

Pushing the cool metal button on the door, she cracked the passenger window open and breathed in the sweet, warm, moist air, free of exhaust from overcrowded city roads.

The SUV negotiated a sharp bend, and Rebecca's heart skipped a beat when the three-story farmhouse came into view. A smile crept across her lips.

Home.

The whitewashed, three-story, clapboard house stood humbly near the entrance to her family's forty acres. The newly painted white picket fence was a stark contrast to the house's green tin roof, speckled with brown rust that told of its age. The green window shades were halfway up, and the windows were cracked open to allow the springtime air to cool the house naturally.

A sweeping porch welcomed visitors entering the front, and a white barn, almost the size of the house, sat behind it. The large moving truck filled with the girls' belongings seemed out of place next to the plain farmhouse and barn.

"This is it," Rebecca said.

Running her fingers over the ties of her prayer *kapp*, her mind swirled with thoughts on how her life had suddenly changed. She was finally a mother, or rather a guardian, of her two teenage nieces, her sister Grace's children. Children would again live in the large farmhouse for the first time since she and Grace had been young.

"It's beautiful," Trisha McCabe, her older niece's god-mother, whispered from the seat behind Rebecca.

"Thank you." Rebecca sat up straight in the leather front seat and smoothed her apron. "I love it here. It's so quiet. If you listen close, you can actually hear the birds eating the seed in the feeder by my garden." She pointed to the area near the front door where a rainbow of flowers swayed in the gentle spring breeze. Four cylinder-shaped feeders dangled from iron poles above the flowers. "The birds love those feeders. I have to fill them at least twice a week."

Trisha's husband, Frank, nosed his large truck up to the side of the farmhouse and then killed the engine. Whispers erupted from the third seat of the truck, and Rebecca assumed her nieces were analyzing the home.

Wrenching open the door, Rebecca climbed from the truck. She inhaled a deep breath and hugged her arms to her chest. Birds chirped and a horse brayed in the distance. The familiar sounds were a welcome change from the roar of automobiles, blare of television sets, and electronic rings of cellular phones she had endured at her sister's home.

Trisha jumped out from the backseat, her eyes scanning the field. "You and Grace grew up here?"

A rush of grief flooded Rebecca at the sound of her sister's name. Unable to speak for a moment, she nodded. "This house has been in our family for generations. Grace and I were both born here and grew up here."

Trisha glanced toward the front door. "The land is just gorgeous. Can I go in and freshen up?"

"Of course," Rebecca said, folding her arms across her simple black apron covering her caped, plain purple dress. "The washroom is to the right through the kitchen."

"I'll be right back," Trisha said before heading in the back door.

Rebecca glanced inside the truck through the open back door and spotted her nieces speaking to each other in hushed tones. Jessica Bedford was a portrait of Grace at fifteen, with her long, dark brown hair, deep brown eyes, high cheekbones, and clear, ivory skin. Lindsay Bedford, on the other hand, was fourteen, with auburn hair, striking emerald eyes, porcelain skin, and a smattering of freckles across her dainty nose.

Watching her precious nieces, Rebecca's heart swelled with love. She'd met the girls for the first time when she arrived in Virginia Beach after hearing the news of the accident that took the lives of Grace and her husband, Philip.

The girls gathered up their bags and climbed from the truck.

Lindsay gasped as her eyes roamed the scenery. "This looks like a painting." She turned to her sister. "Can you believe we're going to live here?"

"Whatever," Jessica deadpanned with a roll of her eyes. She chomped her bright pink bubble gum and adjusted her ear buds on the contraption she'd called an iPod. Her obsession with the electronic devices seemed to exemplify the Amish perspective that modern technology interfered with community and family relationships.

Lindsay pointed to the barn. "Do you have a lot of animals?"

"We have a few cats, chickens, goats, sheep, a cow, and a couple of horses," Rebecca said.

Lindsay's eyes lit up. "Cool!"

The gentle clip-clop of a horse pulled Rebecca's gaze toward the road. A smile turned up the corners of her mouth as Annie and Titus Esh's horse and buggy traveled past her home.

"It's so good to see horses and buggies again," Rebecca said, waving at her neighbors. "Such a nice change from the traffic jams."

"Yeah, but I bet it takes four hours to get to the grocery store," Jessica mumbled.

"It's a much more enjoyable ride, though," Rebecca quipped with a smile. "There's no loud radio to take away from the beautiful scenery around us." She turned her gaze to her garden. "That reminds me. I need to check my flowers."

Moving toward her garden, she found that more flowers had bloomed and vegetables had matured while she'd been gone. Daniel must have watered them for her as he'd promised. Stooping, she yanked a handful of weeds. The feeling of her hands on the green plants sent warmth to her soul. Nothing pleased her more than working in her garden.

It's so good to be home.

Jessica sidled up to Rebecca. Slipping her iPod into her bag, her hand brushed the front of her blue T-shirt revealing Grace's wedding ring hanging from a sparkling chain around Jessica's neck. "I've never seen so many different flowers."

"They're so colorful," Lindsay said, joining them.

Rebecca's smile deepened. Perhaps she'd found a common ground with her nieces — gardening. "My mother planted roses when I was about six," she said. "I helped trim and water them during the spring and summer."

"Your mother planted them?" Jessica turned toward her, her eyes wide with shock. "My grandmother?"

"Your mother helped in the garden too. It's sort of a tradition for children to help in the gardens, especially the girls." She touched her niece's arm. "Do you like to garden?"

"I guess." Jessica shrugged. "I did a little bit with my mom."

"I helped her weed," Lindsay chimed in.

"Maybe you both can help me sometime," Rebecca said.

"Yeah. Maybe," Jessica whispered. "My mother loved to take care of her roses. I had no idea it was something she did when she was Amish."

Rebecca chuckled. "Well, gardening isn't just an Amish thing, but it is part of our culture. We love the outdoors. It's a way to praise God and celebrate His glory."

Jessica nodded. "That makes sense."

"Becky, *mei Fraa. Wie geht's?*" a voice behind Rebecca asked.

Turning, she found her husband, Daniel, pushing back his straw hat to wipe the sweat from his blond brow. He flashed his dimpled smile and her heart skipped a beat. Oh, how she'd missed him during their month apart.

It was so good to be home!

"Daniel!" Standing on her tiptoes, she hugged him. "Daniel, I'm doing great now. Oh how I've missed you."

"I'm glad you're home," his voice vibrated against her throat, sending heat through her veins.

Stepping back, Rebecca motioned toward the girls. "Daniel, these are our nieces I've told you so much about on the phone. This is Jessica, and this is Lindsay. Girls, meet your uncle Daniel."

"Welcome." He tipped his straw hat.

"Thanks," Jessica said, shifting her weight on her feet and glancing around the property.

"It's nice to meet you," Lindsay said.

"I hope you'll be comfortable here with us," he said. "The movers and I have almost gotten all of your boxes in."

"Great." Jessica's smile seemed to be forced.

Taking his hand, Rebecca smiled up at Daniel. Yes, it was so good to be home.

Kauffman Amish Bakery Series

A Promise of Hope
A Novel

Amy Clipston

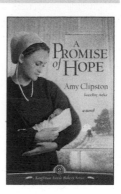

In *A Promise of Hope*, the second installment in the Kauffman Amish Bakery Series,
bestselling author Amy Clipston compellingly
unfolds the tensions, loves, and faith of the
inhabitants of an Amish community and the
family bakery that serves as an anchor point
for the series.

When Sarah Troyer tragically loses her husband, Peter, she is left to
raise infant twins alone. Overwhelmed and grieving, she lives with her
parents in the Amish community of Bird-in-Hand, Pennsylvania. Sarah
is taken completely by surprise when a stranger arrives claiming con-
nections to Peter's past — Peter had told her he was an orphan with no
family. From Luke, she learns her husband hid a secret life, one with
ramifications that will change her own.

Sarah's family, concerned for her and the future of her twins, en-
courages her to marry again. It should make sense … but Sarah's
heart says no. She feels trapped. Should she marry a man she doesn't
love? Or discover if her growing interest in Luke can be trusted?

A Promise of Hope is filled with surprising twists that will grip you
to the very last words.

Available in stores and online!

A Place of Peace

A Novel

Amy Clipston

Miriam Lapp, who left the Amish community of Bird-in-Hand three years ago, is heartbroken when her sister calls to reveal that her mother has died suddenly. Traveling home to Pennsylvania, she is forced to face the heartache from her past, including her rift from her family and the breakup of her engagement with Timothy Kauffman.

Her past emotional wounds are reopened when her family rejects her once again and she finds out that Timothy is in a relationship with someone else. Miriam discovers that the rumors that broke them up three years ago were all lies. However, when Timothy proposes to his girlfriend and Miriam's father disowns her, Miriam returns to Indiana with her heart in shambles.

When Miriam's father has a stroke, Miriam returns to Pennsylvania, where her world continues to fall apart, leaving her to question her place in the Amish community and her faith in God.

Kauffman Amish Bakery Series

A Life of Joy
A Novel

Amy Clipston

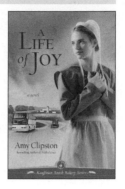

In *A Life of Joy*, the fourth installment in the series, eighteen-year-old Lindsay Bedford has reached a crossroads. Should she stay in the small Amish community she's known and loved for four years or return to the English life in her hometown in Virginia where her older sister is a college student? An extended visit to Virginia might just tip the scales as Lindsay reconnects with friends, joins a new church, works on her GED, and is pressured by her sister to stay and "make something of herself."

Will Lindsay leave her aunt Rebecca and become English or settle in Bird-in-Hand and join the Amish church? Legions of Clipston fans want to know.

Full of well-researched Amish culture, Clipston's book is true to form, delivering the best of the Amish fiction genre wrapped around a compelling story, with characters who will touch the hearts of loyal fans and new readers alike.

Available in stores and online!

Kauffman Amish Bakery Series

A Season of Love

A Novel

Amy Clipston

In the fifth and final novel of the Kauffman Amish Bakery Series, three young women are about to change their lives. Lizzie Anne and Samuel have decided to get married, and Lindsay is about to be baptized in the Amish faith and is courting Matthew. While Katie Kauffman is happy for her friends who seem to have settled their futures, she is also finding herself something of a fifth wheel.

When Lindsay's sister Jessica returns to Bird-in-Hand, she finds that Jake Miller has moved on with his life. He lost hope that Jessica would ever be satisfied to settle in rural Pennsylvania and takes comfort in becoming close friends with Katie. However, it's not an easy road as Jake is Mennonite and Katie has just been baptized in the Amish faith. Her father forbids them to see each other, adamant that his daughter marry an Amish man.

A Season of Love is filled with surprising twists that will grip you to the very last words. As the stories of your favorite Amish community draw to a close, join Lindsay, her friends, and all the people of Bird-In-Hand for one last volume.

Available in stores and online!

Reckless Heart

Amy Clipston

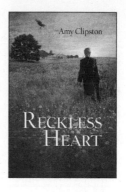

Lydia Bontrager's youngest sister is frighteningly ill, and as a good Amish daughter, it falls to Lydia to care for her siblings and keep the household running, in addition to working as a teacher's assistant and helping part-time at her grandmother's bakery. Succumbing to stress, Lydia gives in to one wild night and returns home drunk. The secret of that mistake leaves Lydia feeling even more restless and confused, especially when Joshua, the only boy she's ever loved, becomes increasingly distant. When a non-Amish boy moves in nearby, Lydia finds someone who understands her, but the community is convinced Lydia is becoming too reckless. With the pressures at home and her sister's worsening condition, a splintering relationship with Joshua, and her own growing questions over what is right, Lydia could lose everything that she's ever held close.

Share Your Thoughts

With the Author: Your comments will be forwarded to the author when you send them to *zauthor@zondervan.com*.

With Zondervan: Submit your review of this book by writing to *zreview@zondervan.com*.

Free Online Resources at
www.zondervan.com

Zondervan AuthorTracker: Be notified whenever your favorite authors publish new books, go on tour, or post an update about what's happening in their lives at www.zondervan.com/authortracker.

Daily Bible Verses and Devotions: Enrich your life with daily Bible verses or devotions that help you start every morning focused on God. Visit www.zondervan.com/newsletters.

Free Email Publications: Sign up for newsletters on Christian living, academic resources, church ministry, fiction, children's resources, and more. Visit www.zondervan.com/newsletters.

Zondervan Bible Search: Find and compare Bible passages in a variety of translations at www.zondervanbiblesearch.com.

Other Benefits: Register to receive online benefits like coupons and special offers, or to participate in research.

ZONDERVAN®

ZONDERVAN.com/
AUTHORTRACKER
follow your favorite authors